THE ENEMY

AN IRANIAN FRONTED SPONSORED *THE ISLAMIC REPUB* (IRF) WHO ARE AN EXTREMIST TERROR THEY SELECTED AND GROOMED SIX ISLAMIC STUDENTS OF HIGH IQ AND PAID FOR THEIR EDUCATION TO MASTERS DEGREE STANDARD, READING AT OXFORD OR CAMBRIDGE. THE SIX STUDENTS WERE GUARANTEED TOP BRITISH GOVERNMENT JOBS THROUGH CONTACTS IN THE RIGHT PLACES. THEY WERE CODED WITH RIVER NAMES AND OBTAINED RESPONSIBLE POSITIONS IN MI5, MI6, GCHQ, ANTI TERRORISM OFFICE, FOREIGN AND HOME OFFICE. THEY WERE NOW IN A POSITION TO SPY ON CLASSIFIED INFORMATION AND PASS IT TO THE IRF. ENABLING TO BE ONE STEP AHEAD OF THE BRITISH SECRET SERVICE!

MAX-CATT IS ASKED BY THE UK GOVERNMENT TO COVERTLY DISRUPT THE PEOPLE TRAFFICKERS WHO ARE ORGANISING THOUSANDS OF ILLEGAL IMMIGRANTS CROSSING FROM THE FRENCH SIDE. MAX-CATT'S MISSION IS TO DISRUPT THE INFLATABLES WILL TAKES HIM TO THREE COUNTRIES AND THE IRF RECRUITMENT CENTRE AT DOVER. HERE THE BOAT PEOPLE ARE ENCOURAGED TO JOIN THEIR TERROR ACTIVITIES IN RETURN FOR FOOD, SHELTER AND TO CHANGE BRITAIN INTO AN ISLAMIC RAN COUNTRY.

THE ZERO STATUS SPY IS FACED WITH DOUBLE AGENTS THROUGHOUT SIS, ONE RIGHT UNDER HIS NOSE WORKING AT BASTION!

*****

 A CIP catalogue record for this title is available from the British library.

ISBN 978-1-915828-11-8

OTHER TITLES IN THE MAX-CATT
THRILLER SERIES

BY

BILL DIAMOND

THE BEGINNING

VENGEANCE IS MINE

NO TURNING BACK

ROTTERDAM

BASTION

THE YALTA PROJECT

ENEMY WITHIN

ROGUE KILL

1

Sir Crispin was in an unusually foul mood and it didn't usually take much to agitate the Bastion boss's overall demeanour. It was Monday morning and the reason for the deterioration in his wellbeing was having had to cancel a Pro-Am golf day at the prestigious Wentworth golf club. The corporate day invitation was sponsored by Spectrum Solutions, a company specialising in Artificial Intelligence and they of course wanted to impress and pamper decision makers and government buyers and in return for the free all expenses paid corporate day they expect the chance of pitching their new technology, especially with lucrative government contracts on offer.

Sir Crispin Norcutt was usually based in Whitehall but the unexpected departure of Cordelia Fernsby, the disgraced director at Bastion, meant the peer was coopted into covering for her until a permanent replacement was found. Miss Fernsby was the murderer of Anneka De Jong, Max-Catt's Dutch girlfriend, and her own sister and she was herself assassinated in Gran Cayman by the Russian Secret Service.

So Sir Crispin had to take up the Bastion reins albeit temporarily. He had no choice really, Bastion was his and Cordelia's brainchild so out of necessity he took back control. Bastion was a UK secret service organisation with the best state of the art technology and the best staff recruited from MI5, MI6 and GCHQ and billions of taxpayers money had been invested in it and with Max-Catt being the head of field operations.

Sir Crispin was gutted to miss the all day golfing jolly as any keen golfer would be but it was his own fault for missing out as he hadn't informed Ella Guthridge, his personal assistant, who he'd nicked from Max-Catt.

'Ella are you sure I didn't ask you to block out my diary for today? I only popped in to pick up my golf shoes!'

'No Sir Crispin you didn't, but you did ask me to get Miss Julia Deakin in for an interview as soon as possible and her only free window was this morning as she has a series of meetings at Box 500 with the Home Secretary and today was clear so I booked her in. Shall I cancel her?'

'No Ella, it was my own fault for not blocking out today myself. Damn it! I've been so looking forward to this day for weeks and I've even bought a new three wood I wanted to try out.' Sir Crispin exhaled disappointedly through his teeth.

He looked out of the window at the early morning Spring sunshine at the buds on the trees progressing well with their development stimulated by the unusual solar warmth from such an early sun. Yes, he was totally pissed off with missing the golf day and on such a lovely day but Ella was right, it was his fault for not blocking out his online diary with just one click! 'It's not your fault Ella.' The boss of Bastion turned and faced Miss Guthridge. Ella felt awful but it was her boss's call to cancel the interview which happened to be for the top job that he was caretaking for.

'Sir Crispin is Box 500 a code name for something?' The temporary boss laughed. 'Box 500 is what employees who work at Thames House call MI5. It's a nickname rather than using the official name. It's the same reason why MI6 is fondly called Big Sis which of course is a play on words, the SIS part stands for Secret Intelligence Service so add the word big and you've got it, like the all-seeing big brother.

'Yes, clever really, but how does Box 500 stand for MI5, I'm intrigued?'

'Box 500 was the official address of MI5 during and for a few years after the Second World War and it has stuck. So now you know the nicknames of both of the domestic and foreign secret services and do you know our nickname for Bastion?'

'Yes it's Fortress!'

'Indeed it is.' Ella went back into her adjoining office and confirmed the interview with Julia Deakin was for 10:30. Sir Crispin's spirits dropped once more and he picked up his golf shoes in a fit of temper and shied them at the wall. One fell to the floor but the other bounced off a sideboard and landed on the domed stopper of a cut glass whisky decanter where it lay until the evening cleaners arrive.

Max-Catt called his first meeting with four new Bastion recruits. The two ex-SAS men, Callum Maclean and Mason Perkins, were personally chosen by Max as he'd worked with them behind enemy lines and knew their capabilities. Jade Jackson and Tazi Emir were the other two field agents, both of whom had transferred from MI6.

They had all passed the gruelling four months of intense training which had included intense language courses and operational studies to become ready for the field. Before their training commenced and being totally unaware of this, they were kidnapped and interrogated by a bogus enemy of the State and forced to give information about Bastion's managing committee that included Sir Crispin Norcutt. Max himself had gone through the kidnapping trial but in his case it had been far too extreme for any human being and his near fatal experience persuaded the Bastion organising committee to dilute the torture procedure as Max had got too close to death by their overzealous methods.

The trained recruits were now operational-ready and Max intended deploying Maclean and Tazi Emir with the task of tracking down and identifying a safe-house of the dangerous Islamic Republican Front or the IRF as they were known. Various incoming intel confirmed that the IRF were rebuilding its UK cell network and the new Bastion recruits were keen to start what they had all trained long and hard for as fully fledged elite agents working for the premier UK secret service.

Max commenced the briefing: 'Colleagues, you are here on merit and have been chosen for your special qualities and for not only passing the concentrated academic tests but the gruelling physical assessments as well which included interrogation and torture tests so well done on those achievements. Colin and Mason, you have shared many a tight situation behind enemy lines with me so I know you can be relied upon. Jade and Tazi you will have to prove yourselves although I'm sure you will be fine but as you don't have field experience I want you, Tazi, under the wing of Callum and you, Jade, are to buddy up with Mason and we'll keep to these teams unless operational demands dictate otherwise.'

Julia Deakin arrived in Ella's office at 10:25 and waited for Sir Crispin to finish a telephone call, noticing that he had a grumpy tone in his voice. The interviewee wasn't at all nervous as she had grown up an orphan and had studied hard with self-motivation that fuelled her drive to get on in life. Instead of using an absence of parents as an excuse for failure or lethargy, her positive attitude to overcome life's obstacles had helped greatly in her career advancement. A difficult achievement on one's own with no support. Julia took on several evening jobs to pay for her university education and as a postgraduate she started out as a junior but soon received regular promotions and advanced to being the head of a government department that required daily liaising with MI5 and MI6.

During the interview, Sir Crispin's perception was spot-on, this lady was cool, calculating and assertive and he realised that he was also being weighed up by her friendly but investigative stare that had the effect of putting him on the back foot. 'You have been put forward by an influential cabinet minister for this unique job. It really is not a run-of-the-mill secret service position as Bastion is still finding its feet so to speak and will need an independent mind to lead it. An outside of the box thinker is essential otherwise the huge state investment will not work the way it was planned to. What do you say to that Miss Deakin?'

'Right up my street Sir Crispin and if I don't get this position I plan to start my own international private detective agency. My boyfriend has said he'll help set me up so either our country will get the benefit of my ability or I'll make shed loads of money privately but I do like the idea of protecting our country that I love. So either way sir I'll leave here a happy person but you will not get a better, hard nosed, decisive person than me to run Bastion. If I sound too sure of myself or even cocky it's because I am, I've had to be! That's me Sir Crispin, just so you know what you'll be taking on and from me you'll also get loyalty but I don't take any shit from chinless wonders in government jobs, in particular the wokey civil servants who in reality are controlling our government and have ministers running scared, too frightened to say boo to a goose!

'Well Miss Deakin I think you've answered everything I might have asked and you certainly seem sure of yourself and have all the required qualifications. Do you have any questions madam?' Julia Deakin glanced to her side and noticed a golf shoe perched on a whisky decanter which momentarily paused her concentration.

'Oh…um…when do I start?' Sir Crispin cleared his throat only because he was taken aback and was really buying time for his reply. 'That is very presumptuous of you Miss Deakin, and I certainly am not going to ask the questions I intended to put to you as they will, I am sure, be treated with contempt so please give me your personal number and I'll call you tonight. I must say I've never interviewed anybody who does most of the talking but I like you Miss Deakin. Directness is stifled these days because of fear of offending others but I don't detect any fear in you! I think that's all then and now you will need escorting out of Bastion as we have extremely tight security here. Good day Miss Deakin and I'll call you later either way.'

'Just one thing Sir Crispin, what the dickens is a golf shoe doing on top of your drinks decanter?'

'It wasn't put there, I threw my golf shoes at the wall and one found its way on to the decanter.' *Very strange* Julia thought. She said a polite goodbye and went back to Ella's room next door who summoned an escort to see Miss Deakin out through Bastion's security, a protocol that was taken very seriously!

2

Max hadn't been back from his Crimean mission very long before he realised the gaping hole that Cordelia Fernsby had left at Bastion. Outside of her Bastion directorship she was a dangerous, callous woman who met her demise at the hands of the Russian Secret Service in Gran Cayman but she was nevertheless very good at her job but sadly greed had got the better of her and had led to her eventual death.

Sir Crispin had temporarily stepped into the vacuum left by Cordelia and was juggling this with his other cabinet office commitments so he couldn't give one hundred percent of his time to Bastion which was what the newly formed elite secret organisation needed and deserved. Certainly his current three days a week attendance at Fortress was nowhere near enough which meant Max was picking up loose ends that needed urgent attention.

As the head of field operations, Max was missing Ella Guthridge's help as well, having lost her to Sir Crispin so he was left to organise the ever increasing and pressing field operations that were flooding in on his own but things were about to change.

Max was called to Sir Crispin's office. 'Good morning Sir Crispin, I thought you had a golfing jolly at Wentworth today?'
'Yeah, don't bloody remind me! I had to cancel it as I had an interview booked in this morning for the Bastion job I'm trying to do part time and I have now found a replacement for Cordelia Fernsby, a Miss Julia Deakin

who appears to be very efficient and a no-nonsense lady. She doesn't know it yet but she's starting on Monday. Bastion can't be overseen by a part time director especially when you are away on missions. By the way your pal Dani Quibi, or ZX3 as was his code name in South Yemen, joined the Halifax Road Mosque in Bradford while you were in Crimea and if you remember you asked me if we could get him to become a member of that congregation because of your suspicions about its possible terrorist links. To be our eyes and ears you said so he's actually been at Halifax Road for three weeks and hasn't missed a single prayer session. Dani has reported nothing suspicious to date apart from that the Imam, Mousa Alami, regularly leaves in the middle of prayer sessions and always in a damn hurry and also gets lots of important visitors apparently.'

'Your pal, Joe Carmichael, at MI6 wants to be kept in the loop with Dani Quibi's activities as well which I suppose is understandable seeing as Dani is an MI6 operative on secondment to us. He has blended in nicely at the Mosque being of Middle Eastern descent and would know the ways of the Muslim religion and now you are back at Bastion you can take over as his handler again and he goes under the name of Sani Yosef. Here's the special double encrypted phone number he uses to make contact and he usually calls after evening prayers from the flat he's renting in Bradford, that is when he has some worthy information to report.

'He did say not to contact him for obvious reasons as various men at prayers have been asked to find out more about him and his background and he is fully aware he's being watched. Of course we have made a false paper trail to authenticate his past residence and work in London which all stacks up and we've even given him a criminal record that shows him still wanted by the Metropolitan police, being his reason for leaving London. The IRF most probably have someone in the Met police who can check Dani's record and see that he got done for stealing a car which is the story you told him to go with so keep your phone with you in case he calls in. He has been given a different disguise this time as he might be recognised from when he was undercover in an IRF safe house where he was discovered and they burnt his arm with boiling fat and then he escaped in a refuse truck?'

'Anyway on another matter, I've received some interesting intel from our Comms room. They have picked up an unusually high volume of chatter to and from the Halifax Road mosque in Bradford. We also have a dangerous suspect we need to arrest who is believed to be a recent recruit of the IRF, Mohammad Kabir. He came to the UK in an inflatable boat just west of Dover and was detained with twenty-four other illegals but soon absconded from the hotel he was taken to. He just melted away like many thousands of them do each year into the populous masses of London. The Border Force now believe they have located him through a tip-off from a nosey neighbour but she backed out and ended the call abruptly. not giving her address. We were, however, able to trace her call but only to an area that encompasses Shelly Street or Knox Road in Walthamstow.'

'MI5 have kept records of calls from that vicinity but can't be any more precise than that as the calls are kept short obviously to avoid detection. This job has been passed to Bastion as it is deemed a terrorist involvement of high risk so here are the details. There are several other field assignments that your assistant, Ella, is typing out for me but I'll need to double check them before I can authorise any of them. There is one in particular that looks very serious though but I'll discuss that with you later. I think that brings you right up to date with everything at Bastion Max and as soon as your new boss starts I'll introduce you to her formally. Okay that's all for now other than to say I'm so glad you're back.'

That weekend Max was moving into his new penthouse in Chiswick in West London. His maximum time to stay in the residential quarters at Bastion had elapsed by several weeks but he was allowed an extension as his new-build apartment was delayed due to some architectural security alterations to the original design.

Max-Catt was still a wanted man by at least two different terror organisations, one being the Taliban who had put out a hefty bounty on his head and the other group was the IRF who have increased their strength in Britain with their new source of recruitment coming from the illegal migrants entering the UK.

The IRF group desperately want Max dead so he has designed and financed a hidden safe room in a reinforced steel cage in his new apartment which has been so cleverly built that it doesn't impact on the modern design of the three-bedroom apartment's layout. Nobody else was privy to this extra domestic precaution, not even Max's family.

It was all a bit disorganised at the Fortress, what with losing Director Fernsby and four new field recruits having just finished their intensive training so most of the outstanding operational workload arrived on Max's desk along with the new pile of ops authorised by the caretaker director, Sir Crispin. However Max had one operation that needed his immediate attention so he called Callum Maclean and Tazi Emir in to his office.

'You two are going on your first field assignment as Bastion agents and I'm putting Callum in charge owing to his operational experience. At last we believe we have an IRF connection with the Halifax Road mosque but it's not certain even though we have had suspicions for some time. Hitherto we've not had enough proof to set up a raid but we have had a recent breakthrough with phone conversations between a runaway illegal immigrant, Mohammad Kabir, to the suspect mosque which indicates that he's most likely joined an IRF cell. He's one of many illegals our border force are listening in on at Box 500 or it's real name of MI5. Any questions so far?' Calum asked quizzically:

'How was Kabir able to be traced?'

'A good question Callum, I asked Sir Crispin that very same thing and was told it was a bit of luck really. A nosey neighbour, a good old fashioned curtain twitcher, saw a suspicious man and described him as having a long beard and walking with a limp, not that that makes him suspicious but he was new to the area and had passed her house many times recently and to quote her '*in a furtive manner'*. Unfortunately she panicked when the police asked for her address as she obviously doesn't want to get involved and she cut the conversation dead. The call was recorded but as it was cut short so quickly that the tracing programme couldn't kick in quickly enough and they could only narrow the location down to two streets in that area.

'So anyway the first task is to find out where the house is so if you can locate Kabir and keep him under surveillance he should lead you to the IRF safe house. If you are able to pinpoint the property don't do anything rash, call it in and we'll devise a plan to take the complete cell. We have reason to believe they use the mosque in Bradford as a communications hub that interconnects their national cell network and that's what we really want to bring down. The name that has cropped up several times is Kamal Hafeez, believed to be one of their top men, who controls all the IRF cells in the south of England. It's him we really want and we are convinced the mosque will lead us to the very top echelons of their national decision makers.

'You'll need night binoculars and any other bits of kit you think will be useful so get them from our Stores and while you're there you can also collect your hand-guns and twenty rounds each. You'll have a choice of three weapons. We have the new acclaimed Smith and Wesson in stock which I have tried in our indoor range and it's bloody good but personally I still prefer my trusted Glock 19. Now remember Callum, keep in touch with me and let me know if you locate Mohammad Kabir. I know you can handle it yourself but this geezer is quite manic apparently and he hates anything related to the West which is strange that these terrorists despise us so much but they all seem to want to live in the UK. Try and find a definite connection with Bradford and in particular the terrorist we want, the leader who we believe was responsible for the failed Westminster Houses of Parliament attack, Kamal Hafeez!

3

The weekend was a busy time for Max and his buddy, Joe Carmichael, had agreed to help him move into his new apartment in Chiswick as Joe lived close by in the bordering town of Acton. Joe hadn't noticed the safe-room that Max had designed even though he kept prompting him with leading questions about the design and how unusually small the master bedroom was for the buildings footprint which went completely over the head of the usually inquisitive senior manager at MI6.

'I love this apartment, my balcony overlooks the Thames and it's a great location here at Strand-on-the-Green. A place to relax, that is if I get the bloody chance.' Max's mood temporarily dropped with the thought of the workload Sir Crispin had put in front of him.

They finished sorting Max's meagre chattels by early evening so Max took his pal to the River Swan Hotel for dinner and a deserved bottle of Burgundy. Max took this relaxed opportunity to discuss Joe's colleague, Dani Quibi. 'I wanted to discuss Dani's involvement with Bastion as you know he's gone under cover for us at a mosque in Bradford. For his cover story, Bastion has given him a criminal history as the IRF will most certainly carry out checks on him.

'He's already reported to Sir Crispin that one of our main IRF suspects is getting an unusual amount of visitors and with Sir Crispin now returning to Whitehall, he has asked me to take over as Dani's handler. So when I get the next update I'll keep you in the Bradford loop. Of course the worry I have is that Dani is already known to some of the IRF members including the boss, Kamal Hafeez. As you know they discovered Dani when he was in a London cell as an undercover agent for us and as a punishment they burnt his arm in boiling cooking oil. Do you remember he escaped in the back of a rubbish cart by the skin of his teeth? Although we have given him a new face and a shorter beard, we can't guarantee he won't be recognised and of course we can't disguise his badly scarred arm. I'd be lying if I said I wasn't deeply concerned. Like you Joe, I care very much about Dani as it was he who saved my four SAS blades in South Yemen.'

'Yes Max, Dani and I built a unique bond and trust when he was ZX3 in Aden working undercover in the Houthi secret service as a double agent and he risked so much for you and your SAS squad.' A worried expression fell across the face of Joe Carmichael.

'I am fully aware what risks he took for us and I'm so glad you were able to get him into Big Sis when he fled from South Yemen as he's a great guy. Okay then Joe, I'll drop you back to your car and try out my new bed.

Next morning Max left his penthouse and timed his commute to Bastion which took him thirty five minutes in rush hour traffic. He entered his office and was pleased to see Ella Guthridge making coffee. She was back! Released from her secondment by Sir Crispin.
'Ella, thank God, you are back. Any chance of a brew?'
'Of course Max, I've sorted your diary for this morning. You have a final briefing with Callum Maclean and Tazi Emir at 10:00 but in fifteen minutes you are to go to see our new director, Miss Julia Deakin. I have already spoken to her when I was moving out my things from my temporary office. She has brought her own personal assistant with her, Miss Sandy Turpin and they both arrived together at 07:45. You have enough

time for your coffee but you mustn't keep the lady waiting.'

'Come in Mr. Hainsworth-Catt.' She quickly hid the lipstick she was using to refresh her appearance but unfortunately and in her haste she smudged the last swipe, giving her a slightly side-winder grin. 'Pull up a chair.' Julia Deakin lent across the desk recently vacated by Sir Crispin and shook Max's hand. 'How do you do.'

Max felt a firm, decisive and business like handshake probably taught in a business school.

'How do you do Miss Deakin.' There was no one there to formally introduce them but they already knew of each other's names through the medium of Sir Crispin.

'I am sure we shall get on..... um, now what do I call you, hopefully not that tongue-twister of a name you possess.'

'I go by its abbreviation, Max-Catt or just Max will do.' Max was weighing up Julia's body language as she was his and he wondered if he should mention she had a permanent lipstick grin but decided not to embarrass her at their first meeting.

'I came here with no begging bowl and set out to Sir Crispin the way I demand things done. My way or the highway! Those were my conditions and they are set in stone. I believe you are your own man so I'm told which suits me fine if the decisions you make in the field are calculated and you can back them up.'

'I spent a good part of last weekend reading your personal file, from Beachley barracks, winning a Victoria Cross, the SAS in Belize, several ops behind enemy lines, saving the Houses of Parliament and a hotel in Winchester and preventing a shopping centre in Luton from being blown to bits. Then there was the drugs busts in the Scillies and Rotterdam, for a twenty-six year old you've been a very busy boy! Bastion is fortunate to have your unique skills and I have also seen that you have a zero rated status which you will know has not been issued to any agent before. You know it enables you to do what you want, how you want and when you want. That's a unique power you hold Mr. Max-Catt so I hope you treat it with the respect it deserves?'

Max paused for thought before answering. 'Miss Deakin whether I am officially zero rated or not I will always do what my instincts dictate which is what has kept me alive on many close encounters with the Grim Reaper. Terrorists do not play by any rules and if we are to defeat them we must also play just as dirty and if that ever changes at Bastion I'd be off down that highway you mentioned! I couldn't work here with tied hands so I'd most likely go back to my SAS regiment but, on the positive side, you don't seem the wokey type to me if I may say so, so I'm sure we'll get the job done that's expected of us!'

'Well that's telling me isn't it Mr Max-Catt and we know where we stand with each other. Now down to business. You have a team going out to track down a wanted suspect, a dangerous terrorist believed to have links with the IRF. I see he arrived near Dover with a bunch of illegals crammed into a dinghy. The IRF are apparently recruiting incoming illegal immigrants who want to avoid the government processing procedure.

Mohammad Kabir is on the run, the anti-terrorism office is looking for him with more urgency as he has now killed three times including a police officer who tried arresting him. I believe the new intel that we have came from a curtain twitching nosey neighbour reporting him.'

'Yes, I believe so. I'll now go and prepare a field team to locate Kabir and hopefully the safe-house he's using.

'Come in you two and sit down and listen good, I've just learned that the man you will be tracking has recently killed three or more innocent people indiscriminately so be careful with Mr. Mohammad Kabir. Got it? Have you collected your kit including the firearms and ammunition?'

'Yes, we both chose the Smith and Wesson and tried it out on the range. Damn good handgun!' Callum spoke for them both. 'Okay, as I said owing to Callum's operational experience he makes all the decisions. I want you to find that absconding illegal who has left a wake of unprovoked killings including a copper. Also locate and mark the IRF safe house which is just as important.

'I'd be damned surprised if they haven't reintroduced coded messages of sorts. It seems the IRF's standards have slipped but that's got to helps us. Start in the first street and section it off then split into two cars. One start at one end and the other at the other end then work inwards towards each other and you should manage a ten house spectrum taking in both sides of the street. Twenty-four hours should give you a good indication of all the comings and goings in both streets but do not do anything further if you see something suspicious, just call up your buddy. It will be laborious work but keep vigilant at all times. Good luck. Oh and rotate your cars between you every four hours and remember you are looking particularly for a man with a Middle Eastern appearance, a long dark beard and a slight limp. Good luck both and Callum look after Tazi!'

The team of two left for their inaugural mission, stopping two streets away from the target zone. Callum got into Tazi Emir's car. 'Okay Tazi, here are the two roads, Shelly Street and Knox Road. There are 320 houses in Shelly Street with the odd numbers on our left and the even numbers on the other side. I'll drive to the far end at and work towards you and at four hour intervals we'll drive to each other's ends to change vehicles.

The slight drizzle had increased to steady rain but visibility from their range of surveillance wasn't affected so they started their watch, knowing that it was likely to take more than a day's observation to pinpoint the IRF's safe-house!

4

Kamal Hafeez had eliminated the former head of the IRF in the south of the UK to take command of operations after Max-Catt had caused a massive setback to the IRF by destroying their Watford headquarters and bomb factory several months earlier.

So the terrorist group had moved their headquarters to a new large four bedroom house in the heart of Tower Hamlets, an area considered to be safe as most of the residents would not want to get involved and would turn a blind eye to suspicious neighbours spreading their fanaticism.

This particular morning Hafeez was livid, an emotion he often expressed with added venom at the nearest human punchbag. 'What the fuck does that dick brain Kabir think he's doing! I've just had a coded message from Mousa Alami, our main coordinator in Bradford, who says Mohammad Kabir has killed three infidels and is bragging about it to anyone who'll listen. That in itself is dangerous to our overall plans in the UK, but to call Halifax Road on an open phone line is nothing short of irresponsible suicide as Halifax Road is our oldest safe house and our national communications centre.'

'Our six undercover river agents who operate across all of the UK's intelligence services use it to pass on vital information for our cause. Damn him! We have to do something about this loose cannon and quick!'

'Get a courier to visit him and I mean Now! Take this message to Shelly Street: Mohammad Kabir, you are to cease contacting Halifax Road mosque immediately! Do not take killing infidels into your own hands. The IRF intend bigger attacks that are carefully planned, targeted and centrally funded. Do not, I repeat, do not disobey this order or there will be terminal consequences. Sign that you understand this instruction and send it back with the courier who brought it to you.

Kamal Hafeez, South Controller IRF.

The courier arrived by motorbike in good time to his destination as the short distance from the Cavell Street headquarters to Walthamstow was not a long journey. The door code at Shelly Street was changed daily and the courier keyed in the new combination and entered the safe house. 'I have come from headquarters and I must hand deliver a written letter to Mohammad Kabir. Is he here?'

'No, he's out and about causing more trouble most likely. He's a damn liability and will get us all caught. We have been discussing his activities between the cell members only this morning and decided unanimously to report him to Hafeez.'

'That's what my dispatch is about and between you and me, Hafeez is going ballistic because Kabir has been using an open phone line to call the Halifax Road mosque which could send the IRF into another turmoil especially with Max-Catt running this elite Bastion crap!'

'How long will he be?'

'No set time, he's a weird one!'

Tea was made and the messenger waited for Mohammad Kabir and was getting frustrated as an hour had passed. He regularly went to the front window and cursed the rogue member and was pissed off further thinking about his return journey that would now be in heavy London traffic even though it was a short distance back on a motorbike.

A hundred metres down the street the two Bastion surveillance agents had finished the first block of four hours and drove down the street to swap each other's cars. They didn't speak but gave a nod as they passed each other. Twenty minutes after the change Callum noticed a man at Tazi's end of the street who was definitely sporting a limp.

A check with binoculars confirmed the limp had a long dark beard who didn't seem to care much about the now persistent rain. It was Mohammad Kabir, the man they wanted. The beard limped towards Callum and when he was about a hundred meters away he turned into a house with an overgrown Hydrangea bush in its front garden. The man had passed Tazi Emir who now had to act fast but not on behalf of Bastion to send a coded message to the Halifax Road mosque.

Bastion agent is in a silver BMW one hundred meters down the road from Shelly safe house and has just found out our safe house location. Send someone from the Shelly cell with a weapon to surprise him from behind by approaching from the block-of-flats end. He must be taken into safe house and killed but not in the street. His body mustn't be found until Shelly Street is evacuated which should be immediately. This message is from code River Severn. Do it now!

Hafeez didn't allow his temper to detract from what needed doing and Severn's coded message was sent from the mosque straight on to Shelly Street cell leader, Akrami, who knew exactly what to do.

'Salimi arm yourself and go to the tower block end of our street but go via Knox Road and come back into our street back towards this house. You will come to the rear of a silver BMW with a man sitting at the wheel, use your gun to bring him here but don't kill him in his car. He won't be expecting you and will be totally surprised. Our orders are that we must kill the infidel agent in this house then collect our personal things and evacuate here immediately. We are to split up and make our way to our back up safe house.' Salimi slipped out the back door'

The messenger from headquarters had Kabir pointed out to him when the rain soaked limp arrived and he was still towelling himself dry when the messenger handed him the written warning. 'I need you to sign that you've read it and understand the instruction so read and sign it and give it back to me.'

'Go fuck yourself, you don't tell me what to do messenger boy.' The tension heightened and the room went silent. Akrami walked behind the visually angered Mohammad Kabir, raised his gun and nonchalantly fired two shots through the back of the troublemaker's head.

'I'm sorry he didn't sign your note but he's better out of the way especially now with the evacuation.' The motor cyclist left without speaking another word and returned to his headquarters.

Callum was watching the helmeted person leaving the same house as Limpy went into. He was studying the guy who was about to leave when he nearly jumped out of his skin when a tap on the driver's window startled him.

Callum was facing the tip of a gun's silencer but it was what was attached to it that worried the Bastion agent. 'Get out of the car and I'll only ask once. Any sudden

movement and I'll shoot you. Now get out but slowly.'
Callum noticed how the gunman's hair was dripping with rain off his nose, an obscure thought given the serious event that was unfolding. He did what he was asked while thinking of how to overpower his captor and he also realised he was heading for the hydrangea bush.

Callum knew he was walking to his death once he was inside the house and probably facing torture first. No one wants to be their own executioner's assistant so, with a gun pressed hard enough to feel in his kidneys they slowly walked towards the shrub fronted house. A stooped man with a rainbow coloured umbrella came towards them who couldn't possibly see the two walking towards him as his umbrella was masking the top of his body. As they were about to pass, two bullets came through the umbrella and hit the unsuspecting Salimi in the neck and left shoulder throwing him backwards.

He wasn't dead, well not until Tazi Emir leant over him and shot the helpless man twice more in the head at point blank range. 'Come on Callum, let's get in your car and get out of here. We'll pick up mine later.' They was no hesitation from Callum, just an unanswered question about what had unfolded since Limpy showed up in Shelly Street!

5

Bini Akrami was naturally nervous when he was asked to report to Kamal Hafeez's office at the headquarters.

It had taken three hours for the seven residents of Shelly Street to disburse after the emergency evacuation and make their way singularly to the headquarters.

'You had better tell me all about the events in your own words as I have been told by my courier you shot Kabir. Why?'

'I had to kill him before he got us all killed or captured by the security forces as he was a fucking liability, just ask any of the Shelly Street team. We only just evacuated by the skin of our teeth as police were swarming all around the area after Salimi was shot four times and left in the gutter just up the road from our safe house.'

'How did you know we had someone watching our house Kamal?'

'I'll ask the questions but thankfully we had a tip off from one of our river agents. Look I get it about Kabir, in fact you probably saved me the trouble anyway.

'Now take your team tonight to Rorke Street in Limehouse. There's plenty of room there and I'm putting you in charge of that temporary cell. There are three other IRF members there who only moved in last week. We have the property on a year's rental and it has four bedrooms so there's a lot of room for your seven men until we can set up a different arrangement as we'll need Rorke Street to train and accommodate the new stream of illegal migrant recruits who are already willing to join in the IRF jihad and many more of our brothers are using that easy route of entry into Britain on the shuttle service of inflatables that leave the Calais coast and land in the Dover area. We have already recruited over a hundred brothers from that source by setting up a recruitment shelter near Dover so once they land on the beach they are told to make their way to our recruitment shelter.'

'They are offered a safe place to live, food, a mobile phone and a week of intense education about our aims to bring down the British government and replace it with an Islamic state governed by Sharia Law. There are already Sharia councils that act as guidance for many Muslims but as yet they have no legal status or binding authority under UK law and although there are now well over a hundred of them in the UK, with this number growing all the time, they are not legally recognised but that is what we hope to alter and it's only a matter of time.'

'Sorry, I'm digressing. So you know what to do, move your team to Rorke Street in ones and two's at a time at different intervals and my assistant will tell the Rorke cell to expect you.' Hafeez, having sorted the evacuation of Shelly Street, then needed to speak with his comms man at the Halifax Road mosque.

'Mousa we've been compromised in Shelly Street and had to evacuate. Also Mohammad Kabir who kept calling his pal at your mosque is no longer a problem for you or me and I just hope the infidels haven't traced his calls to the mosque as you are our central communicator and we can't afford to lose your vital hub. I therefore want you to get a coded message to all our 'river' undercover agents. Severn, as you know, is now well ensconced in Bastion. They all get Saturdays off which is tomorrow so I'll book a private Turkish bath for eight persons at the Asian Spa in Bethnal Green for 10:00. I know the manager there and he's a follower of our cause so I want all the rivers agents to attend and tell them not to be late!'

Mousa Alami, the imam of the Halifax Road mosque, made notes of Kamal Hafeez's instructions. 'I've got all that and I'll send out the order to all six of our under-cover agents By the way what happened to that loose cannon, Kabir?'

'Bini Akrami shot him after he got getting limpy with my messenger. Anyway keep vigilant, we don't know what damage Kabir did by calling your mosque.'

The imam sent out the messages using local shops strategically located in order to drop off or pick up messages. Which are activated when the river coded undercover agents receive a simple dot on their phone which is too small and insignificant for prying eyes but big enough if one of their agents is looking for it.

(*Severn*) Tazi Emir, Bastion transferred from MI6.
(*Trent*) Kamal Malik, Foreign Office.
(*Clyde*) Mohammad, Home Office
(*Thames*) Borak, GCHQ
(Avon) Faraz, MI5
(Wye) Akrami, National Counter Terrorism Office or NaCTSO.

The six river agents received their single dots and collected their messages: *Be at The Asian Spa in Bethnal Green. bath no 7 at 10:00 tomorrow. You will be taking a steam bath. Don't be late!*

6

Max can I please have a private word before our official debriefing regarding our aborted operation?' Callum Maclean was on the phone to Max within minutes of returning to Bastion. 'Yes come up now Callum.'

'What the hell happened out there, you shouldn't be back this soon?'

'That's what I want to see you about and before you speak with Tazi as something isn't adding up with what transpired today. Firstly we got into position at either end of Shelly Street as you instructed and swapped positions with our cars after four hours of surveillance to avoid suspicion. About twenty minutes after the first changeover, a man with a limp and a beard, fitting the exact description of Kabir, came along Shelly Street from Tazi's end and obviously passed his car then Limpy went into a house about halfway down which I identified with an overgrown Hydrangea shrub.'

'The thing that's bothering me is that I heard nothing from Tazi who was told to alert me if the man who we both knew to be Mohammad Kabir, passed by his car. If I could identify Limpy from the far end of the street then so should Tazi. I texted him after and got no reply.'

'Nothing happened for ten minutes until a guy pointed a gun at my head through my car window and forced me to walk with him towards the Hydrangea house. Anyway a guy came towards us with his face covered by an umbrella and as we passed he shot my abductor through his brolly and to my utter amazement my rescuer was

Tazi! He hadn't killed the guy with his first two shots and my attacker was writhing in the gutter but Tazi didn't hesitate and put two more bullets in him from point blank range. We then decided to use my car to return to Fortress and Tazi didn't offer any further explanation for his actions and it was as if his mind was preoccupied. What I don't get is why he didn't warn me as he should have when Limpy passed his car.'

'That was what we bloody agreed to do if either of us noticed our target and another thing was how calm and prepared he was to meet me and my armed shadow before we got to the house! It all just seems strange to me so what's your take on this Max? It's not what we were used to in the SAS where at least we knew our enemy!'

'We live in strange times that don't always add up Callum and even the ex-boss of Bastion, Cordelia Fernsby, sold out to the Russians but you are right, it does seem very odd that Tazi didn't alert you. I'll see Tazi on his own and see what he has to say. I'll be in touch as we need to check out the house where Mohammad Kabir went to. I want to go myself later this afternoon with just you and Mason so please be ready to leave at 16:15. I will see Tazi now and then check in with the new lady boss.'

'Tazi come in and take a seat. Give me your take on this morning's events at Shelly Street and leave nothing out.' Tazi's story was the same as Callum's account until Limpy limped by. 'I saw Mohammad Kabir go past me and I was about to text Callum as instructed, but I saw a furtive looking guy slip out of a house and run straight past me. It was raining hard and he only had a light coat on so I watched him disappear up Knox Road which runs parallel to Shelly Street. I was just about to get back into my car when I saw the furtive guy reappearing around the corner from the block of flats end behind Callum's car. I used my binoculars and could see him stealthily moving towards the rear of Callum's car so I got my umbrella out and moved up the street. Then Callum got out of his car and I could easily see there was a guy pointing a gun at him before covering it up under his jacket. Then they both started walking, with Callum in front, towards me but the armed guy was too close behind Callum which made it look totally unnatural so I turned off the safety catch on my gun and quickened my pace while keeping my umbrella down. When we were about to pass I fired off two rounds at the armed guy who fell to the pavement and rolled towards the gutter. I fired two more shots as he was still moving….' Max interjected.

'Were either of you or Callum in any danger from this man?'

'Well he had a gun so I wasn't taking any chances. Then we left quickly in case others turned up.'

'Why didn't you call for back-up?'

'It wasn't my call as you had put Callum in charge!' An air of condescension crept into Tazir's tone.

'Okay Tazi, you may well have saved Callum's live today. That'll be all, thanks.'

Max phoned Julia Deakin to say he wanted to discuss the Shelly Street events with her but first he was going to look at the Hydrangea landmarked house with Callum Maclean and Mason Perkins. She understood and said she would see him as soon as he got back and Max and his team of two were armed and ready to move out within ten minutes.

Callum's car crept slowly into Shelly Street and stopped thirty meters past an overgrown Hydrangea bush and Mason moved in from the other end of the street and went down Knox Road stopping nonchalantly at the side gate of 148 Knox Road and was soon over the locked side access. He waited behind a garden shed, looking into what he calculated to be the target house.

Within two minutes the front door was battered in and stun and smoke grenade were thrown into the house and Callum and Max rushed into a smoke filled room, their attention momentarily diverted by breaking glass caused by Mason who came crashing in from the kitchen. As the smoke cleared the three searched each room. Max-Catt went up the stairs followed by Mason while Callum covered the ground floor. The two first floor searchers were in a back bedroom when three armed police rushed in through the front door. 'Armed police! Raise your hands and drop your weapons.' Callum did as he was told but replied 'We are Bastion agents.'
'Yeah and I'm Mickey Mouse.' Max and Mason heard the ground floor commotion and came down doing what Callum had done, dropping their guns to the bottom of the stairs. 'I am Maximus Hainsworth-Catt and I am in charge of field operations at Bastion. I could even have shot you from upstairs and not have been answerable for it so please look at our ID's and be friendly with it, there's good chaps.'

The detective inspector took Max's ID and was immediately assured and told the Bastion agents that the police had heard the sound of the stun grenades from the murder scene at the gutter just along the street. Callum thought it best to stay silent about being an eyewitness at the gutter shooting which Max thought was the right thing to do.

During the search of the house Mason found a body that they now checked over with Max looking at the soles of the corpse's trainers and noticing that one was clearly worn more than the other indicative to the wearer having a permanent limp.

'Inspector I believe this dead man is a wanted illegal immigrant by the name of Mohammad Kabir so check his DNA with the border agency and you will see that it is that same as that at the scene of three killings in Stratford which included a colleague of yours. The terror group that took him in must have killed him themselves I would think probably because he was, in my opinion, compromising this safe house. The pavement body found further along the street is another illegal import who was probably working from this not-so-safe house but that's for you to find out. It's his killers I'm interested in, the IRF terror group.'

Max searched the corpse's pockets while reminding the agitated police inspector of Bastion's overriding powers which he grudgingly accepted but which didn't stop his high level of pissed-off-ness. Max found nothing on the body as it had been cleaned. 'We are finished here, good luck inspector and if your forensics find anything of interest I want to know about it immediately right?'

'Yeah right, leave us to clean up all the shit.' The DI was evidently not happy with Bastion. 'It's what these fellows do best, don't you think Perks?' said Max with a grin. 'Most definitely sir.'

Max got back to Bastion a little after 18:15 and reluctantly declined a couple of beers with Callum and Mason as he needed to see his new boss and update her with the events of the day. Tazi's had already left the building to respond to his *period-dot* command to collect a message which he did by calling into a newsagent on the outskirts of Uxbridge. He picked up a copy of Motorbike World, paid the newsagent and then left the shop. The centre page of the magazine held his message which he read and confirmed he had understood it. He was now going to have a Turkish sauna the next morning at 10:00.

Max knocked and entered Julia Deakin's office where she was making two coffees and spoke whilst percolating. 'Okay Max-Catt, shoot! What has your team been up to today. I've seen all the intel flooding in almost on an hourly basis about Shelly Street which seems a popular place to be today with two dead bodies being discovered! Anything to do with you or your boys Max?'

Julia lent over her desk and passed her lead agent a cup of coffee. Max hadn't realised how much of a dry mouth he had and wished he was downing some real ale with his ex-SAS blades. 'Sorry Miss Deakin, I was miles away. Yes a lot went on in Shelly Street today. The bad news is that we didn't get any of the cell members who were obviously tipped off because they evacuated the house and left us one of their own, a dead Mohammad Kabir, our original quarry.' Max went on to explain what Callum and Tazi had already reported.

Julia Deakin's concurred with Max that the two stories didn't add up and they both wanted answers. Why didn't Tazi call for back up or text Callum once he'd spotted the suspect? Was it true that he saw another man running towards Callum and how did Tazi anticipate so quickly that the gunman was going to escort Callum to the safe house?

'Although I suppose Tazi did save Calum's life by shooting an armed man who must have been part of the Shelly Street cell.' Julia was considering all the angles in this bizarre chain of events.

'What do you think Max and by the way please call me Julia when staff are not around and I'd like to call you

Max or Max-Catt which is less informal. Anyway as I was saying, what's your take on it all? You must have given it some thought as clearly something stinks or they bungled an important operation with bad decision making.'

'I have spent so much time with Callum behind enemy lines where we've had to trust each other with our lives which is still the case today. This is not favouritism in any way but my money is on Maclean for not cocking up and I think the answers are firmly with Tazi Emir. My biggest question is why he pumped two more bullets into a dying man lying in the gutter who was no apparent threat to him and I will go over it in more detail with Tazi on Monday morning.'

'How have you settled into your new home?' Julia changed the subject out of the blue!

'I still have a few boxes to unpack but I'm getting there. I was supposed to go home to my family's estate tomorrow but decided that with us being on alert over the Shelly Street fiasco I'll be staying at Chiswick on standby which will give me a chance to finish unpacking and hang my clothes up.'

'I think that about wraps things up for now but make sure I get the full Shelly Street report by Tuesday at the latest. Have a pleasant weekend Max and I'll see you on Monday.'

Max left Bastion for the weekend, hopefully to finish unpacking at his new penthouse on the river at Chiswick.

7

Tazi Emir (River Severn) took two different modes of transport to get to the Bethnal Green Spa Baths, making extra sure he wasn't followed which had been drummed into him since he was a young IRF recruit.

The IRF had invested large sums of money in what they called their river agents who now, after having been privately educated to university level, were all ensconced in various UK Government departments.

Tazi was half an hour early so waited in the baths cafe, drinking Turkish tea and watching the door. Second to arrive by taxi was Kamal Malik (River Trent) who ignored Tazi for obvious reasons and went straight through to the changing area.

Tazi made himself comfortable on the two seater sofa and scanned a morning paper, reading the headlines that two males of no fixed address were shot dead in Shelly Street in Walthamstow in East London. Tazi of course was involved in one of those deaths himself and guessed the meeting in the baths had something to do with the shootings. He mused: *Bringing the whole six of us undercover river agents together is scarcer than the proverbial rocking horse shit!*

Akrami (River Wye) came soon after Kamal and also went straight into the changing room again ignoring Tazi. Faraz (River Avon) and Borak (River Thames) arrived together and went through to the changing room with Mohammad (River Clyde) being the last to arrive as intended by their staggered timing. The six had all changed into swimming trunks and went into the steam room number seven where two senior members of the IRF joined them, Kamal Hafeez from headquarters and Mousa from the Halifax Road mosque in Bradford. Hafeez's bodyguard, a mountain of a man, stood outside the steam room and it was his job to persuade any uninvited guests to use another facility. Before Kamal spoke he checked the spa entirely as the steam was nearly at its maximum and visibility was no more than two yards. Satisfied they were on their own, the IRF leader told Mousa that they must tighten security between the cell network communications and then started the meeting.

'As we have never met, it's good to see all your faces instead of just messages with river names. Khan, of course, recruited you and made your educational arrangements up to Masters degree level and through those qualifications and our government contacts you all got in where we want you in the heart of the British establishment and have achieved what was expected of you and now you can start repaying your debt to the IRF and our cause.'

'Our organisation is eclipsing the Islamic State and most of the other groups who are trying to establish our blessed faith throughout the world. Yes, we are fanatical but it's the only way to accelerate our idealism and we shall spread Islam quicker than the traditional Muslim brotherhood ever can.'

'We now have an established recruitment stream set up from a ready source of believers who are arriving on a regular basis into the UK illegally from channel crossings and in vehicles. We have a secret registration and recruitment station in Whitfield on the outskirts of Dover and a contact in the smuggling gangs. The main organisation is based in Tirana, about seventeen miles from the Adriatic, and are called Sail to Freedom and they can be found through a third party contact on the dark web so I'm giving you this sensitive information because all of you will be indirectly involved. The smuggling gangs give the illegals our Whitfield address and tell them to make their way there as soon as they land or abscond from a hotel or holding centre.'

'They are told that they'll get fed, housed, given a mobile phone as well as pocket money and will be kept safe from the UK Border Agency providing they sign up to the IRF's rules and ideology which will give us a steady but regular recruitment source helped by the fact that at least half of the illegals are devoted Muslims anyway. Our job is to then convince them that our radical ways will accelerate the establishment of our ultimate goal which is a UK Caliphate!'

'Because we lost our explosives assembly plant and laboratory in Watford in one hit which was carried out by the IRF's nemesis, Max-Catt, we plan to open smaller integrated safe houses, each having a trained explosives specialist who will be do his work remotely so our isolated armoury store will be kept secret.'

'The IRF are ready to start a new terror campaign for our extreme faith and a new jihad will begin as soon as next week and we will strike simultaneously with small cells. Each one of you must play your part in feeding us updated information as to what the British secret services are planning, what they know or any counter measures they are taking which is of vital importance to us. This now leads me on to the IRF's communications procedure that must be adhered to with immediate effect.'

‘We have lost five safehouses in the past nine months including the southern headquarters in Watford which meant the loss of our main bomb and explosives assembly plant. We are now more or less back to where we were before that infidel Max-Catt intervened and on that subject, Tazi, as you are working with him now I expect you to send me his whereabouts in advance, his work patterns and better still to let me know if he’s moved out of his safe residence at Bastion…’ Tazi interjected.

‘Can I have a private word with you after our meeting Mr. Hafeez?’

‘Yes Tazi, of course. Anyway, as I was saying, eliminating Catt is an IRF priority and a must before we start the new wave of terror we have planned. Our Taliban brothers still have a huge reward on Catt’s head and have asked us to dispose of him, a joint collaboration if you like. To that end we have hired the help of an ex-US navy seal, Brad Zimmermann, who is purportedly the best mercenary hitman available.’

‘His fees are breathtaking but he guarantees the end result and we need that as several attempts have already been made and each time we have failed. Max-Catt always seems one jump ahead but not this time but before I call Zimmermann in, I need to know where Max-Catt is staying for at least a week in total and that'll be down to you Tazi.’

‘Now for the crux of this meeting and why you were messaged through our pick up and drop off method which is evidently working well and I must emphasise the prohibition of any further phone calls to headquarters or our communications centre at the Halifax Road mosque as the latest listening devices available to Bastion and GCHQ are able to trace standard network phone connections to a two hundred yard radius after just fifty seconds of continuous airtime. They have done this in the past and most recently this has caused the evacuation of our Shelly Street cell, moreover we have lost two brothers who were shot dead and all our losses have derived from careless calls but that is stopping from this moment on as the central committee has directed that any member of the IRF found guilty of breaking the communications protocol will be executed.'

'One such call was from a new boat recruit who was trying to meet up with a friend who had come in on the same inflatable to Dover. His call was traced to Shelly Street and the cell members only just escaped thanks to our Severn agent, Tazi, before the security forces raided the house. So no ifs or buts. Do the six of you understand? No more calls! Always check your text messages for the *period dot* and only use your river codes and never use or refer to your real names. Is that clear?'

There was no reply, only six silent nods. With perspiration dripping off the end of Hafeez's nose and through the steamy fog he screamed. 'I said is that clear?' The six river spies answered in unison, sounding off a series of affirmatives. 'Okay you can all leave now but singularly and always check you are not being followed. It was even risky meeting here but I deemed it essential and worth the calculated gamble. You stay behind Tazi.' The silent giant remained on guard at the door but no one, not even the spa's staff, dared to enter number seven.

'Right Tazi or I suppose I should get used to calling you Severn, what is it you want to see me about?'

'Yesterday I had to instruct the comms in Bradford by way of a coded message addressed to Mousa for him to contact you at headquarters and you know this already. What you don't know is that I killed Salimi! I was on surveillance duty partnering a Bastion agent called

Maclean and we had separate vehicles and were at each end of Shelly Street. Mohammad Kabir passed my car and entered our safe house. Of course I recognised him but I didn't want to alert Maclean at the other end of the street before I contacted Bradford to get the cell members to evacuate. I got a text from Maclean saying he'd identified Kabir and questioned why I hadn't alerted him as it was obvious I'd seen him when he passed my car and I didn't know at that point if he'd been summoned back up to the house so I had to move quickly.

'A few minutes had passed before I saw another man moving up behind Maclean which must have been the response from my warning message. Maclean was evidently ordered out of his car at gunpoint and was obviously being taken to the house. I weighed up what was best for the IRF, a single brother dying as a martyr or me being exposed so I decided that with all the investment and time that had gone into the rivers educational programme and landing a top job at Bastion the decision was easy. I had to prove to the obviously suspicious Maclean that I was on his side by saving his life. I had to kill Salimi. No real choice and I hope I did right!'

'You did right, Severn, no question. When the heat has died down over the Shelly Street debacle, I want you to go to the Bradford mosque for a couple of days so do it next weekend when you won't be missed at Bastion and I will arrange for Brad Zimmermann to meet you there as I need you to complete a personal dossier on MaxCatt for him. Try and get as much information as possible, in particular where he's living, his movements or anything that will help Zimmermann eliminate the infidel.'

'I will sir, you can reply on me.'

'I believe I can Severn, I do believe I can!'

8

Monday morning at Bastion started pretty good for Ella Guthridge and Max as they were starting the day with some machined expresso coffee fully loaded with a good shot of caffeine. Just how Max liked to start his day. They were discussing the new workload that had arrived from Julia Deakin and their conversation stalled as a strange perceptive tension followed Callum Maclean and Tazi Emir into the general office. It wasn't quite at the elephant in the room stage but there was definitely an atmosphere and both Max and Ella sensed something wasn't right between the arrivals. Max had seen enough personal vendettas in the army and knew it had to be stopped. It was obvious this tension had built up from what had happened when they were partnered on surveillance duty at Shelly Street.

'Bring your coffee into my office please Callum.'

'Okay what's going on between you and Tazi. I know he should have alerted you when your target passed him but he did save you from certain death. If you had gone into that safe house you wouldn't have come out alive that's for sure so I think because of that we have to give him the benefit of the doubt. Patch up your differences with Tazi now and we'll keep a special eye on Mr. Emir just to be sure.'

'I guess you're right Max, you usually are. He did save my life and I am fully aware of that. Perhaps we have been spoilt always being able to trust the judgment of our SAS comrades to watch our backs.'

Callum now felt pretty bad with himself for giving Tazi a hard time last Friday. He went back into the general office where Ella was glued to her work screen and Tazi was at a spare desk reading up on what might be his next assignment. 'Tazi I don't think I thanked you properly for saving my life when you shot that terrorist. Will you shake my hand?' Tazi's face broke into a warm smile and he received the handshake with good grace.

Max called into see his boss and gave her the field report on the aborted operation at Shelly Street. 'There's nothing in there which I haven't already told and with regard to Tazi, I think we have to give him the benefit of the doubt. Yes he should have called for backup and yes he should have alerted Callum Maclean and most definitely no, he shouldn't have shot a dying man lying on the ground, but all that said, he did save the life of his colleague and a Bastion field agent at that. Callum sees it this way now and I believe he'll thank Tazi properly for saving his life at Shelly Street.' Max's tone had turned conciliatory. 'That's good news as we don't want discord within Bastion and we have enough enemies without in-fighting.'

'On another matter, I have received intel that's just arrived in from the Home office. The CIA has confirmed that a mercenary hitman, Brad Zimmermann, is on his way to the UK. He's an ex-US navy seal and he left the USA on a flight bound for Heathrow yesterday. The CIA are sure he's responsible for many top profile assassinations but are unable to get the proof required to bring him in. They believe he has been offered a lucrative contract in the UK and have sent us current pictures of him taken from his passport at the US border control at JFK airport. He's purportedly one of the best there is in the world.

Heathrow airport security monitored him through border control but as he was not wanted by any police force they had no reason to hold him but I shall circulate his details throughout our departments. His visit may not even concern Bastion but we must be on alert.'

Max nodded his concurrence while mulling over the forensic reports from Shelly Street which confirmed that Mohammad Kabir was responsible for three indiscriminate murders proven by his DNA. It was strongly believed he was shot by his own people although a police inquiry was ongoing.

Max picked up his next assignment. Bastion had collated intel from France, Turkey and Albania about a particularly active and ruthless people smuggling gang who supply boats for transport into Britain mainly along the southeast coast. It was a lucrative business at ten thousand US dollars a head per migrant. Once the Bastion operation had been authorised by Miss Deakin, it was passed down to Max's office for him to organise a logistical and operational field plan. The operation was not desperate per se, but the longer the smugglers were operating, the more untold human misery they would inflict not to mention the severe impact upon the UK's economy, housing, and social balance.

Most illegal immigrants were aware of the risk they faced crossing the English Channel but the reward, if they made it to the UK, outweighed the gamble. Such is the promise of a new life that is dangled in front of them by the smuggling gangs. The mostly, economic migrants would chance their luck from Calais in the stifling or freezing lorries they stowed away in which carried the same degree of risk as the water route, but still they came in their tens of thousands every year.

Bastion were going to send a team to Albania where intel had located the area where one of the biggest smuggling organisations were operating from. The name of the illegal company was *Sail to Freedom* which ran a substantial back street organisation and they had representatives selling boat space on the African continent and the Middle East, including Afghanistan, Syria, Iran and Albania, to name just a few countries who already had a long waiting list of takers to buy a slot on an inflatable dinghy bound for the English coast. The sellers know there is an unquenchable demand and raise the price in calmer weather.

Max-Catt was already thinking of the team he would take with him. He had a closer-to-home requirement for Jade Jackson, the fourth member of his field team and would speak with her later about the job he wanted her to do. He decided, not as punishment but for an ulterior motive, to leave Tazi Emir behind and just take his two ex-SAS men, Callum Maclean and Mason Perkins, with him to the continent. Max worked on devising a plan having researched in more detail what was known about these Albanian mafia gangs who have no conscience and even less heart. He pondered his thoughts with venom: *I will enjoy at least denting their evil business in human misery but sadly, regardless of how successful we are, I know they'll be back or other gangs will soon take their place!*

Max was told verbally by Julia Deakin that the operation code named Buttercup couldn't be acknowledged by the UK government as the action was to take place without permission of entry from a foreign sovereign state.

Firstly Max called Jade into his office to explain her solo job, based at Bastion. 'Jade I am going away very soon on a secret mission and am taking Mason and Callum with me but you are staying here as I want you to watch and photograph anything unusual about Tazi

Emir. I know he's a colleague but I feel there's something odd going on with him. It's important he doesn't suspect you are watching him and he's not shy in the art of killing someone so be very careful! I'm not saying he's guilty of anything at this stage but I just want you to find out what he's about, his background, his pre-University days and anything else you can find and I hope you realise the importance of this job.'

'Yes sir, I'm a little shocked but life in the spying game is full of surprises which I'm learning very fast.'

Okay Jade, I'll brief you later. In the meantime go to Human Resources to look at his personal record and I'll phone them now to authorise the release of his personal data. Thank you Jade.'

Next on Max's agenda was to get Callum and Mason in to explain their forthcoming mission and they both arrived in their commander's office knowing there was an operation pending.

'We have an overseas operation named Buttercup, a sweet name but that is where the nicety of it ends. It's going to be like the old SAS days when we were escaping from the Houthi rebels. I am not taking Tazi as I need to dig deeper into his background following on from your remarks Callum, I think it's worth having a closer look at him and Jade will be watching him while we are away.'

'I have only just received instructions regarding Buttercup so I'll get as much data as I can find before I put a plan together but we do know that a high percentage of illegal immigrants that do a runner before being processed join the IRF who willingly take them in. A secret location fronted as travel agents in Whitfield on the outskirts of Dover is where the IRF meet, feed, clothe and recruit them, giving them a place to live in return for signing up to the IRF and we shall soon be shutting that place down. Once I have knocked up a plan we will discuss Buttercup in greater detail which will be a covert operation which means that if we get caught we are on our own. The UK government officially will deny knowledge of the infiltration into France, Turkey and Albania and they will deny our action to avoid political ramifications. That will be all gentlemen and I don't need to remind you not to discuss Buttercup with anyone apart from the three of us.'

Tazi's perception was spot on as he felt isolated for not being asked to attend Max-Catt's operational briefing and nobody telling him what was going on. Instead he was given a desk task that resembled a glorified filing clerk and he just hoped the Shelly Street debacle hadn't brought suspicion on him. Tazi was beginning to despise Max-Catt and his team of infidels.

The undercover river spy had been given his own mission to get personal details about Max-Catt so he started by asking Max's assistant, Ella Guthridge. 'Ella, I'm making a coffee, would you like one?'

'I never say no to a coffee, thanks Tazi.' Ella also wanted to keep Mr. Emir onside as she'd been asked by Max to dig a little deeper into his background as well as Jade. 'Here you go Ella. By the way, do you know what the secret meeting was all about between Max, Callum and Mason? I feel quite left out.'

'No I can't help you there but I shouldn't worry, it happens all the time here so don't take it personally.'

'You are right of course. Somebody said Max has moved out of his personal quarters here and bought a place nearby, lucky sod. Do you know where Ella?'

'No but why do you want to know?'

‘I’m not that interested but I’m looking for a place myself and am interested in property prices around here but of course I’d have to find somebody to share the purchase.’ Tazi thought he’d better back off and not show too much interest in Max’s personal background and changed the subject. ‘Do you fancy a drink one night this week Ella?’

‘I don’t think my boyfriend would like that but I don’t mind a coffee and a chat like now though Tazi.’

Tazi was expecting a period-dot text on his phone to indicate that there was a message to pick up from the newsagent’s system that would confirm when Brad Zimmermann had arrived in Britain. This information would decide whether Tazi travelled to the Halifax Road mosque at the weekend but there were no dots so far in Tazi’s messages. He doubled checked as the isolated dot was hardly visible on the phone screen then the double agent went back to what he considered to be an unimportant filing job and he wanted Max to explain the reason for his confinement to a desk.

‘Sir I’m not happy with being left out of meetings that include my equals as I got better results all round in our training apart from the practical tests so why am I doing clerical work and being excluded from meetings? I want to know!’

‘You will be informed on matters when I decide to and let me remind you of three major issues that cost us the capture of a complete IRF cell. I know you saved Callum’s life but you didn’t alert him when our suspect target had practically bumped into your parked car. You will stay at your desk until I say and when I see an improvement in your field activities and attitude. Is that clear?’

‘Yes sir!’

9

Brad Zimmermann was court marshalled out of the US seals for beating up two US marines to within an inch of their lives. A friend of his needed them sorting out for taking his wife from him, well actually borrowing her for a few nights actually and the threesome were caught literally with their pants down. All three pairs!

The husband was informed by a mutual friend that these swinging marines were in the mess bragging of their shared triple delights and the incensed husband made enquiries and found Zimmermann and the two thousand dollars he paid him to inflict near mortal wounds on his wife's trio of lovers seemed a good investment.

Zimmermann got arrested for grievous bodily harm and did eighteen months in an Oklahoma centre of correction and while inside he was given a hundred cigarettes to straighten a fellow inmate out and soon realised he could benefit from such a lucrative business when he got out of prison but not by beating the crap out of people but using his superior expertise with a sniper rifle! Zimmermann was trained to the highest level of marksmanship as a US navy seal and regularly won monthly and regiment shooting competitions when he bothered to enter. He was the best!

Contracts came in thick and fast after his release from prison as it was the best place to market illegal skills and cost nothing in advertising.

Zimmermann soon got the name of the '*vendor of death*' together with his reputation of producing clinical work on a no-hit-no-fee basis and his reputation rapidly spread around the world and he always collected his fee. Zimmerman also had the global codename of Phonoi pronounced Fonoy after the Greek spirit of killing and murder as apart from his rifle skills he was military trained in unarmed combat killer and was a man who charged high prices but guaranteed his work.

He had arrived in the UK having negotiated a contract to eliminate a dude named Max-Catt who the hitman had been told was an elite agent with Bastion. After researching the ex-SAS man, Zimmerman demanded a fee of five hundred thousand dollars plus expenses which took the deal to nearly a million US bucks. The festering thorn in the side of the IRF was Max-Catt and the deal would be worth every cent to take their Nemesis out as he had cost them dearly in thwarted targets and the loss of the safe houses that Max had uncovered and the fact that Max was ex-SAS made the deal even sweeter for Phonoi.

Coincidently Zimmerman was offered another contract in the UK and would complete the smaller job first before dealing with Max-Catt. It was a comparatively straightforward job and based on that he planned to be with the IRF in Bradford in Yorkshire by the weekend having fitted in the bonus hit.

Although Brad Zimmermann was more than capable of researching his own targets, the US hitman called Hafeez on his encrypted line: 'Hi is that Hafeez?'
'Yes, who is that?'
'Phonoi! I'm in the UK as we speak and of course I'm in disguised from my passport. I will take three days to complete another job and will be with you on Friday night as agreed. No need to worry about accommodation for me as I always stay in five star hotels and will check in to one as soon as I've completed my first task.

I'm just checking that you are ready your end and I'm sending you my offshore bank details as my fee must be cleared in my account before I do the job and I expect my expenses to be paid within twelve hours of completing the task. I don't do quibble so make sure you have the funds for immediate transfer and I don't apologise for sounding curt, I just am although I see it as being businesslike. I will meet with you where you advised on Saturday morning at 08:00 and I'll need the personal dossier on Max-Catt so make sure you have it! Thank you. Goodbye....' Kamal Hafeez looked at his phone as if the reception had been lost but it wasn't, it was just the businesslike Phonoi.

Hafeez sent a coded single dot message to Tazi Emir who would know that it meant a visit to Bradford was on for the weekend and to take with him a dossier on Max-Catt who he hated with even more venom since Max had rebuffed him. Tazi had to get as much detail on Max as he could for the guy who would see the demise of his boss he so hated which he would do with new added effort.

Things had quietened down at Halifax Road since the shambles of Shelly Street and certainly since the communications lecture. The imam, Mousa Alami, took the afternoon prayers with an increased turnout due to all the IRF activity going on and the overspill from the loss of the safe house in Shelly Street, Mousa had almost forgotten about the new member, Sani Yosef who was actually Dani Quibi, and was there undercover for Bastion having been seconded from MI6 with the blessing of Joe Carmichael.

'Sani can you come to my office after prayers as I would like to see you.'
'Yes of course Mousa.'

With prayers over, Sani collected his shoes and went to the imam's office. 'Ah come in Sani, thank you for coming. I've been meaning to talk with you for a few days but I have, as you know, been called away. Anyway I have noticed you have a hundred per cent attendance for prayers and have demonstrated to me that you are a devout Muslim. Am I right?'

'I try to be but I must admit to wrongdoing before I came here and I have a police record!'

'What do you think of the Western ways? Would you like to see them change to our Islamic path? Perhaps Sharia as the law in our UK? Are you fed up of waiting to see changes? We can pave the way eventually for a Muslim led government here in Britain and we can make the Islamic dream a reality.'

'Wow those are powerful questions and before I answer can I ask that if I say yes to your questions, would you cancel my membership at this mosque?'

'Certainly not.' Mousa Alami balked with surprise of the question. 'Then yes I would be behind any movement to make Britain a Muslim country.'

'Would you join a modern jihad?'

'Yes, if there was one.'

'There is and it's called the IRF!'

'What do I need to do to join them? Do you run it from here?'

'No more questions Sani. Kamal Hafeez, the southern area boss, may want to interview you and he can point you in the right direction as to where you'll be best placed to serve the IRF as they are about to start a campaign and I am told they are looking for a good standard of recruit. He's coming here, to this mosque, to meet with an American next Saturday so, if you're interested, you might like to make yourself available this weekend then you can be introduced to Kamal. Well thank you for our little chat and perhaps we'll see you on the weekend to explore your ambitions further.'

‘I’ll be here, thank you Mousa.’

Mousa waited for Dani Quibi to leave his office before sending an encrypted message to Kamal Hafeez explaining that a bright member of the congregation could become an important convert for the IRF. Hafeez got the message and responded confirming that he would be coming to Bradford on Saturday to meet Phonoi and would take the opportunity meet up with the new member and interview him.

Dani Quibi left the Halifax Road mosque and returned to his attic bedsit near the centre of Bradford and phoned Joe Carmichael at MI6 who had been Dani’s handler when he was an asset in Houthi occupied South Yemen and when Dani, then code named ZX3, had to flee Aden, Joe got him a job at MI6.

‘Joe I can’t get hold of Max-Catt, my new handler, so can you send over a courier to collect a classified message. At last, after three weeks of observing me and my hundred precent attendance to prayer sessions, the imam, Mousa Alami, called me in to his office to question my faith and ask if I would join the IRF jihad. The big cheese is coming from the IRF’s headquarters to see me at the mosque on Saturday and I expect he’ll give me an interrogation and press me on my background so I hope my paper trail holds up as well as my disguise. He was the guy who instructed the burning of my arm so please make sure Max gets the message as soon as possible. Oh…I nearly forgot, I don’t know if it means anything but an American is coming to the mosque next Saturday morning to meet with Hafeez who is one of the main IRF leaders.’

‘Look, I’ll won’t stay and chat as you never know who might be listening so keep well my friend and I hope to see you soon…’. Dani broke off the call and Joe sent a courier with a sealed note to Bastion which Max signed for and was thrilled that at last Dani might be getting into the inner sanctum of the IRF and was intrigued to learn that they were entertaining an American at the weekend. *Is it a coincidence or could the Yank be Brad Zimmermann?* Max thought.

After some investigative research from the Home and Foreign Offices, Max had collated some interesting information that would dominate his plan to seek out the boat smugglers and called Callum and Mason just before they were leaving Bastion 'Sorry it's late lads but I have had some good intel from our government sources. Firstly I thought the inflatable RIB's were supplied by Germany and France but recently, owing to cooperation with the UK, these two EU countries have clamped down on the supply so the people smugglers are now sourcing most of their boats through a Turkish company called Aydin Boat Supplies who are based in the port of Mersin. So first we need to destroy the factory that supplies the smugglers, covertly of course, then move on to the smugglers themselves and the main suspected gang has a legitimate business in the Port of Durrës on the Adriatic coast.'

'The name of their company is quite sick as they call themselves *Boats to Freedom* and we shall be doing a job on them as well. Then, to complete our trilogy of destruction, it's back to Dover, well actually Whitfield which is on the outskirts of the city where the IRF take in illegal migrants and hide them from the UK border force and in return they work for the IRF as terrorists. Of course most of the migrants just want to work legally but we know the IRF take many of them in and they get radicalised into the IRF's cause.'

'If we succeed in taking out all three of our targets we will damage the inhuman slave trade beyond anything the British government has managed to achieve over the last fifty years when the first boats came across as people in Britain just don't know how long the boat people have been trying to get into these sceptered isles.'

We shall make ready with our equipment and I'll work out the logistics within forty-eight hours.' Callum's eyes lit up. 'Bloody hell Max, it'll be like the old times in the SAS. What do you reckon Mace?'

'Can't wait to see what shit our boss here is going to get us into.' Max silently chuckled. What Mason said reminded him of the unique comradeship that the special forces had back at Stirling Lines in Hereford. Max was looking forward to knocking out as much of the smuggling gangs activity as he could but he knew damn well that if all three targets were a hundred per cent successful, it would still only be a dent in the smugglers trade but he was going to enjoy being able to disrupt them for a decent period of time at least and it may just make them wonder when they might get their next attack. That thought buoyed Max up as he changed his evening plans to his two comrades for a few drinks.
'Come on you two, I'm going to stand you both a couple of beers. We'll taxi from here…!'

10

Mr. Tandi Formento had just finished a global conference which had subjected him to untold pressure and his ultimate decision could change the balance of power in the Middle East. He had made unswerving decisions and these had left him as a shadow of his former self. He flew directly from the high-octane conference to London for a respite and to rejuvenate his soul and took up an invitation to stay with his cousin in Maidenhead.

The host cousin was a wealthy merchant banker and had invited Tandi to stay at his Thames fronted house which to say it was of substantial proportions would not be, in anybody's reckoning, an overstatement.

Tandi was the chair of the Financial Action Task Force, an organisation which had been set up by countries throughout the world that were most effected by money laundering practices. Their aim was to stem the global movement of unregistered transactions and terrorist financing which was prevalent in so many countries, a watchdog for the world against corruption would be a fair analogy and it was Tandi Formento who was their driving force and instigator to place Iran on the organisation's blacklist! To say it pissed off the Iranians would be quite a mild description of their reaction especially since the imposed United Nations sanctions were biting into the Iranian economy so badly.

'Carlo what a luxurious place you have, it really is the dog's bollocks! It's taken you twenty minutes to show me over and look at this garden with the Thames at the end of it and is that your own pontoon and river cruiser?'

'Yes Tandi, would you like a trip upriver?'

'Yes that would be great. I'm so looking forward to doing nothing for a week and thank you for the invite. It's so peaceful here and I am desperate for this break'

'You sounded really stressed out when you phoned me from your conference in South Africa so what was going on there? I know you are chair with the FATF organisation and that must be stressful but you sounded bloody awful. You even put the phone down on me!'

'Yeah, I am so sorry about that. I suppose I should explain to you, my dear cousin.

'It was the night before the voting on my important proposal in which I insisted we have Iran placed on the FATF blacklist until further investigations have been completed. Whilst I was on the phone to you there was a knock on my hotel room door which I answered while still talking to you. There was nobody outside but an envelope had been slipped under the door. It had a short but menacing message: *Don't go ahead with your proposal regarding Iran! If you do there will be terminal consequences for you!*

That's when I ended our call as I chased down the corridor to the Reception but the postman of the not-so-glad tidings had gone. Yes I was frightened but it wasn't going to deter my recommendations to my fellow member delegates as I had spent the first two days at the conference persuading those who thought it was a step too far for Iran. We already have The Democratic Peoples Republic of Korea and Myanmar on the FATF's "*naughty list*" and I had some tough decisions to make at the Cape Town conference along with the other delegates. It was difficult getting some of them to agree with my recommendations but we got my proposal through unanimously in the end. The threat came to nothing and here I am with my favourite cousin and his lovely wife. Can we now change the subject as I don't want to miss another minute of relaxation here.'

Carlo Formento pushed off from his pontoon mooring and cruised to Windsor. 'See that big castle Tandi? It's the largest concentric castle in Europe and the longest ever lived in!'

'Well hark at you, the font of British historical knowledge. I suppose you know who built it as well?'

'Actually yes I do, it was William the Conqueror and it took him sixteen years to do it. It's a bit like the Elizebeth Line that runs from Bond Street to Heathrow.'

'Are you saying that Tube line took a long time to build?'

'Something like that. Come on Tandi let's moor up and go and have some lunch and I'll treat you to some British real ale as you sound as if you could do with one or two after the threat to you in Cape Town.'

Using the fake name of Charlie Faulkner, Brad Zimmerman, was nosing around some boats moored up as nobody seemed to be about in the hire shop. 'Can I help you?' A voice behind Charlie startled him at first. 'Yes, I'd like to hire a cruiser for a day so can you fix me up please?' The man in a pale blue boiler suit was still wiping his oily hands on a cloth that looked oilier than what he was wiping on it. 'I'm only the marine mechanic here but Lucy is about somewhere and has probably gone to the karzi.'

'What's a karzi, is it a place near here?'

'You're a yank right? Nah a karzi is what us Londoners call the mens room, the bog, the crapper or if you want it posh, the powder room but you Yanks call it the bathroom which makes me laugh as who shits in a bath?'

'Yeah, I get your point. Shall I wait here or go back into your shop?'

'Yeah the shop is where she works.' Charlie Faulkner returned to the shop where the lady had returned from her pee break. 'Sorry, nature called. Can I help you?'

'I hope so, can I hire a boat for this afternoon?'

'Sorry sir, the minimum hire is for three days as the cost of the changeover doesn't make it viable just for a day. So sorry!'

'Look, I'm a realtor from over the pond and I am acting for some very wealthy dudes who will pay big bucks for a place within twenty miles of London but it must be backing onto the Thames and some guy suggested I cruise the Thames from Maidenhead to Runnymede and see what's on the market. I'm on a fat finder's fee so I need to check this out so how much for three days then?'

'A thousand pounds is our minimum hire charge for three days.'

'OK miss but I'll only need it for today and a thousand pounds won't be a problem for these rich dudes and it'll go on my expenses.'

'Good, I'll show you what's available but we have a few out on loan at the moment.'

They walked back to where Charlie had met the grease monkey. 'This one's a nice little cruiser, it's only two berth but for what you want it for it would be ideal,' Lucy pointed to the '*Kingfisher*' that was moored on the company's long pontoon. 'She's ready and ready to go if you want to take her now?'

'We also need a further thousand pounds deposit but you'll get that back if there's no damage.'

'Okay I'll take the Kingfisher. What time do you close?'

'This time of year it's six o'clock but as you have paid for three days you can sleep on it tonight if you want.'

'I think I'll be finished with it by tonight but I will not be finished by six if I'm going the full distance I was recommended to go. Can I leave my car here and leave the Kingfisher moored up after you close and I can collect my deposit in the morning.'
'Sure, just post the keys into the shop's letter box but you will have to leave your car on our roadside forecourt as the gates to the boat yard will be locked and I'll give you the combination so you can let yourself out.'

All the paperwork was completed and Charlie paid in cash and said he'd be back the next day. He collected a large briefcase from his hired car and headed back to the Kingfisher where the mechanic was waiting with his filthy rag hanging from his arse pocket. 'Right then, I'll go over the running of boat for you. Have you any experience with boats.' 'Yes I was in the US navy for seven years.'

'Good, so I'll just show you the dashboard and reserve water tanks and how to empty the toilet or the bathroom as you would say and then she's all yours.' Charlie thought if he keeps the piss-take up he'll be the next visitor calling on the Thames fish. 'Okay it all good so you can leave me now.' The marine mechanic left without another word, untied the Kingfisher and threw the two mooring ropes at Charlie and the Kingfisher gracefully pulled away and turned towards Maidenhead and Windsor.

Tandi Formento enjoyed his lunch in a riverside pub and after two pints of real ale brewed upstream at Henley, Carlo took them back along the river and skilfully moored his long cruiser alongside his personal mooring. They sat for the rest of the afternoon in the sprawling garden halfway between the boat and Carlo's house discussing the implications of the Cape Town conference while watching the tranquil scene of various sized vessels chugging up and down the Thames in a never ending procession. One of the boats in the procession was the Kingfisher that stopped opposite Thames Retreat, Carlos' house.

Charlie Faulkner knocked two pegs into the ground on the pedestrian path side of the river then got back on board and he closed the curtains on the pegged side. He trained his binoculars across the river and he thought he made out Tandi Formento so he set up his camera which had state-of-the-art facial recognition and a matching verification tool which used biometrics to identify human faces. A red indication pulse started flashing as it had found a match The name below the highlighted frame was Tandi Formento, Charlie's target.

Charlie untied his mooring ropes and chugged off around the next bend in the river then moored up and got his head down for a few hours.

This break was exactly what Tandi needed after three days of mental exhaustion. His jet lag and the two pints of real ale were making him want to nod off as Carlo's wife Annabel showed Tandi to his room. 'Towels are on your bed and just call if you need anything else. I'll give you a knock at seven if you haven't already come down for dinner. You looked shattered Tandi!'

'Thanks Annabel, that's kind. Sorry for being an unsociable guest but I'm whacked and I'll see you later but can I treat you and Carlo to dinner somewhere nice?'

'I am cooking my specialty for dinner, venison pie with rice pilaf, roasted vegetables, creamed spinach and mashed potato followed by baked Alaska and I doubt you'll get that on the menu in a restaurant twenty miles outside of London and you can watch the moon twinkling on the river while you eat. How does that sound Tandi?'

‘Sounds mouthwateringly wonderful and perhaps you should open a riverside restaurant called Chez Formento.’ Both smiled at that thought as Annabel quietly closed her guest’s door.

It was getting dark when Charlie Faulkner woke up. He went to his oversized briefcase and removed a Fold AR-15 sniper rifle that is deadly accurate at four hundred metres and pretty mean at six hundred metres too which folded nicely into his briefcase giving him every bit the look of the estate agent as he claimed to be. He assembled the weapon, loaded it with five bullets and laid it on the cabin table then took a piss in the Thames before casting off for the third time in seven hours, turning the Kingfisher round and slowly moved towards Thames Retreat.

Tandi had shaved, showered and felt much better and was thinking ahead to Annabel’s sumptuous dinner as he crashed into bed and went out like the proverbial light.

It was a gentle but continuous tapping on his door that stirred him from his deep slumber and for a second Tandi didn’t know where the hell he was but a glance around the opulent bedroom soon gave him his bearings. He dressed and went to the drawing room where he received a warm smile from his cousin, Carlo. ‘I’ve fixed you an aperitif, a whisky sour is your tipple if I recall correctly Tandi? Let’s take our drinks out to the patio before we get called for dinner.’ Tandi enjoyed the subtle lighting that stretched a warm glowing beam across the Thames. ‘You sit there Tandi and hopefully the moon will show itself and you can marvel at the shimmering Thames.’

11

Charlie Faulkner had moored up again on the towpath side of the river opposite Thames Retreat in almost the same spot as before and his timing was perfect as he had full view of the three diners. Although he was pretty certain which one was the balding Tandi Formento, he made sure by checking again with his biometric camera. The device confirmed the match and the target was marked. Charlie showed all the traits of a true professional as he was about to do what he did best which was to kill!

He slid open the steamed up rectangle window of the cruiser and rested his AR15 on the window ledge before zooming in the focus on the night sights which brought the horizontal and vertical target lines into defined cross hairs while making one more small adjustment of a quarter of a degree which allowed for a slight cross breeze. This extra tolerance wasn't necessary from that range but Charlie Faulkner was the consummate professional killer! He slowly brought the sight round to bear on his target and waited until he had a clear head shot, knowing that the optimum shot would be when Tandi placed the food from his fork into his mouth.

Tandi wouldn't be moving his head while doing this action so when the fork had reloaded, Charlie Faulkner breathed in and his hand slowly felt the trigger with the squeeze imminent. He stopped! *The bloody double glazing.* He hadn't factored in the patio double glazing which could alter the trajectory of the bullet and may miss the target even though his rifle was high powered. He removed his trigger finger and wiped his brow and thought that he really had to get closer to the glazing as he knew that a good sniper wants clean air between him and his target. *'Don't cut corners Brad boy'* Professional thoughts hammered his brain until he gave way to them, another sign of a killer who is at the top of his game.

Now for the fourth time he slipped the ropes of the Kingfisher and navigated her slowly across the width of the fast flowing Thames, pulling alongside Carlo's cruiser and tethering against the side of it. Charlie secured the two vessels together side by side and hopped over onto the moored one and, with his AR15 in hand, stepped quietly onto the private jetty of Thames Retreat.

The assassin stealthily moved up the slightly rising manicured lawn and stopped quickly as the patio sliding door opened. Charlie had no cover apart from a Greek looking statue or a single bush and opted for the shrub, diving behind it. The sniper then caught the unmistakable whiff of a Havana cigar wafting on the night air whilst also getting distracted by the loud incessant croaking of frogs and had to get his concentration back to the job in hand when a women came out into the garden with two glasses and a decanter on a small tray and placed it on an outside table.

Now that the target was in the garden it alleviated the risk of a deflected shot which of course was good from the assassin's viewpoint. Charlie stood up and stealthily moved closer towards the statue which he stared at and thought it looked strange with its big balls and little dick resting on them. Charlie shook his head and fought off another ludicrous distraction and, keeping the unknown shrub between him and the after dinner drinkers, he moved back to the pontoon and hopped over Carlo's boat and climbed onto the Kingfisher. Making no sound, he went below deck and slid open the window and took aim.

He required a slight adjustment as the target was thirty metres closer from its previous setting and after making himself comfortable and steadying himself he rested the rifle barrel on the window base and brought the crosshairs to bear on his target as before but this time instead of waiting for the fork-loading, Charlie waited for Tandi Formento to sip his drink which gave the same steadying of the target's head. Charlie's finger was caressing the trigger so he took a deep breath and squeezed. The shot was well aimed and hit the unsuspecting target between the eyes and the velocity took the target and his seat backwards, both facing upwards towards the sky!

The slight putt of the silenced shot was soon lost in the air and Charlie didn't wait to see the outcome he was experienced enough to know his target was dead. He slipped his rope quickly from the anchor boat and allowed the current to take him without engine or lights downstream. Charlie started the engine about a hundred metres away. The marksman guessed river police will be used as well as the road coppers so he needed to ditch the boat quickly, knowing he wouldn't have time to take the boat back. He moored up on the path side like any other overnight stayer.

The sniper disassembled his Fold AR15, placed it back in his briefcase and jumped onto the riverbank, tossing the boat keys into the murky Thames. Charlie Faulkner looked out of place walking along the towpath at night in a suit, swinging a briefcase and sporting an umbrella but he didn't look so out of place when he reached a bridge that allowed him to get onto a main road. He called a cab easily enough and was taken to his hire car at the boat rental yard. The fare was twenty quid for a four minute journey and Charlie thought that was a rip off but not in the greater scheme of things when he considered the fee he was getting for killing Tandi!

Faulkner collected his car and drove towards London but just before the M4 motorway junction 8/9 he hit a roadblock! It was too late to turn off anywhere and he didn't fancy trying to outrun the police and he couldn't turn around anyway as there was a car too close behind him and others were backing up behind that. As a police officer approached his vehicle he knew he would have to blag it out. 'Good evening officer' he jauntily said as a torch flashed into his face and around the backseats of his hire car.

'Where have you come from and where are you going to sir.'

'I am from the USA officer and I am looking for real estate for an American client of mine. I know London and he wants me to look at some apartments in Connaught Gardens for him. I'm an estate agent in New York and I'm on a damn good finder's fee if I can find my client the right property here in the UK. I am just returning from visiting Windsor castle but took the wrong damn road and I finished up in Maidenhead where I had a pub dinner. Why? Are you taking breath tests for alcohol?'

'No sir, please step out of your car for a moment.' The briefcase and umbrella were on the passenger seat and the police officer gave another search with his beam and went to the boot asking Charlie to open it which was empty of course.

'Okay sir you may go, but remember to head east on the M4, follow the signs for Heathrow sign but don't turn off, keep to the right and it's straight on for the city.'

'Thank you officer.' The obliging copper waved Charlie Faulkner on and he headed east towards London. He pulled into an underground car park in Hammersmith, locked the car and then took the Tube to Hyde Park Corner and checked into the West End Tower hotel on Park Lane, a five star hotel that would be his home until the second UK contract had been executed.

In his eighth floor room he pulled off his fair beard and hair piece along with his light metal rimmed glasses and placed them in a bag. He fell into a luxurious king size bed $875,000 dollars better off plus nearly $50,000 in expenses and laid back thinking: *How ironic, my money being laundered in one of the countries who blacklisted my paymasters. Karma or what!*

Next morning the assassin woke up as Brad Zimmermann. He showered and watched the news on the television in his room which was all about the assignation of Tandi Formento, killed by a single sniper's bullet. The television news went on to report that the victim was on vacation in Maidenhead at the time of his murder, visiting his cousin's home. The media reported that *it was too early to say what the motive was and that the authorities believe it may have been connected to the recent Cape Town Conference where Tandi Formento was instrumental in placing Iran on the FATF blacklist.*

Zimmermann now had the proof he needed to collect the other half of his payment.

Pleased with his work, he enjoyed a five star breakfast and left the hotel and with his bag in hand he went to Hyde Park and behind a glade of bushes he set fire to the bag of evidence, turning it into smouldering ashes. Nobody nearby appeared interested as nothing is ever out of the ordinary in London. *'Bye Charlie for now, you did a good job! I'll see you again when I take out Max-Catt.*

From the floating ash in the park, a new dangerous Phoenix was rising in the shape of Mr. Bradley Zimmermann.

The folded up rifle would stay wrapped up in a spare duvet which was bagged and shelved in the double wardrobe in the hotel and would be ready for the next contract that he would know more about when he met up with his contact and paymaster, Kamal Hafeez of the IRF!

12

Julia Deakin's temporary personal assistant went through the interconnecting door of her boss' office and the Bastion director indicated for her to go back into her adjoining office with a quick hand wave. Madelyn Davies got the message and retreated back through the door, a little embarrassed that she hadn't knocked in the first place.

'Sorry Max, could you please repeat that as I had an interruption.' 'I have the draft plan of Operation Buttercup ready and I would like to go through it with you before I have my final briefing with Callum and Mason so is it okay to come up now?'
'Yes, do. I'll postpone my conference call with the Home Office right now.'

Max collected his sealed folder from Ella Guthridge who had kept it in their safe where all of the field operational documents were stored. 'I won't be long Ella and no calls while I'm with the boss please.' A smile and an affirmative nod was her answer of compliance. As Max turned to leave she got a slight whiff of his cologne that set a gymnasium of thoughts bouncing around her flirty mind. *Max-Catt you are a real handsome dude but you are unfortunately out of my league I fear!* These trivial thoughts soon passed as Ella needed to get the requisite form typed up for the logistical kit requirements given to her by her boss ready for the forthcoming Buttercup mission.

'Come in Max-Catt.' He nodded a greeting to Julia Deakin and passed over the top secret Operation Buttercup file. Starting with his planned trilogy of targets, he explained that he would work backwards from the launch area of the boats on the French beaches to the source of the boats and hopefully collate additional information of the sophisticated organisation as they got deeper into the gangs territory.

Max pointed out to Julia that his mission would take him to Turkey, Albania and France but not necessarily in that order and when he had finished explaining his draft proposals after an hour, it was necessary to stress to his boss that an unknown element that the team might confront could mean that at least eighty percent of the plan would have to be fluid.

Miss Deakin gave her approval of the operation by rubber stamping the documents and retaining a copy for herself. 'Make sure you keep me posted with updates as the government, particularly the Home Office, is very keen to get any positive news on the ever growing illegal channel crossings. Most levelheaded Britains understand how these thousands of unknowns have impacted on the social fabric of the UK as the dinghy crossers lie about their age and throw their passports and phones in to the sea before landing on British shores. Invariably they are young men travelling without their families and are in fact just economic migrants and not asylum seekers as they claim to be.

'Look after your team Max and remember that the government will disown you if you are caught. I'll need to see you again before you leave to be updated on any amendments you might have made to *Buttercup!* By the way, that's a nice aftershave you wear!' Max did a half smile as an acknowledgement to her remark and left his boss's office thinking: *Oh God, I just hope she isn't an-*

other Cordelia Fernsby with crazy sexual demands. Perish the thought. With his stamped approval tucked under his arm he returned to Ella's office.

'Ella ask Callum and Mason to be in interview room two in fifteen minutes please as I'll be there waiting for them and if you have time would you kindly bring me a strong Columbian coffee please.'

Ella gave thumbs affirmatives to both request as she was taking an incoming call. 'Good morning, is that Ella Guthridge?'

'Yes who's calling?'

'It's Joe from Big Sis, sorry Ella, MI6 to you. I can't get hold of Max as his phone is off. Is he about as I have some urgent news for him!'

'He's just got back from a meeting with the director and now he's on his way to another meeting so hang on a second.' Ella switched the call to hold and chased after her boss. 'Max, Max, I have Joe Carmichael on the line and he wants to speak to you urgently.'

'Thanks Ella, I'll take it in my office.'

'Hello Joe, what's the urgent news I was just going into an operational briefing so I can't be too long.'

'Okay I understood Max but Dani Quibi couldn't make contact with you so he asked me to pass this message on. At last the imam at the Halifax Road mosque has approached him and questioned his loyalty to the faith to sound him out he thinks. Dani is also to be interviewed by the IRF big boss this coming weekend. He will play it by ear but he'll accept any opportunity to advance into their inner circle. That's about it. Of course he'll have to keep his disguise up as he was known to several IRF members when he worked undercover with them before.'

'Brilliant news. I hope he'll be careful and they don't see his scarred arm.'

'He's a shrewd guy, is Dani and I keep wanting to call him by his old code name of ZX3. Okay Max I know you want to get off so we'll speak soon.' That put a spring in Max's step as he walked to interview room number two.

'Okay you two toe rags, let's go over Operation Buttercup. I am going to change the original plan slightly and we are going to start on the French coast along the stretch of beaches of the Pas de Calais. Our intel section who work closely with the Foreign Office has given us some vital information. Therefore our first port of call, excuse the pun, will be Wimereux which is twenty miles south of Calais. We will be travelling covertly in two RIB's piloted by the SBS as it has to be a covert landing to enable us to get our weapons and ordnance into France. The British government pay France millions of pounds to help prevent the inflatables from launching but unfortunately they adopt the '*Nelson*' philosophy in that they see no ships! Everybody knows that French hearts aren't in it and they don't want the illegals in their country any more than we do. We are fighting against the antiquated European Convention of Human rights that was established in 1950 to protect genuine asylum seekers but unfortunately most that make the channel crossings are male economic migrants of working age.'

'So we are charged with secretly finding out what is going on at the source end and if we can throw the odd spanner in their sordid works then so much the better, eh chaps? We will be dropped off the French coast twelve miles out by a Royal Navy patrol boat and then taken by RIB with a silenced motor, courtesy of our SBS friends. We will reach the selected beach in scuba suits for stealth and pull the waterproof float assisted containers that will carry our kit including a change of clothes.'

'Now for the latest intel received! We are to go to a cafe-bar at 214-16 Rue du Moulin in the coastal town of Wimereux and rendezvous with an unknown woman. She will approach as she wants to stay anonymous but she has a cast iron motive to help. She will identify us by our three phones being placed in the centre of our table together. Once she has given us the information, we will never see her again!' There were no questions from Callum or Mason so the briefing concluded.

Max went back to Julia's office and said his team would be leaving in three hours to drive down Dover to board a Royal Navy patrol vessel. Max mentioned to her to keep Tazi busy with non-sensitive desk work. Miss Deakin wished him well and reminded him to send back regular communications. She leaned into Max and on tiptoe gave him a peck on his cheek much to Max-Catt's surprise: 'Take care Maximus, your country needs you!' Max was a little taken aback so just smiled a nervous farewell.

At 19:20 the team of three Bastion agents boarded a fast navy patrol boat. The captain had been advised of his cargo and the RIB's were stowed in readiness with two SBS blades arranged to drop them a hundred metres from the shore. They left Dover immediately and were speeding across the English Channel at full speed and it was dusk when they came into sight of the Normandy coastal lights but they were still in international waters for diplomatic reasons as they watched their RIB being lowered down the port side of the navy vessel. A rope ladder was unrolled by the two SBS blades who climbed into the inflatables to start the engines which amazed Max at how quiet they were.

The three were invited by one of the SBS blades to get into the RIB's, two in one and one in the other along with their kit. He then threw the holding rope to a naval rating that allowed the small four man inflatables to chug quietly away, leaving the navy boat to stay on station to await the SBS blade's return.

The RIB's cut engines a hundred metres out from the shoreline and Max looked towards the beach through his night vision binoculars and focused in on an unbelievable sight. There were five massive inflatable boats, about thirty metres apart, half in the sea and half on the beach obviously waiting for the incoming tide to float them.

The inflatables were going to be filled no doubt with illegal immigrants and these hopeful passengers were arriving from a kettled crowd further up the beach and marshalled by the smuggling gang. Men in five orderly lines left the massed group after being checked and given a lifejacket each and made their way to a designated inflatable.

'Bloody hell lads, we've caught them red handed as five large RIB's are being filled and launched on this very beach. Okay, we are going to stop them but we don't want to engage in a firefight with the smugglers or harm the passengers. We'll have to move quickly as well as once the tide is in they'll be loaded and gone with their next stop being Blighty! We'll swim to the front of the boats and simultaneously fire our automatic rifles with the silencers off and aim above the boat occupants heads which should create panic and scatter the passengers and give us time to puncture the five inflatables while making sure we don't hit the occupants.

'It will require SAS precision and once we have shot the rubber boats we'll lob an incendiary grenade into each one. By that time the illegals would have scarpered back up the beach to safety and most likely we will have armed smugglers chasing us down the beach which is when we scuba out to the safety of the dark sea and we'll swing in a large arc to that outcrop of rocks over there,' Max pointed, although in the dark, to the rocky

part of the beach. 'We need to go now so if there are no questions let's do it!

The scuba clad Bastion agents slipped over the sides of the RIB's and the two float assisted containers were lowered into the sea. Mason pulled the lighter, smaller box with both Max and Callum pulling the much larger waterproof container as the RIB's returned to the RN patrol boat leaving the three Bastion men on their own!

The team of three were now on their own and knew what had to be done with teamwork and total coordination. They were ten metres from the rubber boats and were easily guided by at least twenty mobile phones currently in use when the signal from Max started the fireworks!

13

The noise from three none-silenced automatic pistols that fired orange tracers into the sky above the boats caused the anticipated panic as the would be passengers scrambled over each other in a panic. The Bastion men now turned their aim to the soft reinforced rubber bellies of the inflatables and very soon the five vessels had deflated and dipping below the waves. With the five boats now evacuated, grenades were lobbed into each of the deflating vessels as the smugglers armed guard arrived but was stopped in his tracks as the incendiaries boomed, breaking the silence of the night!

The five blazing boats resembled a Nordic Viking pyre and the sight, although spectacular, illuminated the bobbing frogmen with the illegals running up the beach and passing the armed gang members running towards their burning assets.

It was time for Max and his team to swim round to the cover of the rocks and the three were soon gone under the breaking waves with their containers trailing behind them just above the surface of the sea. Max's team moved up the beach to the outcrop as they couldn't hang around the beach as French security would soon be flooding the area to investigate the five bonfires.

They changed into smart casual clothes, looking like pretty normal civilians at a first glance but underneath the clothes were three killing machines, made that way by the UK Special Forces.

After disposing of their scuba suits, they carried their ordnance and essential kit boxes along the beach and buried them above the high tide line, marking the site by coordinates and a stone pattern. From a map of the town, they located the Le Papillon café which was just off the promenade and a little way inland up a low gradient hill.

Le Papillon looked to be a well-used seaside bar and was warm and lively when the team entered. Max, who was a fluent French speaker, knew the excited chatter was all about the five burning immigrant boats and it was generally thought to be the work of a rival gang doing a bit of tit-for-tat reprisal. Max smiled at the various conspiracy theories that he heard and would have loved to tell them what really happened!

They found a table in a corner and placed their three phones close to each other in the middle of it as a secret signal for their contact. Callum went to get three beers and after the second round of Biere la Trotteuse, a favourite Normandy ale, any tension they had felt earlier evaporated. Max was thinking that they could easily forget what they came for, especially when an accordion squeezed into life and the atmosphere took on all the hallmarks of a good old session with the Trotteuse going down well.

A tap on Mason's shoulder broke the ambience when a young French woman asked if Mason had the time. She had seen the stack of mobiles on the table and guessed it was a signal. Max took his phone and read the time in perfect French then the woman spoke. 'After two minutes leave the cafe and turn right and after fifty metres cross the road and you will see my red Citroen parked there. Please get into it, the doors will be unlocked and I'll be in the driver's seat.' Then she was gone out of the café and the team drank the dregs of their beer, abandoning any chance of a drinking session.

Max got in the front and the other two slid into the back of the little red Citroën. 'I know you men are here from the UK to help stop the boats, I have spoken with your Foreign Office and I will tell you that I was once part of that despicable inhuman business, which is driven by poverty, along with my younger brother who joined me in that heartless organisation.

'Wimereux is the end of the evil chain that starts in Albania. I had to get out by making the excuse that I had cancer and was dying but I would have done anything to get out. If you saw or knew what I have seen, what misery is caused, it would sicken you! Reluctantly they let me go and promised they would kill Maurice, my kid brother, if I went to the police. Maurice is only seventeen and they used him as a message runner and he also helped in the boat warehouse. They killed him one night and said he had disobeyed their strict secrecy laws and they threatened that they would sell me to one of their contacts in Africa if I didn't keep my mouth forever shut. I am in hiding and have changed my appearance but I can't leave Wimereux as I have a sick mother to look after.

'I do see the two main partners from time to time as they work with '*Boats to Freedom*' and they live here in Wimereux. Their names are Charles Petaume and Didier Laterne and this is their address,' The anonymous women handed Max a note. 'I followed them home from a restaurant one night for the sole purpose of bringing them to justice and revenge for my baby brother. You must go now and please be careful as these are dangerous men and they have a large gang here in this town.

They usually launch inflatables from the next bay with lots of spotters looking out for police although it's well known the law only carry out perfunctory searches along the coast here as the French authorities really don't want the illegals any more than your country does. When I sent a note to the British Embassy in Paris saying I had information about one of the main gangs I thought I was wasting my time but here you are, but now please go!' The three men thanked whoever she was and the Citroen was soon driving back up the hill to who knows where.

A taxi took the three agents to 177 Rue de la Republique, the address given to them by the mystery woman and the home of Monsieurs Petaume and Laterne, an expensive detached house, in an expensive district, with a long front garden, a typical Norman steep, a dark grey tiled roof with garret windows. The three SAS trained team knew how to get people out of fortified houses and they assumed this one would be secured and alarmed with up to the minute surveillance equipment so Mason was ready with the stun and smoke grenades in his jacket pocket.

Max ordered Mason to go round the back of the house and on two minutes synchronised from zero, he was to smash a rear window and lob in the stun grenade then wait five seconds before lobbing in the smoke grenade. Max would do exactly the same at the same time at the front of the house.

The raid was on and counting down. They only had handguns so surprise would be essential. A back window was punched in with a stone by Mason whereas the front window was smashed with a round concrete ball used to stop cars from driving onto the front lawn which was a very handy window buster. The shock waves from the stun grenades were felt around the house with curtain ends flapping outside the windows, blown outwards from the blasts. Callum didn't wait and with his Smith and Wesson in hand, he dived through the front window where he found three men and a woman rolling on the floor coughing violently and holding their throats from inhaling the smoke.

Callum fired his silenced Smith and Wesson into the ceiling just to let them know what fire power was around the groggy house occupants. Max climbed through the window but didn't make anywhere near as dramatic an entrance as Callum's spectacular dive and roll entrance. The woman was persuaded to stop screaming and the men were soon secured with reinforced tape by Mason and Callum while Max's Glock kept overall control. 'Which one of you three are not Petaume or Laterne and anybody giving the wrong answer will be shot.' 'I'm not either of them. I'm Franke Radisson.' Glares from the obvious targets were tangible. 'Okay Franke, I believe you. The piss soaking through you trousers speaks volumes in corroborating your answer. Take Franke and the little lady upstairs and secure them in separate bedrooms SAS style.'

'You two other lads are coming with us and I suppose the keys to that lovely car parked outside are somewhere around here so let's go!' The gagged and taped captives were pushed out of the front door with one being bundled into the boot with the other sitting between Callum and Mason. Max went into the garage and using the fob on the car key ring, the double roller door went up. Max came out and put a garden spade in the passenger side. Then Max drove towards the nearby seafront. 'How did you get cut Callum, you're bleeding badly?'
'Fucking glass window.'
'Serves you right for diving in like Rambo. You've watched too many bloody movies mate.'

'Fuck off Sir.' Mason and Max couldn't help bursting into fits of laughter. The gagged man must have thought he was having a nightmare but for his ears which were still on fire from the stun grenades. 'Okay pal, where is the cove you launch the boats from? Don't fuck with us or I promise you hard times ahead,' As expected there was total silence and a dagger stare!

'Okay my friends, we will see. By the way, nod if you are Laterne.' Max was looking for an answer in the rear view mirror but no answer came, only a death stare from the prisoner. Max returned his gaze to the road and drove towards the coast, leaving the built up area behind. They were on the coastal road and stopped at a car park overlooking the Channel. 'Callum check the tide tables for Wimereux.' Maclean knew not to question his boss who he had unwavering trust in but he mentally questioned such an obscure command. 'High tide is in one hour,'
'Oh good, not long to wait then.' This added to Callum's perplexity. The trunk occupant was taken out and the procession walked down the concrete steps to the beach. It was dark but the slight moonlight silhouetted the jutting rocks casting an even darker shadow than the open area of the beach. Max chose an inlet in the rocks where the moon couldn't penetrate.

'Okay Callum dig me a hole, I want to play in the sand.' Max threw the garden spade to him. Callum looked at Mason who was equally dumfounded but he dug for ten minutes and cut out a hole as instructed by Max to a depth of a metre. Mason gave Callum a break and went down another half metre. 'I'll say when to stop,' Still nothing was said to the snarling captives. 'That'll do Mason, great job you two. You remind me of the infamous Burke and Hare digging duo! Callum cut their gags please but leave their hands tied.' Max turned to the secured Frenchmen.

‘Okay I want to know where the building is that is used to store the inflatable boats before they are taken out for launching. I know it’s a reception centre to hide the illegals when a launch is imminent so please tell me!’ French expletives and threats spewed from both the captive men but as Max spoke fluent French he understood the obscenities. ‘You must have a death wish as we are a large Albanian run gang that is spread across Europe. You are dead men walking so let us go or this will be your last chance not to write your own death warrants!’ The secured captive screamed the threat into the face of Max-Catt and was soon gagged again.

‘Okay big mouth, get in!’ Nothing happened. Max took him to the deep hole and lifted him as if he was nothing more than a bag of spuds and started to lower down either Petaume or Laterne, it didn’t matter much which one it was but, whichever one of them it was, he forced his foot against the top of the hole resisting Max’s lowering action. Before Mason could move to push the captive’s legs forward, Max kicked the side of his knee resulting in a muffled wail from whoever he was. Once he was bent over in agony, Max kicked both his legs from under him and he dropped like a lead weight into the hole that was almost tailor made.

Mason then filled the void back up with sand. Now all the parties present knew what was occurring. Mason was making a neat finish patting down the sand around whoever’s neck as if playing sandcastles and enjoying a flashback to his childhood on the beach. He hadn’t quite finished when a bright light bounced up and down above them. ‘Everybody get to the rocks, between those two big ones and Callum assist the other bloke and lay flat but keep hold of him and if he raises his head smack him.’

Max's last job was to rapidly build up a pile of sand around the protruding head of the partially buried man then he had to dive for the cover of the two rocks just as a police patrol car drove by. It stopped and the man standing in the back of the police pickup swung his halogen search light around and lit up the mound of sand that shielded the partially buried man. The policeman seemed to be studying the bank of sand and it seemed ages while the torch beamed on the sand cover but eventually, he guessed it was just another abandoned sandcastle built with no imagination. The patrol was so close that the group could hear what the man working the searchlight said. 'Come on Jacque, the tide will be in any minute so it's time we got off the beach!' The pickup turned in a wide circle and Max watched the bright red rear lights disappear up the beach access road ramp and was gone.

'Right where were we? You two know my questions so I won't ask them again.' Callum cut the gags once more so the captives could answer. Max kicked away his quickly made sand cover to expose the head of the man buried on the beach who was still cussing away. Mason pointed out that the sea was only twenty metres away and the tide was coming in fast but still no co-operation from the captives with the shouts from whoever and his mate intensifying so Max got Callum to gag both again as he didn't want rescuers coming to see who was in trouble. 'Look you two if you decide to tell me what I want to know just shake your heads but if you shake them and start shouting again you'll both get a heavy slap for your trouble.

No heads shook and five more minutes passed and with it another ten more metres of sea encroachment and loss of beach. The man in the hole shook his head. Mason removed his gag. 'Yes speak.' 'We'll give you a million euros to let us go!'

'Just the answers!' Silence resumed and the gag went back on the sand compacted man. Ten more slow minutes passed and the sea was now lapping at the chin of the head!

You had better be quick with your answers.' Max thought *this guy is a damn stubborn dude or a very good poker player.* The answer came quickly after that but not from the compacted man. Nature had the only answer and decided what it was to be for him!

14

One of those freak waves that happen every so often which catches sunbathers out or vehicles when the driver is so sure of his tide tables only to see one metre of water lapping around his car. It does happen!

Just such a freak wave caught Max-Catt out which came in so quickly that it covered the hole and the team's knees and the big problem for the man buried in the hole was that the tide didn't recede as it might and the hole wouldn't be exposed again until the tide went out again which of course be too late for the hole occupant which was irony as he drowned in the stretch of water where he had been paid to send so many hundreds of illegal migrants to their watery deaths!

Max and his team were not unduly concerned for the scumbag's life. In fact they themselves had to get off the sand and scramble over the two big rocks that earlier had shielded them from the patrol to get further up the beach as the incoming tide was chasing them up to the sea wall.

They drove to the next bay and collected their containers of weapons. 'Now I want your name or you'll join your friend in the sea. I'm fed up with your games and as your pal can't answer nor will you in a few more moments. Ever heard of Russian roulette? I will ask you questions with one bullet in the chamber of my gun and if you don't answer I will shoot until the bullet gets fired so let's play!' Max emptied his gun of all the bullets except one and aimed it at the surviving Frenchman's head. 'What's your name?'

'Laterne, it's Laterne.'

'Where is the warehouse with all the boats.'

'Look I can get you two million euros and you can just walk away with no questions asked!'

'That wasn't my question, last chance.' Max pressed the barrel of the Glock19 to Laterne's temple.'

'Don't shoot. Please! It's not far from here, only a kilometre up this coast road and it's just an ordinary house but you can't miss it as there's a fishing boat at the side of it but at the back is the boat warehouse where we assemble and install the outboard motors. We have a series of spotters all along the coast when a launch is to take place who let's know if there are any police patrols about.'

'We have a choice of eight or nine launch areas. Look I've told you everything now release me please! I have children. By the way tell me how you found us, was it that snitch Pierre Laporte?'

'Who is in charge? Max ignored Laterne's question.

'Me and Charles Petaume were but as he's now dead it's only me at this end of the chain. Please let me go I've told you everything.'

'Nearly finished. How many illegal immigrants have you smuggled over to the UK in the last year?'

'It must be around three thousand or so but of course a third don't make it but that's not our problem as so many jump aboard the boats and will not wait for the next launch as they know that once they are in the boats we don't have time to get them off.'

'Mason pull over into that side street.

'Okay Laterne out you get.' Max-Catt took the Smith and Wesson from Callum and, walking behind the people smuggler, he put a bullet through the scumbag's head at point blank and exited through his left eye with a wake of compressed spouting blood!

Max didn't feel good about killing a defenceless man but he quickly assessed what damage Laterne could continue to do with endless human suffering and gave it no more thought.
Callum helped Max to roll the dead smuggler under a bush and when he was found the police would know of Laterne's illegal activities and put it down to a reprisal from a rival gang.

The team drove away to a gas station in town and bought two five litre petrol cans and three bottles of beer. They drank the beer and set off back the way they came along the coast road, looking for a house on the left with a boat outside. Mason saw the boat and guessed that it was the landmark they were looking for.

'There Max, slow down, on your left there's a boat. Let me out and I'll check around the back of the house.' Max pulled up a little way past the house and, like Mason, he guessed that must be the place. Perkins slipped out of the car and inched around the side of the fishing boat and from there he could see a huge building with security lighting and camera on each corner. *This must be the place.* Mason guessed. He went back to the car and declared his discovery. 'You stay here Callum.

Mason led Max past the boat and quietly pointed out the building. 'Okay Mason, I can see it's well illuminated and probably alarmed too but I'm not really bothered about the cameras as what we are going to do to the building should destroy any footage but put your scarf over your face as a precaution though. We will need to short circuit the electrics to kill the alarm as we don't want to disturb anybody do we?'

As Mason was the electric expert he soon found the supply box feeding the building. Two minutes later they were in darkness and used their torches to lead the way around the big warehouse. The side door was impregnable but when they went to the back of the building they saw a possible entry point, the goods in and out access. The building had hangar type doors for deliveries with a wide access onto a road that ran parallel to the coast.

Max had wondered how the gang had got ten metre RIB's delivered with little access from the front and now had his answer! Built into the hangar doors was a pedestrian door but after ten minutes of brute force they had made no impression on it.

'I could kick myself for not brining any tools with us to break in and we would need ladders to get to the high windows.'
'Well we can't stay here all night talking about it. Was there anything in the garage in Wimereux where those two tossers lived?'
'That's a point, there were machine tools and disc cutters and other stuff.
'Alright, it's only a few miles away so let's go back.'
They drove into the driveway of the house on Rue de la Republique and while Max opened the double garage, Mason took water to the two taped up captives they had left in the house then escorted the woman to a toilet/
'You have two minutes in there and after that I'm coming in for you.'
He repeated the same to the guy who was thinking Mason had come back to kill them which loosened his bowels, helping him do his business without any effort.

Max had collected an electric disc cutter, a crowbar, two five litre containers of petrol and a fifty metre extension cable from the garage together with a big halogen lamp and loaded all the kit into the car and sat in silence with Callum waiting for Mason. 'Where the fuck have you been?' Max impatiently barked at Mason. 'I those poor bastards to the loo and gave them water p. Oh and nicked a good quality bottle of Scotch.' Nothing more was said and Max just shook his head.

Back at the warehouse, Max drove round the back
right up to the building. 'Okay sparks, go and get us power, here's the extension, it's fifty metres so there will be enough length from the box.'

Max held the drum while Mason uncoiled the cable to the box on the other side of the warehouse and Max was soon cutting through the steel with Callum holding a coat over his boss to muffle the sound which took longer than Max expected but eventually he was able, with the help of the crowbar, to prize the steal flap outwards allowing Callum to reach in and feel for the fire escape bar on the door.. Two good tugs downwards released the door outwards and the three were in. They were amazed with what the halogen lamp revealed as Max arched the lamp left then right, up and down.

The warehouse was massive and there must have been thirty or more deflated RIB's in crates with '*Aidin Boat Supplies Mersin Turkey'* printed on the sides. Max videoed the manufacturer's name while Mason and Callum supplied the lighting. At the far end of the warehouse were hundreds of plastic wrapped orange life jackets stacked on shelves on five levels across the whole width of the end wall. The torches then arced over the nearside wall where scores of crated outboard motors were stacked three high along the thirty metre length of the building and bundles of paddles in their hundreds filled the high shelves above the intruders. After five minutes of filming everything the ex-SAS men went into action!

15

They carried the petrol containers into the warehouse. 'Okay boys you have been trained to be top saboteurs by using the best techniques so you know where to pour the petrol for optimum effect. Do your job. Go to it!' Max was unscrewing his petrol can when Mason shouted. 'Max there's a 150 litre petrol tank here but I don't know if it's full but we'll soon see.'

'Brilliant, okay soak the selected areas you two and pass me your empty containers and I'll refill for you. Go!'

The tank wasn't completely full but they got another forty litres out of it and a barrel of oil was used to coat the timber crated RIB's with the thick oily substance to feed the bonfire. 'Okay guys you know how petrol explodes and how quickly the fumes will surround us so pass me those three empty beer bottles I asked you to keep from the gas station.'

Max had kept back half a can of petrol and filled the bottles with petrol soaked rags. 'Okay you two, take the car twenty paces down the road and leave the door open for me. Go!' The guys understood Max's reason and ran to the car. Max went back into the warehouse and lobbed the first Molotov cocktail to the back of the warehouse towards the stacked wooden pallets and as expected there was an immediate 'whoosh' and massive flames snaked up the pallets attacking the plastic covered life jackets. The whole end wall was now a sheet of flames moving rapidly outwards and coming down the side walls from both ends. Max helped the hungry flames by hurling his other two homemade Molotov's halfway along either side wall. He couldn't stay to see how the flames developed as they covered the warehouse at an incredible speed and devoured everything in their path almost instantly. Max left the door open so the draft fanned in oxygen to increase the flames potency and fuelled the inferno with more life.

Max ran to the car and was half in it as Callum screeched away They turned right and right again back on to the main coast road towards the town.

As they entered Wimereux they pulled over to make way for the three racing fire engines coming towards them. Max stepped out of the car and looked back at an orange glow in the distance and after hopping back in he smugly announced 'drive to Calais, we are going home lads.'

The team only had to wait an hour for the first P&O sailing to Dover. They parked their borrowed car just outside the port and walked to the booking kiosk passing several illegals migrants just hanging around and waiting for an opportunity to smuggle onto a a lorry heading for the UK.

The three split up with Max going through on his own with Callum and Mason leaving it another half hour before buying their tickets just as an added precaution. They all met back up in the cafe at the port terminal and waited for the call for foot passengers to embark the ferry. As it was only a one and a half hour crossing they were soon in the international waters of the English Channel. Then, in near perfect French, Max made a call 'I would like to report there are two human traffickers in an upstairs room at 177 Rue de La Rèpublique, Wimereux!'

16

Jade Jackson phoned through to the head of the Bastion Human Resources department. ‘Is that Mrs. Janice Turnbull?’

‘Yes, who’s speaking?’

‘It’s Jade Jackson, I’m in Field Operational Services, my boss is Max-Catt.’

‘Yes, I do remember your initial interview with me. Well how can I help you Jade?’

‘May I see you?’

‘Of course, give me half hour and come to my office.’

Jade wondered what she would find but didn’t expect any devious activities on Tazi’s Bastion records but that was not what she was looking for.

‘Come in Jade and take a seat. It’s nice to see that you have settled in and I trust you don’t have any work issues.’

‘No, not at all. Did my boss call you and request to give me access to the personal record of Mr. Tazi Emir, one of our field team?’

‘Better than that, Miss Julia Deakin the overall boss of us all, cleared that access. I guessed that was what you had come for. You can’t take the file out of here but if you would like to take it to that comfy sofa you can read it and make notes if you wish. Can I get you a coffee? Some of the personal records are long and mostly boring, well they are if you have read as many CV’s as I have.’

‘Thank you Mrs. Turnbull and I’d love a coffee, white with no sugar if I may.’

Jade was interested in two elements of Tazi’s profile. How was his educational journey financed, starting with one of the best private boys schools in the UK then on to Cambridge University to gain a Master’s degree? The other question that Jade wanted an answer to was his private address which she phone photoed and made notes of his schooling. ‘Thank you Mrs. Turnbull, here’s the file back, you have been most helpful.’

‘You’re welcome Jade,’

Back at the field operations general office, Tazi was working on second rate non-sensitive stuff that Max had set him. He was aware the atmosphere had frosted since the Shelly Street debacle and realised he had to keep his head down and be a good boy until things settled and got back to normal. He had the feeling of being watched which was correct as Jade was on his case!

‘Good morning Tazi, are you getting lonely without the rest of the team being here. Bet you wished you were on the operation with them don’t you? Do you happen to know where they are or what they are doing?’

‘They tell me fuck all. That’s what.’

‘Wow Tazi, I’m sorry, I didn’t realise you were so upset.’

‘It’s not your fault Jade as it seems they have cut you out of the field work as well, but I bet you haven’t got this shit for work! Cross checking hundreds of addresses for one they are trying to match. It’s like being back at school.’

Jade used this as an opening to her investigation. ‘You seem a clever bloke Tazi, what school did you go to?’

‘Winchester.’

‘What the Winchester private school?

‘Yes.’

‘Wow your parents must be mega rich.’

‘Not really, I had a scholarship sponsor from a private firm.’ Tazi realised that he perhaps shouldn’t mention his educational benefactors and closed the conversation which Jade had already perceived from his baulking reaction so retreated from the enquiry and quickly changed the subject. ‘Listen, don’t let it get you down, I’m sure it’ll be fine soon. Max-Catt is a bit pissy because he failed to round up the members of the IRF cell in Shelly Street. Would it cheer you up if you came to a show on at the West End this Saturday which I have a couple of tickets for?’

‘Thanks Jade, that’s thoughtful but take a friend as I’m going to my parents at the weekend.’

‘No bother, as long as you don’t mope around as you mustn’t let it get to you. Take my number in case you change your mind, but do it before ten o’clock tonight otherwise I’ll have to sort out a friend. Where do your parents live?’ ‘Just outside Bradford, a place called Bingley.’

‘Ah that’s where you get the Yorkshire accent from.’

‘Is it that obvious.’

‘Eee-by-gumm, not at all.’ They both laughed at Jades’ friendly teasing which seemed to relaxed Tazi. ‘Okay Tazi, remember if you change your mind give me a call by tonight and keep your chin up.’

‘Thanks for the chat Jade, you seem to be the only friendly person I know in our section.’

Jade went back to Julia Deakin’s office, knocked and entered upon invitation. ‘Can I have a quick word Miss Deakin?’

‘Yes of course, take a seat. What can I do for you?’

‘Can you get me the parent’s address of Tazi Emir. They live in Bingley near Bradford? As you know I’m checking out his background more thoroughly for Max-Catt.'

'Sure, I'll get our intel department on to it right now and it should only take a few minutes. I'll call you when it comes through. By the way Max-Catt will be back this morning from Buttercup.'

'That's good and was the mission successful?'

'No idea Jade but I do hope so.' Jade Jackson left the Bastion director's office and returned to her investigative duties, pleased that her good looking boss and her colleagues were retuning today.

It was 14:10 when two things happened at the same time in Bastion. Firstly Jade got a call from Miss Deakin. 'Jade the address for Mr. and Mrs. Mohammad Emir is 27 Colliery Terrace, Bingley, Yorkshire. Sorry, I have to go as Max-Catt has just walked through the door.' Which was the other thing that happened at that moment.

'Max, welcome home.' His boss didn't ask him and instead she percolated two coffees. 'I believe yours is 8 strength Columbian blend if I remember correctly.'

'Spot on Julia, thanks.' They both sat down and Max apologised for his unkempt appearance, unshaven and probably not smelling too sweet either. 'Well what have you got for me, did you exercise your zero status?'

'Accidentally yes. I buried a man up to his neck in sand on a beach and a bigger than expected wave brought the incoming tide over him quicker than I anticipated. We all got wet on that beach and it served the callous tosser right as he had sent thousands to the same watery end in overcrowded inflatables. So yes I used it to good effect!'

'I of course will require a detailed written report for Operation Buttercup but give me the verbal gist now.'

‘Okay, in short. From our own intel I met an anonymous lady in the Papillon café in Wimereux in Normandy, a coastal town south of Calais and she gave me the names of the two bosses who ran the launching end of the boat trade.

We got it out of one of the bosses the whereabouts of their warehouse which we razed it to the ground and in doing so we destroyed scores of inflatables, hundreds of lifejackets and over a hundred outboard engines. I also got the names of the boat and engine suppliers who are somewhere in Turkey but the source of the chain points to Albania which is where we are going next, tomorrow in fact after a good night’s sleep.’

‘Bloody good show! The Home Secretary will be relieved we are at least doing something against the inhuman operations purveyed by despicable people.’

‘It’s more than we hoped for Julia, it’s a bloody great vacuum we’ve made and we aren’t finished yet. We’ve cut a big tail off the smuggling beast and tomorrow I’m going for the head of the monster.’

‘I can see they have riled you so I’ll let you go and shower which will please both of us.’ Max smiled as he passed back the empty mug to Julia. ‘I’ll see you with my plan before we depart which will probably carry over to this weekend so I’ll let you know my logistical requirements for both Albania and Turkey and we’ll wrap the two up together hopefully. I’m going to shower and sort out the second and third phases of Buttercup. As I said I’ll see you before we go with the same team who came to France with me.’

Jade missed seeing Max, she was already on her way to Kings Cross railway station having booked her ticket online for Bingley in Yorkshire and took with her a worrying thought. *What if Tazi changes his mind and travels back to see his parents in Bingley and sees me!*

She put the thought behind her as she settled down for her journey northwards to Yorkshire.

Max was feeling better thanks to an extended shower and as the water cascading over him it reminded him of the unexpected wave that erased the human sandcastle on the Normandy coat but he brushed the thought away, deciding it was the Frenchman's own stubbornness that had caused his demise.

After cleaning himself up, Max-Catt met up with Callum and Mason. 'We're off again boys early tomorrow morning so no piss up tonight, not like our SAS pre-operational custom back at Stirling Lines! This isn't the SAS now my luvly boys!

We fly on an easyJet flight to Tirana in Albania and will make our way to Durrës on the Adriatic coast to a company in the port called '*Boats to Freedom*'. What sick bastards calling it that. We shall be doing more or less what we did in Normandy but we will be in very dangerous territory there, not like friendly France. The British consul in Tirana has been informed about us and arrangements for us to covertly pick up three fire arms has been arranged. Then after the Albanian mission we shall fly directly on to Turkey where we will acquire our demolition products and living off the land so to speak. No questions? Good! Get some rest tonight and be ready at the underground car park by 05:30 tomorrow.

Eat and sleep well. I'm off home to do the same.'

17

Tazi was in deep thought for most of the day on how to get information on Max-Catt for the Yankee hitman who he was supposed to be meeting this coming Saturday. The best idea he had was to leave work early that afternoon on the pretence of feeling rough. So he hired a car and went to the junction where the public road joined the private access road to Bastion and there he waited for his boss's black Porsche to show up to, hopefully, follow Max to his home.

'I'm feeling like shit Ella, it must be those Thai prawns I had last night, I need the loo every five minutes so if anyone asks for me would you tell them I've gone home.'

'Sure Tazi, no problem but don't forget to sign off.'

Tazi left and took a taxi to a hire car office on the edge of Uxbridge where he picked up a nondescript rental car and returned to the Bastion road junction where he waited for Max-Catt. Playing the spy, he sported a pair of sunglasses and a baseball cap and, with hands tapping on the steering wheel, he playing the waiting game.

Max-Catt was an hour later than usual as he had the first phase of Buttercup to type out in more explanatory detail than his verbal synopsis given earlier to Julia Deakin which actually meant that Tazi needn't have left his office early. After over two hours of waiting, Tazi heard the unmistakable throbbing of a 911 Porsche approaching the junction. The black beast arrived and, surprisingly to Tazi, Max took the road to join the M4 motorway, turning east towards London. Tazi followed Max all the way to the Chiswick flyover but due to the volume of traffic he got pushed back to five cars behind the Porsche and was now facing a red traffic light which he accelerated through just in time to see the Porsche turn off.

Tazi followed the Porsche to an area off the main road towards the river front and saw it turning into private mews development with double gates.

Tazi parked up and waited until another car entered the private cobbled drive and while the resident waited for the electric gates to open, Tazi smartly approached the driver's side of the waiting Jaguar. 'Excuse me do you know Maximus Hainsworth-Catt's address, I have a parcel for him to sign for?' With apparent distain and a facial look as if he had a piece of shit under his nose, the Jaguar driver uttered one word 'No' and drove through the gates.

It was twenty minutes before an elderly lady came out of the pedestrian gate at the side of the vehicle access so Tazi asked her the same question as he had the snooty Jag man. The lady smelled of lavender and wore thick make-up that was accentuated by the deepest red lipstick that had unfortunately missed her lips on the left side of her face which gave her a grotesque smile, but at least she was helpful. 'Look at the buzzer list darling, the name will be on there.'

'Thank you madam.' The lady shuffled off and Tazi entered the private grounds before the gate closed. He went, as suggested by the elderly lady, to the buzzer box but there were no names indicated on it, only coded numbers to press for each apartment.

Damn it. I've come all this bloody way' but there on the top line of the buzz box was the concierge's number. Tazi pressed in the four numbers and a robotic echoed voice spoke. 'Ponting-Forsyth here, can I help you?'

'Yes, Royal Mail here, I have a special delivery for a Mr. Hainsworth-Catt and it needs signing for. I only have the address of these apartments as Thames Mews, Strand on the Green but no apartment number. I need to write it on the parcel or he'll have to collect from the Chiswick Post and Sorting Office.'

'Wait a moment, he's one of the new builds, a penthouse I think and only just moved in.... here we are Penthouse 3. Is that all?'

'Yes thanks.' The poshly named caretaker had gone but that mattered little to Tazi who finally had Max-Catt's address and was pleased with his initiative that afternoon! *Not bad for a glorified filing clerk* Tazi Emir sarcastically thought!

18

Next morning the same three Bastion agents left for Luton Airport in a Bastion car. The chauffeur had changed from the original one who never spoke but the new chauffeur, Fred, was totally different and kept up a conversation to the edge of distraction but even so it was better than his mute predecessor.

When the team reached Tirana they went through the airport security separately. Callum was pulled to one side and searched, having the contents of his backpack unceremoniously dumped out onto an inspection table. The overweight, sweating inspector fumbled through Callum's clothes and personal items but then he grew bored and gestured to Callum to pack up his belongings and go.

The team took a beaten up taxi to the port of Durrëss taking the SH2 motorway and the fare amount to 4,000 LEK which sounds a lot but you wouldn't get three beers with that amount in London.

'Can you stop please' Max requested from the back seat of the cab which shared with Mason and a spare wheel. They were in Rrashbull, a suburb town of Durrëss. Max paid the driver by card which made him swear under his breath and through the black teeth that were still hanging on somehow to his diseased gums.

'Why are we getting out here Max?'
'Don't look, just take my word for it. There is a silver BMW back there on the other side of the road that has

followed us from the airport. It stopped when we did so it's too much of a coincidence and it's still watching us. Don't look round. We are going to act normal but not lead him to our target in the port. So we'll check into a hotel here and take a twin and single room. We'll go to the dining area and have lunch after we've checked in. We will not be staying here tonight however but I'll explain more over lunch. Come on.'

They crossed the road and asked a passerby where the nearest hotel was and because they were dropped off near the SH2 highway there were a few to choose from but it really didn't matter as they would not be staying. They selected the Orange Blossom hotel which boasted four stars emblazoned over the revolving entrance. They checked in and made sure they got their passports returned to them and Max paid for the three of them for one night.

A young boy escorted them to a cafe style dining room where mostly truck drivers were eating in groups.

They ordered from the menu of the day as there was not an *a-la-Carte* to choose from. 'I'm having stew and dumpling.' Mason advised his pals.

'Yes Mason, good choice, I'll join you as that's all that's on offer.' Which caused Max and his teammates to laugh.

'Right, discreetly look to see who comes in after us for lunch and make a mental note. You've both been trained in the SAS and now in Bastion on facial recollection so use those skills. That reminds me why haven't either of you realised that we have been followed since the airport. Don't slack while on an operation. Where were your observational skills?'

Callum and Mason realised they were on the butt end of a bollocking from their boss but both realised he was absolutely right. Mistakes made are usually costly.

‘Anyway forget about that now but remember it for the future. Be aware and observe your surroundings. Right! As I was saying, Mason you take the stairs to the first floor and wait then by the lift. Callum and I will give you time to get to the lift and then we’ll come up in the lift. We will press the button for the first floor and the lift will stop there to collect you. We will get out to join you but will allow the lift to ascend to the fourth floor. The watchers will be observing this and will think that we are going up to our rooms on the forth. I’m banking on that they will have slipped the receptionist some dosh to find out our room numbers and will give it a few minutes before following us up but instead we will go along the first floor corridor to the far stairs on the other side of reception where the dining hall is. Then we’ll go through to the kitchen and out through the rear door which I checked out on a trip to the loo so if you’ve finished your rhubarb and lumpy custard Mason, let’s go.

Mason pressed the lift button on the first level and the door slid open, Max and Callum came out and Max reset the lift for level four. The lift door slid closed and continued its journey to the fourth level. The team ran to the end of the first floor and took the service stairs down to the reception area. Max assumed and hoped the followers were calling the lift back and had checked earlier that there was no line of sight from the lobby area where the lifts were to the dining room entrance.

The walked into the diner where they had eaten earlier and went through a swing door into the food preparation area. ‘Good morning everybody.’ The surprised kitchen workers looked perplexed as the three well-built foreigners passed them and headed for the back door that accessed the staff car park.

The three jogged across the road and turned two corners before they thought it safe to stop. The bar on the last corner was the chosen place to plan their next move. They ordered three coffees and Max opened the Google maps app on his phone which displayed a street plan of Durrëss. After a few sips of coffee and deep concentration, Max made a decision. 'Okay, we will leave Rrashbull separately. There are plenty of shops here to buy disguises so get a hat, change the colour of your jacket and ditch any recognisable attire you are currently wearing and Mason get those gaudy green trousers off for a start. Make your own way to the town of Durrëss and we will meet in two hours from now on the junction of Rruga Curila and Rruga Kertüsa.' Max pointed out the location on his phone map.

'Callum, you take a taxi, I'll take a bus and Mason you take a train. Most young people here speak English so you shouldn't need your translator app. We'll leave here separately and I'll see you both in Durrëss in two hours. Mason you will need to walk to the railway station so you set off first. Go now.'

19

They are not in their rooms, they have vanished Alteo!' Roan was calling his boss in Tirana.

'What do you mean they have vanished?'

'We watched them go into the lift apart from one of them who took the stairs and they went to the fourth floor so we naturally assumed they were going to their rooms after they had eaten in the diner. We got into their rooms but they hadn't been used.'

'You had better find them or Gjoni will make us pay. They have destroyed our launch and holding facilities in France and that has put our operations back six months at least. We also run the risk of losing the business to French gangs who will muscle in on the vacuum that we have left and, needless to say, Gjoni will be furious!'

'We only know what happened to our Calais partners as one of the gang, Claude Dupont, phoned me yesterday who was in the Wimereux residence of his two bosses, Laterne and Petaune, our partners, when three raiders attacked the house. He and an administration clerk, Charlotte, were tied up and the raiders took the two bosses away with them and went on to destroy all our supplies in the warehouse. They killed Laterne who was found under a bush on the coast road but Petaume is still missing and we presume he's dead. Claude Dupont and the women were questioned by police and then released which is when Claude phoned me with the news. He told me that we had lost five, ten metre RIB's that were to take nearly two hundred heads to

Dover. The attackers came from the sea and after they had destroyed all the RIB's rioting on the beach broke out as the migrants demanded their ten grand payments back.'

'Claude said he heard one of the three saying they are off to Albania next to do the same so I immediately put surveillance on the closest airport and identified the three British men arriving and you have gone and fucking lost them! Make your way to our warehouse now and keep your team alert and call me if to spot them. You might be in big shit with Gjoni who you know doesn't accept failure or mistakes!'

'I have told you Alteo, the three just vanished. They didn't see us, I swear so please put in a good word for me!' Roan was begging as he knew what Gjoni was capable of and liked to make examples of people who failed him.'

'I will have a word for you but finding them again will help you greatly. When you get to the warehouse make sure Durrëss is secured by our men and guarded around the clock and when you get there with your team make sure the three don't leave Albania. We have to make an example of them and if you fail this simple task you had better leave Albania as you know what Gjoni will do to you!'

Roan, who was in charge of a team of six, knew Alteo was deadly serious about the consequences of failure and understood that he must up his performance so catching the Bastion team would go a long way to full redemption with Gjoni!

20

Callum was sporting a black trilby hat and blazer and looked like something out of a fifties movie. He continuously checked his watch as he was the first to arrive at the port destination which was not surprising as he had come by taxi to the rendezvous point which was where two main artery roads in the port town intersected. Callum was relieved that he had the meeting place right which was confirmed when Max appeared around a corner with only his height and build giving his identity away. Max was also now in new attire comprising of jeans, a bomber jacket with a simulated-fur collar and a baseball cap. 'No Mason yet?' Max enquired but he didn't get an answer from Callum.

A further twenty minutes passed before Mason joined them when they then intentionally found a sleazy bar. Callum ordered three Birra Pejas, a local beer, and took them to the corner table that his teammates were sitting at. The bar was busy and it was a very rough dive which was just what Max was looking for.
'We appear to have lost the followers.' Max remarked as he sipped his beer which was surprisingly good or was it his nervous thirst he mused.

'How did those guys know we were coming by plane to Tirana airport as no one knew of our plan apart from us three and Julia Deakin?' Mason asked that very good question. Max-Catt took another mouthful of beer before giving his take on the matter. 'I was considering that myself whilst on a bus which, incidentally, had little or no suspension. I think the leak it must have come from either the woman or the guy we left tied up in the mansion. I do remember we wrongfully discussed destroying the suppliers at Durrëss and as soon as the police freed them either he or she must have phoned their associates here which I'm guessing is where the tipoff came from!'

'Damn! You are probably right Mason and it was me who stupidly discussed our plans in front of them. Bollocks! So the gang here will be on high alert.'

'At least we know that they know Max but don't beat yourself up as we can't predict every eventuality.'

Callum's reasoning didn't appear to improve Max's frustration or make him feel any better for his schoolboy error.

'Well it's too late worrying about what we should have done as we are here now and have a job to do!' Max countered his negativity. 'We are all ex-SAS and we were taught to make the best of what we have and to complete the task ahead of us so that, my bonny lads, is precisely what we are going to do. The fact that the Albanian gang are aware we are here in Albania will, I am sure, make them have many guards in force at the supply warehouse so it isn't going to be a walk in the park raid like Normandy was that's for sure.'

'I used my no-limit credit card in four different cash points on my way here and I have about five grand in Stirling so I'm going to ask around this joint if anyone wants to earn some really big dosh in exchange for their help. There looks like there might be plenty of takers here for some criminal activity and easy money don't you think boys?' A grin came over the faces of the three teammates as Max surveyed the bar's dodgy clientele and picked out his first target.

'Hi, do you speak English?'

'A little.'

'Do you know anyone in this bar who can get me a handgun for cash?' Max came straight out with it as he figured that was the best way in such seedy surroundings. 'I don't but I know someone who can.' The guy made a call. 'Someone is coming here to see you in ten minutes!' Max bought the guy a drink and gave him the equivalent of fifty quid for his trouble then went back to his table and waited for the fixer. After fifteen minutes a bearded man entered the bar and Max watched him go to the man who had fixed up the meeting and was now standing at the bar who pointed over to Max and his team.

'You need a gun?' He spoke good English. Max was drawn to a massive scar that ran the complete length of his right cheek. 'Yes, I need three actually with thirty rounds of ammunition, a twenty five metre length of blasting fuse and can you also get me two stun and two smoke grenades and finally a tranquilliser rifle with six knockout darts for an average human.'

'I can get the fuse cord, the guns and stun grenades immediately but it'll take me a couple of hours to get you a stun rifle which I'll need to source from the Tirana zoo but as I have contacts in most places that will not be a problem. I can't get the smoke grenades though, well not for several days. If what I can get for you is okay I'll be back here by 17:00 this evening so are you able to wait?'

'That'll do fine and how much?'

'Five grand but only in pounds sterling.'

'Okay..er, what is your name?'

'You don't need to know me as it's safer not to. Give me two grand deposit and the rest when you get the gear!'

'No, I'll give you a grand now and the rest on receipt of the goods.' The anonymous fixer grunted an acceptance and told Max to be outside the bar at 17:00 then left without another word.

'You two stay around here and, if I'm not back in time to meet Mr. Fixit at 17:00, check the goods and pay him the balance with this four grand,' Max handed Callum the packet of money. 'I should be back but I want to check out the importing warehouse along the main quay at the docks but I'll try and be back in time to collect the required goods.'

Max then went to a local car hire firm and booked a pickup for the minimum hire of twenty four hours which he drove to the port of Durrëss and parked in the car park. He asked a dock worker where the 'Boats to Freedom' warehouse was and was pointed in the direction to it which Max soon found as it towered over the others nearby.

As Max had thought there were men milling around trying desperately not to look like guards but Max could tell from experience if someone was wearing a concealed shoulder holster and these dudes most definitely were.

Max didn't want to draw attention to himself so he walked by, not stopping or staring, and went to some nearby storage containers stacked along the waterfront almost opposite the target factory and from between two containers took several photos and a two minute video of the building and its surroundings as he was looking for a way to get into the building. He assumed, unlike in France, that the building would have guards at night especially after being tipped off but hopefully not as many as there were now.

Max-Catt got back to the bar in time for the weapon and cash exchange. Mr. Anonymous Fixer took them to his car which had somebody in the passenger seat which put Max on edge as he wondered who this other guy was as there had been no mention of anyone else being involved. Mr. Fixer gestured for Max to get into his vehicle and he introduced the passenger to Max. 'This is the guy who has supplied the rifle with the tranquilliser darts and he insisted on meeting you to give you instructions on how to use it. He's a qualified anaesthetist so listen to what he tells you.'

The anaesthetist started speaking in good English to Max. 'People who are ignorant of the facts use these weapons indiscriminately are likely to kill somebody.'

'We use a dosage to tranquilise a lion for example that weighs much more than a human so it takes a lot more serum to knock it out. That is why police don't use darts to bring down crime suspects as it's too risky and only experts can calculate safe doses with accuracy and you also have to know the health of the intended target such as heart conditions and so on so I have supplied you with enough serum on each dart to knock out an average human male weighing about 190 pounds.'

'I have made six darts of imobilon, a mixture of etorphine and phenothiazine which produces methotrimeprazine. The darts have hollow needles that enter the skin of the target and upon impact the phial of tranquillising liquid is automatically injected into the body. Why am I here to warn you? Because there are too many imponderables to make a certain calculation without weighing the victim and knowing their general health. Too much could kill, too little will not tranquilise enough so I have provided an average dosage and, just so you know, any target with a weak heart will most likely die through shock trauma to the body. Also do not shoot two darts in any one target which is my strictest advice!'

Max-Catt thanked him for coming and said he would heed his warnings and that he actually had had some training with a dart rifle during his army training.

Mr. Fixer wanted to get on and passed a box to Max containing a bundle of blast fuse on top of which were three handguns and two stun grenades, a little smaller in size than Max was used to but they would suffice as a distraction and momentary shock.

Mr. Fixer produced the 9mm ammunition separately from the glove compartment of his car and handed Max a small but powerful looking air rifle with a plastic case containing six tranquilliser darts. Max inspected the purchases and was satisfied he had the genuine articles. The guns didn't have silencers but that wasn't too much of a problem as Max and his team didn't plan on hanging around after their raid. Max nodded his approval and told Callum to hand the money to Mr. Fixit who flicked through the notes, counting them quickly.

The three SAS trained colleagues waited until the purveyor of illicit goods and his passenger had gone out of sight before they handled their new weapons, the Russian military issued Makarov PM handgun, not as smooth as Max's Glock19 but better than nothing. They put the box of goodies and rifle into the pickup and drove nearer to the port.

At 17:30 Roan reported that they hadn't found the three saboteurs even though they'd combed all the bars in town. Alteo instructed Roan to take his men to Durrëss and help with the protection of their warehouse. Roan knew the building well enough and was pleased Alteo seemed to be in better spirits than he had been earlier.

It was starting to rain and neither Max nor his two passengers didn't want to leave the comfort and shelter of the truck. Callum's long mackintosh that he'd bought to change his appearance didn't look so stupid now. In the hired pickup they pulled into a large gas station and purchased four, five litre containers and filled them with petrol. Max noticed the gas station also sold gas bottles so he purchased three of them as well for good measure as there was plenty of storage space in the Ford Ranger.

They waited in the hired pickup with the rain pattering on the cab roof beating out an incessant echoing drumbeat which was getting heavier and which didn't look like it was going to ease up anytime soon.

They decided to wait until it was dark before they checked out the warehouse and if phase two of Buttercup ran as smoothly as Normandy had they'd be delighted but there was not much chance of that happening with so many goons on guard!

21

The black nimbostratus clouds gave them an earlier start than they could have envisaged for the time of year and of course they needed the dark, which was their only friend outside their team. Callum and Mason followed a hundred paces behind Max to break the threesome look to those who might be interested in a trio of blokes.

Max disappeared into the line of shipping containers where he knew there was a good observational vantage point between four stacked containers. He placed three wooden pallets, that were in abundance on the quay-side, into the chosen space and this hide was completed by the time his team of two arrived and between them they rigged up a bright yellow tarpaulin to cover them against the now heavy rain.

Mason parked the pickup behind the long line of containers and out of sight of the line of warehouses across the wide dockside supply road. Each of the team had their Makarov PM handguns safely in their pockets and carried ten rounds of 9mm ammunition each.

As Max was the best marksman, he would use the compressed air rifle and they were soon ready to embark on the difficult raid with Max scanning the huge warehouse that was at least four times the size of the Normandy one.

The Bastion leader knelt down and looked over the pallets through his SAS standard night binoculars. He could see two men huddled under what shelter they could get from a lean-to that served to keep the heavy rain off a line of stacked rubbish bins and they didn't look too interested in actually guarding the place. 'I can't see the left side or the rear of the building so I'm going to check these out. You two wait in the pickup and I will not be long.' Max, with binoculars in hand, moved off.

Skirting the left side of the building, Max saw a single guard sheltering from the heavy rain in the recess of the front entrance which he assumed to be the reception office. The Bastion man moved towards a smaller neighbouring warehouse and climbed the boundary fence, dropping down the other side in one swinging movement.

Max made his way to the boundary fence with the Boats to Freedom factory and as there were stacked oil drums along the boundary fence that was where he made for. Max didn't need his binoculars from this range and saw two more uninterested and bedraggled guards sheltering under a broken umbrella and wishing they were at home with one trying desperately to light a damp cigarette which was stubbornly refusing to ignite so the guard threw it away in temper.

Max crept to the end of the drums but still couldn't see behind the long warehouse so he retraced his steps to the far side of the smaller warehouse and climbed its rear fence where he came across an access road that split the second row of industrial units. He moved back once more towards the target building but this time from the rear and from there he had only a fence between him and the rear of the target warehouse. Max-

Catt hoisted himself up and saw a solitary guard smoking a cigarette and pressing himself against the leeward side of the warehouse where he had more shelter than the other guards but even so it was not great but he did have the benefit of the height of the building giving him shelter from the rain that was driving in from the sea blown by the prevailing Adriatic winds.

Max counted six guards in total plus any that might be inside the warehouse. Although he only paid for six stun darts the anaesthetist had supplied eight so he had two extra. Max-Catt had already worked out his plan of attack which he couldn't have done accurately until he knew how many outside guards there were. He then made his way back the same way he had come and got into the Ford Ranger, drenched through.

'Okay here's the plan. There are six outside guards and I recognise one of them from the gang that followed us to the hotel. I'm going out again and you can come with me Mason as we're going to tranquillise all six of the outside guards and you follow up with your pistol if the darts don't have the effects they should. I've thought about this and there's really no other way. Callum, you lucky bugger, can wait in the dry.'

'We shouldn't be long. Come on Mase, let's get the job done. Give me a hundred paces start then follow me across the road. I'll be climbing over the next unit's front fence and we'll move around the far side.' Max left the truck and took the rifle with the eight boxed darts in his pocket.

No one at the *Boats to Freedom* building was interested in a madman out in the storm crossing the road a hundred metres away and the same lack of interest was shown in Mason who duly followed in Max's footsteps.

Max waited for Mason and once he'd caught up he followed Max over the rear fence of the empty building. Max made a step out of a few concrete blocks and carefully peeped over the fence eighty metres from the single guard at the rear of the target warehouse.

Slowly Max loaded a single dart into the air rifle and took aim at the guard's neck as the rest of his body was covered in thick clothing so options were scarce. Max breathed out and made sure the sight crosses were in line and slowly squeezed the trigger. There was no noise, only a slight thud as the dart left the rifle and entered the target's neck exactly where Max was aiming for. The man shouted and held his neck but didn't know what had happened to him and nobody apart from the two Bastion agents heard him shout. He staggered about for five seconds then dropped to his knees and keeled over sideways. The sedation had worked as the expert said it would for a man of average body mass.

'Max a guy has just come out of the building with a tray of coffees and I can see he's given two to the men sheltering by the rubbish bins and he's on his way to the back of the building to where I assume you and Mason are.'
'We'll be ready for him Cal, thanks for the tip-off.'

A man carrying an umbrella came round the corner as Callum had warned and his umbrella was almost horizontal in order to protect his face and the tray of coffees from the heavy driving rain and wind that was gusting at 30 miles an hour. The coffee carrier hadn't noticed his fallen colleague until he raised his umbrella which was the first chance Max had to fire a dart at him which wasn't such a good shot as he was a moving target and the dart hit the target in his right cheek and the shock and pain from this propelled the tray of hot drinks to the ground.

Max reloaded his third dart and the two Bastion raiders moved to the left corner of the building and Max could see the two side guards still huddled, clasping their coffees as hand warmers against the bitter wind. Max waited for the nearest one to take a sip before he darted him in the neck and Mason was there with his Russian handgun as back up. Just like the last tranquillised victim, this recipient screamed and held his neck while the other coffee drinker stared in utter astonishment at his gyrating pal. As the tranquilliser kicked in the drugged victim fell unconscious to the ground and the second guard stood over his recumbent pal wondering what the hell was wrong with him.

Any thoughts for his colleague instantly vanished as he clasped his own neck then staggered several paces and collapsed. Mason was busy cleaning up by taping and gagging the four fallen victims while Max went to the front corner of the building and darted the guard at the entrance. Mason had taken the umbrella and coffee tray round to where the side guards were that they had passed first and they thought it was their coffee coming to them as promised. Mason raised the umbrella exposing the Makarov PM barrel aiming at them then he made the first one gag and tape his pal and then he secured the second guard. All that was left now for Mason to do was to secure the guard at the entrance and then they could concentrate on the unknown quantity inside!

Mason went through to the Reception holding the umbrella as if he was the returning coffee carrier and was shocked at the warehouse's massive size. There were two guards sitting at a table chatting who were not particularly interested in their surroundings and they must have felt pretty relaxed as there were six armed colleagues outside protecting the building or so they thought. Mason approached as he did with the outside side guards by dropping his umbrella and, to the surprise of the two men at the table, it wasn't their coffee carrying mate.

After taping and gagging the last two *Boats to Freedom* employees, Max and Mason moved the two internal guards outside and called Callum who brought the Ford Ranger to the entrance when they took all of the kit from the pickup inside the warehouse then the two inside Albanians were put in the back of the truck. 'Take these two and collect the others from both sides of the warehouse and take them to the back. Are they all secured and gagged?'

'Yes, all bound up nice and tight.'

'Okay secure them in back to back pairs and then return to me in the warehouse and be quick as we have the devil's work to do and we might have visitors very soon.'

Max did a quick look around the massive warehouse and, like the one in Normandy, it was full of crated inflatables stamped with *Aydyn Boat Supplies, Port of Mersin, Turkey.* There were also hundreds of life jackets and outboard motors almost like for like as Normandy except ten times more of everything including 48-hour survival packs which were not stored in Normandy. Max thought that it must be a separate enterprise to sell these kits at ridiculous prices to the illegal immigrants who were not allowed to take their own food on the Channel crossing. Max got to work and had already uncoiled the blast fuse to almost half the length of the building and had positioned the three switched on gas cylinders with a metre of gas tube fitted to each one around the warehouse and by the time Max had completed these tasks the other agents had returned.

'It's still pissing down out there.' Callum shook himself off as he hadn't dodged the rain this time.

'Where are the petrol cans' Callum asked.

'Over there and we should empty one at the back of these gas bottles and run a trail down the sides of the building but can't stay around to watch the pyrotechnics like we did in Normandy as these gas cylinders will explode causing a nasty firebomb.'

The building was laced with petrol on both sides and for good measure Max placed two large bundles of wooden paddles against the gas bottles and all three agents retreated to the front door. Max lit the blast fuse and watched it travel through the building then sent Callum and Mason to the pickup to ready the vehicle. The fuse hissed its way along the sparkling line then it caught the vapours of the petrol fumes halfway along to its gas cylinder targets which started separate fires that licked up to where the crated inflatables were stacked almost to the eaves of the building.

Max wanted to see the fuse reach its end before he retreated to the pickup and he could smell the gas that was being pumped out of the gas canisters and knew that at any moment the gas fumes mixing with the petrol vapour and oxygen would send an explosion in all directions. Max was mindful of this and crouched behind the Reception wall. Whoosh! A blast took the door off next to where the Bastion leader was crouching, throwing him backwards before he was able to struggle back onto his feet. Looking over his shoulder he could see a wall of flames and black spiralling smoke that found its way to the roof trusses before retuning down the walls. The place went up twice as quickly as Normandy had which was down to the inclusion of the gas cylinders. Max got in the back seat of the pickup and Mason screeched away from the burning warehouse.

They all heard an ear piercing explosion that shook their Ford Ranger even though it was now a hundred metres away.

They headed back to the car hire centre to return the Ford Ranger and then took a taxi to a hotel at Tirana airport where they booked a flight to Adana Sakirpasa airport which was ninety three kilometres from the port of Mersin.

The next flight was not until mid-morning the next day so they booked an evening meal at the hotel but first a deserved beer in the bar was in order. All the TV channels had one breaking news story about a massive explosions and fire at the port of Durrëss with the footage showing a skeleton of a building that was once the Boats to Freedom company. It was also reported that several security guards were bound and gagged and left in a safe area away from the fire.

The three ex-SAS men looked at each other, chinked their glasses and smiled! 'Two down and one to go lads. Cheers.'

22

Jade Jackson left the railway station at Bingley and took one of the many cabs waiting in a line to collect the offloading train's passengers who squeezed out of the station looking to be collected or to walk to their Bingley destination and in Jade's case it was one of the queuing cabs. In her briefcase were copies of Tazi Emir's personal file with all the important bits of information she thought she might need which had been authorised by Max-Catt and endorsed by Julia Deakin, the Bastion director.

Max-Catt had good reason to suspect one of his new field agents that was borne out by the strange behaviour he had shown at the Shelly Street debacle so Max wanted to know more about this secretive loner and had charged Jade Jackson with the task. Jade had joined Max's new field team from MI6, the same as Tazi Emir but from different MI6 departments. She felt a little uneasy spying on a colleague but knew that guilt shouldn't interfere with her work and she must uncover the facts about him. It was Jade's turn at the taxi queue and she was asked where she wanted to go to which she replied 27 Colliery Terrace in Bingley, the family home of Tazi Emir, as she slid into the back of the taxi.

'Here we are miss, that's fifteen pounds please. If you want a return taxi phone Bradford and Bingley cabs or any other licensed company. I am not touting for business but it's just that there are some very bad men in Bradford so please be careful.'

‘The grooming and raping gangs have been active for years and the police do jack-shit about them. They are frightened of being dubbed racist which is a load of bol.., sorry miss. Anyway some pretend to be genuine taxi firms but are dirty bastards and force sex on vulnerable girls or sell younger girls to other gangs of men which is sadly rife in Bradford and Rotherham. I am a second generation Pakistani and a good Muslim and they are getting good Muslims and Islam a bad name. There are so many gangs grooming young white teenage girls and they should all be put in prison and the keys thrown away. I don’t want to frighten you miss but only use taxis that have Hackney Carriage licence numbers issued by the council.’

Jade had heard of such gangs and thanked the driver for his concerned advice, promised that she would heed his warning and gave the considerate driver a good tip and a wave.

She didn’t actually call at 27 Colliery Terrace, Tazi’s parents home but instead knocked at the next door neighbour’s house to get some general information about Tazi.

‘Good afternoon, I’m from the Bingley Herald, a free weekly newspaper, and we are running a column each week on Bingley residents that have excelled in their work or at school. Tazi Emir’s name has been put forward and as a neighbour I wondered if you might give us a little bit of insight into his background, where he went to school, did he play with your children that sort of thing so can you help?’

‘No sorry, we only moved in two years ago and don’t know our neighbours that well.’

The door closed in Jade's face but undeterred she went to the other side of 27 and tried there asking the same as she had at 25 but with better results. 'Yes Tazi was a very clever boy, a good Muslim and never missed his prayers. He was a bit of an introvert but always polite. I understand he got his education fully paid for by a Middle Eastern oil company from Iran I think. His mother is a friend of mine and she's always proudly talking of Tazi's scholarship being completely funded including his boarding costs and all his university costs too. He went to Cambridge university you know. Yes, he is a clever and a very lucky boy. He went to the Halifax Road mosque in Bradford to pray and a mosque worker would collect him when his father was working shifts but that was when he was younger and living at home. It would be lovely to see him in the paper so what edition of the Herald will Tazi be in?'

'We don't know yet as we will have to get his parents' permission first but thank you so much for the information.' Jade had recorded the full conversation.

Now it was time to meet the parents. 'Good afternoon, are to Mrs. Emir?'

'No, I'm Miss Emir, what do you want?'

'Sorry I should have identified myself. I'm Jackie Spence from the Bingley Herald. We are running a column on Bingley residents that have achieved above average grades or done well at their careers, that sort of thing. We are working with the local comprehensive schools as a promotion for the area and your son, Tazi, has had his name put forward as a successful Bingley boy.'

'He's not my son he's my brother's son! I'm Tazi's aunt and his parents are not home at the moment.'

'Perhaps then you might tell me some interesting bits about Tazi's background.'

'Well, I suppose you'd better come in then.' Jade followed Miss Emir into the house.

'What is it you wish to know?'
'Anything, what he was like as a boy, what his achievements are, you know, a bit of his background would help.' Jade had her notebook and pen out and pretended to scribble snippets of the conversation down but all the while she was recording it.

'I'm sorry for assuming you were Tazi's mother, I hope I didn't offend you.'
No, not at all. My name is Myingeeta Emir and the reason I'm living at my brother and sister-in-law's house is that my father threw me out for not going to Islamabad and agreeing to an arranged marriage. I was only fifteen at the time and besides that I don't even like men, any men! Not in a romantic way anyway as I'm a lesbian and my father is old school and has said that I have brought shame on the Emir family name.

My other four brothers thrashed me with a stick having been ordered by my father to do so and Mohammad, my oldest brother, was the only person in my family I could turn to. I have a secret girlfriend but if her family found out she would be ostracised like me so we meet in a hotel twice a week.' Jade was amazed at Myingeeta's revealing outburst. 'I'm so sorry, that's so terrible, you poor thing.'
'You don't realise what it's like growing up in a Pakistani family if you're gay. It's so cruel to be made to be someone your body rejects. My nephew, Tazi, I'm sorry to say is more radical than my four brothers and even my father. He spat at my feet the last time I saw him about six months ago and said he wouldn't come here while I was in the house.'

'He thinks it's a disgrace to his beloved Islam and I believe he got his extreme views from the Bradford mosque he attends in Halifax Road, that is when he is here as he lives in London where he works for a government agency. He preaches to me saying Islamic males who have anal sex, [liwat] are to be punished according to all the major schools of islamic law and teaching. Sadly he despises me and I know my sister-in-law wants me out of this house bit I owe so much to my elder brother for supporting me against all the family.'

'Sorry, please excuse me, you want to know about Tazi but please do not write anything I have said. I lost control for a minute but it has been such a release for me to tell somebody who is sympathetic.' Myingeeta sniffed into a tissue and continued. 'Tazi has done well, he's working in London at some top government job and I know from the age of about twelve he had his education paid for by Iranian sponsors!'

'My brother was approached at the Halifax Road mosque by a Mr. Khan many years ago who promised a good education for Tazi at a prominent public school and would continue with his education right through to a masters degree. Look I don't even know you and I've poured my heart out. I am sorry but all my friends have ditched me because their fathers, brothers and husbands say I'm tainted but, between you and me, I'm saving up money with my girlfriend and we are moving to London to be together and we will drop the religion that doesn't tolerate us.'

Jade felt terrible and hadn't realised what a predicament some girls were going through simply by blind ignorance. 'I'm glad you shared your personal dilemma with me and I'm sure that your strength and fortitude and of course your love for your partner will see you both through this incredibly difficult time and you have my word that nothing will be published about you and I'm not going to print Tazi's achievements now as he doesn't deserve it after spitting at your feet. No, this will be our little secret. Here take my number and please let me know once you and your partner have a home together in London.'

'I'd like that and it's been such a relief to be able to open up to someone even if it was to a complete stranger and thank you for listening. Can I make you some tea?'

'No thanks, I've got a really busy schedule today but we'll drink tea together in London, I promise.'

23

Jade walked the length of Colliery Terrace towards the main road in order to call a licensed cab, heeding the advice the thoughtful cabbie had given her.

A taxi pulled up and opened the car window. 'You are waiting at the taxi stand so do you want a cab? I'm free.'

'Are you council licensed?'

'Of course look at my badge on the back of my car. Where do you need to go?'

'Bingley railway station.'

'I'm going past there anyway so I'll only charge you a tenner.'

It had just started raining so that really swung her decision and Jade hopped into the back seat of the smart new Mercedes taxi. 'Okay thanks.' The driver asked if she was visiting the area as he detected a southern accent. Jade was busy sorting her notes out and didn't enter into too much dialogue with the cabbie and it wasn't until they pulled into a street with some boarded up terrace houses that Jade became concerned. 'This isn't the way to the station! It's in a built up area near the town centre so where are we?'

'Don't worry miss, I know a quick way.'

'No, this is wrong. Stop the car and let me out now!'

'I have some friends who want to meet you first. They will drop you off at the station and they'll pay you if you are nice to them. You'll be fine. They live just at the end of this street.'

'Pull over now!' The driver ignored his prisoner-passenger and turned his music up louder. Jade tried the doors but, as she had guessed, they were locked. From what the driver had said the gang she was about to be handed over to wasn't far away.

'I've never shot a person in the back of the head but, trust me buster, if you don't stop this car now I'm going to get my first experience. Stop!'

The driver ignored her and actually accelerated his car so Jade fired two shots from her Bastion issued Smith and Wesson M&P9 handgun which has all the features of the bigger guns but is easier to conceal and ideal for the lady shooter. The bullets went past the driver and slammed into his dashboard stopping the music in an instant and which almost made him lose control with the car skidding to a halt. He was enraged with the damage to his three month old Merc but Jade wasn't finished and went mental. 'Take me to your friends buster and any messing and I'll blow your scummy shit brains out!' Jade baulked at what she had just said as she rarely swore but that cabbie had poked the wrong female bear.

'No I can't, really I can't!' Jade fired off another two shots at the front windscreen, missing the head of the driver by the width of a cigarette paper. 'My next shot will be in you buster.' The driver didn't speak but drove another fifty metres and stopped the car. 'Which door?'

'That blue one there.' The cabbie pointed to it.

'Okay buster get out and knock on the door and say you have a present for them when they open the door. If you give them any warning signs, verbal or otherwise, I'll shoot you first. Go.'

The dodgy taxi driver knocked on the door and when it was opened he said what he had been told to say. Jade then came to his side and pressed her gun into his hip as they followed the door opener inside the house which smelled strongly of stale curry. They were led into the main living room where three gang members were watching daytime television.

Before the residents had time to get excited over a fresh, young and attractive white girl Jade drew on her Bastion training which was not up to SAS standards but pretty damn thorough. She had replaced the almost empty gun with a ten cartridge magazine. 'Okay you dirty fucking scum listen good! The first guy to move will be the bravest of all of you shit.... ' Jade's speech was disturbed by a noise coming from the stairs as someone was running down them fast. A man, with a beard that had grown down to his chest, rushed into the room but didn't expect to be facing the barrel of a loaded Smith and Wesson. 'I'm glad you can join our party, sit over there.' Jade had kettled the now five which included the angry taxi driver to one end of the room and, exercising good practice, she kept her back to the wall.

'So is this all of you?' Nobody answered.

'Fatty, I asked is this all of you.' It was at this juncture that the gang were looking for any female weakness and Jade could sense her captives were growing in confidence so it was time for action and Fatty received a shot that shattered his chubby left knee. He fell off his chair and was rolling over in agony and screaming expletives in Urdu.

'Will somebody now kindly tell me is this all of you in the house? You' Jade pointed the pistol at another front row target and cocked the gun to fire another shot. 'Yes we are only four here plus Akram the driver who brought you.'

‘Ok you seem the brightest scum here so tape up your pals quickly and I’ll check each and every one after you have done it and if they are not perfect I’ll shoot one of your kneecaps off like fatty. Do it.’

Mr. Sensible had taped the hands of two of the gang when the third who was about to be tied pushed Mr. Sensible to one side and rushed at Jade with a long blade but she was trained to expect the unexpected and was ready. She fired into the thigh of the brave but stupid scumbag but his attack had gained momentum which carried him to the feet of Jade. He slashed at her leg but a retaliative smack across his temple with her gun barrel rendered him unconscious and bleeding profusely. Jade couldn’t believe what she was doing.

‘Carry on binding please Mr. Sensible which includes fatty and him.’ Jade pointed with her gun to the knifeman. Finally after checking all the bonds she taped the very nervous Mr. Sensible then calmly called the emergency services asking for two ambulances and an armed police unit to come to 148 Granville Terrace, Bingley.

The street, that was at least a quarter boarded up, had not seen the likes of the blue police lights and sirens since the Scargill miners strikes. In dramatic fashion three squad cars arrived which poured out twelve armed police officers just seven minutes since Jade’s call so she felt it safe to leave the gang and opened the door to them and, not wanting to complicate the situation, she holstered her firearm.

‘Armed police! Did you call us?’

‘Yes, please go inside.’ The police rushed passed Jade led by Detective Chief Inspector Lowden who ordered a space for the medics to get in through the hallway which was made narrower by the large emergency kits carried by the green clad medics.

DCI Lowden turned to Jade to ask her to explain the unlikely scene of a group of five taped up men, two of whom had serious but not life threatening shooting injuries 'Where the gun?' The DCI asked.
'In my holster.' Jade replied.
'Give it to me.'
'No, but allow me to explain. I am Jade Jackson, a field agent at Bastion and I'm working undercover.' Jade showed Lowden her identification and he knew Bastion had superiority over all the security services.

Some of the services hated this, especially local coppers, but not DCI Lowden who had the greatest respect for what Jade had done. He had heard of the work Bastion had achieved, not least of which was saving the Houses of Parliament from a terrorist attack. Jade explained the situation and showed the DCI how she shot up Merc which made him inwardly chuckle. Their cordial chat was then broken when a female police officer interrupted their conversation. 'Sir, sorry to interrupt but we have found two fifteen year old girls upstairs in a bedroom both under the influence of drugs which the medic who attended them believes has all the signs of heroin.'
'Thank you for that sergeant.'

'You do realise you were targeted by the taxi driver for sex? We knew there was a gang operating in Bingley as we have had many reports and hundreds of complaints mainly from late night revellers who want early morning taxis and this bogus taxi is obviously one of those. I just hope this is an isolated gang and we have got them all. It will be a fantastic breakthrough for us and will restore some safety to Bingley. Could you please make a statement of all the events from you being picked up

by the taxi and up to us arriving here and also why you were in Bingley, all the way from London.'
'Investigative work.'
'You can sit in my car to write it out and then I'll have you dropped off at Bingley station for your train home. How's that?'
'Yes, thank you. I'll do that now but unfortunately I can't elaborate why I'm in Bingley as it's Official Secrets Act protected I'm afraid. Please tell me though chief inspector, why have these rape gangs been getting away with their grooming for so long?'
'Because the bloody police chiefs along with local councillors are frightened of being called racists and the politicians don't want to lose the Muslim vote. That's the real truth but I think the tide is turning thank God.'

DCI Lowden thanked Jade emphatically for bringing a wanted despicable gang into custody.
'Could you please take my number chief inspector and let me know the outcome for those wretched children. It beggars belief.'
'Of course, now let's get you back to London.' With Jade's statement completed she was whisked off to catch her train to London.

She got out of the police car at the station drop off and went into the platform cafe to wait forty minutes for her train to Leeds where she would change for the London train to King's Cross. Jade sipped her coffee with satisfaction for coming through her first sortie but she couldn't help thinking of those hapless young teenage girls kept by those scum grooming and rape gang.

Yes, Jade Jackson was pleased with her first day as a spy. Before she wrote out her report for Max-Catt, on the not so perfect Tazi Emir she wondered whether to include her excursion to Granville Terrace!

24

The time was agonisingly slow for Tazi Emir as he looked at the clock on the office wall every ten minutes and wondered if it had stopped working as the hands were definitely taking their time. He hated what he was doing and detested who he was working for, the infidel elite. He wanted action and had an idea how to get some. His leader wanted information on Max-Catt's out of hours movements, where he lived, where he socialised, anything really that might be helpful for the contract killer, Brad Zimmermann.

Tazi was very good with modern IT methods and was able to knock up almost anything to resemble any forgery. He had seen for himself Max-Catt's new home and on his visit there he remembered what the concierge had told him, that Max he lived in the new building on the residential site. Tazi pulled up the London Borough of Hounslow website and opened their planning department's pages that included technical services and building inspections who were responsible for not only planning but for the safety of buildings and standards. Tazi was able to write over an original document of the building regulations department and drafted a letter.

Dear Occupier, our technical officer Mr. Amir Chanmireh, will be calling on Friday to inspect your property following reports of hairline surface cracks that may only be superficial, but they are appearing in a load-bearing wall in your apartment. If they are a structural defect, they may be dangerous so please allow access to our officer immediately. By order.

Paul Brady, Chief Technical Officer, London Borough of Hounslow.

Tazi printed out the official looking letter and made himself an identification badge in the name of Amir Chanmireh which he slipped into his own Bastion identification card that hung around his neck. He was ready to become a council technical services inspector.

Eventually the slow handed clock arrived at lunchtime and Tazi was on his way to Chiswick, Strand on the Green to be exact.

When he reached Max's block of apartments he rang the concierge. 'I am from Hounslow council Technical Services department and the building contractors have been notified about a possible structural problem and will be meeting me here on site. I need to get into Penthouse 3 of Thames Mews so can you let me in to the property please. Here's the official letter we sent the contractors and to the block management directors including the asset managers giving notice that we would be arriving today for a vital inspection.'

'I can't just let you in Mr. …ur.' The concierge looked at his list of occupiers. 'Mr. Hainsworth-Catt has moved into Penthouse 3.'

'If you do not let me in now and there is a partial collapse of the building in that block you will be held responsible. What is your name?'

'Look, I'm only doing my job, I'm not being funny mate and I don't want any trouble. How long will it take as I've got a delivery of topsoil arriving for the communal garden.'

'It could take up to an hour as it depends on how serious the fault is and I have to make several tests and then make out a report.'

'Look, if I let you in would you stay there until I get back from the soil delivery as I'll only be half an hour at most.'
'Oh I'll be longer than that, I'll stay for at least forty-five minutes.'
'Okay come with me, I'm not happy about it but I'm not being held responsible for any claims or accidents. Bloody officialdom.'

'Here you are Penthouse 3. I'll come back in half an hour to lock up. Is the geezer from the builders coming here too?'
'Yes I'll call him and let him know I have access.'

Tazi Emir was alone in Max-Catt's attic penthouse. He locked the door so as not to allow entry from the outside even with keys. Tazi methodically went through all the rooms and drawers and took a couple of photos of Max from an album for Brad Zimmermann to identify him by. He then found what he was hoping to find, spare keys to the apartment, the building and the entrance gate which he made impressions of by pressing them into Blu Tack that he'd thought to bring with him for that very purpose. He was aware Max was somewhere in France for a few days at least so he wasn't expecting him to return anytime soon. Tazi then drew a map of the apartment and the location from the building's main entrance door in case the attack on his boss was done at night. Tazi was pleased that he had thought of all scenarios.

Tazi stayed in Max's apartment until the caretaker returned and then went back to Bastion later than he'd planned. Lunch breaks were frowned upon at Bastion and his absence didn't go unnoticed by Julia Deakin. Nothing was said however as she knew there was an ongoing investigation into Tazi Emir unbeknown to him. He went to his desk and did the boring work that made his frustrations even worse but he had to keep a cool head for himself and for the IRF.

Julia Deakin had interviewed nine applicants for her personal assistant's position and she chose the one who was best qualified and could start after the weekend. Mrs. Penelope Stanwick, Julia's temporary assistant from the communications room, could now go back to do what she does best, detecting unusual radio and phone chatter on Bastion's suspects list.

It was Friday evening and close of play at the fortress. Tazi went to his drop off messaging facility at a newsagents in Uxbridge and picked up a selected magazine. Tazi paid the newsagent who was also his go-between coordinator and wrapped in a ten pound note was the message for the Halifax Road mosque which doubled up as the central communications hub for the IRF. I have imprinted the target's apartment keys. I'll get the duplicates made and bring them to the mosque tomorrow.

I will also bring a plan of target's residence with layout of rooms. I'll explain to Phonei how to get into the target's complex and apartment.

Severn.

The message would be collected later in the evening and taken by motorbike to Bradford.

Jade waited behind to see Julia Deakin who was finishing a call with the Home Office 'Yes Jade, good to see you back. How did you get on in Bradford?'

'I have typed out a report so do you want to see it before Max-Catt?'

'I should really leave it for him to read first as he instigated the investigation but you can give me the gist without the full report details.'

'I did have to shoot someone!,' The look on Julia's face was that of total incredulity. 'I got into a cab that had a dodgy cabbie. I was warned at the station to watch out for unlicensed taxis and also there are some very bad men about in Bradford and the cab I used must have had a false licence plate. Anyway he was only bloody taking me to a gang which I'm sure you know what for. He even bragged he'd get paid well for me. The bastard had me locked in the back of his cab and drove me to a gang's house. I pulled my gun on him and shot up his dashboard good and proper but it didn't end there. I made the driver knock on the gang's door and at gun-point we went in. There were five men including the cabbie but, long story short, I got them all securely taped up and called the police. Two tried it on and I shot one in the knee and one got it in the thigh. Sadly the police found two young teenage girls in the house who a medic thought were hooked on heroin. To deal with the situation I called in armed police and ambulances and gave a statement to a DCI Lowden and then returned to Uxbridge.'

'Good God Jade, blooded on your first fact finding operation?'

'Sorry ma'am, it's just that my dad is so correct in what he says. He was a career soldier who fought for Britain and is saddened by all the diversity crap that's over-played. People can't see we are losing our freedom of speech in our own country. Who is telling our coppers during armistice week and remembrance Sunday not to wear poppies or to do the bloody Macarena at the Notting Hill Carnival. It's not the plods on the beat, I'm sure. It's someone from high up the greasy wokey pole who must be telling them not to offend the minority. My dad is damn right! Our country is lost to extreme Islamic activists that blow up our buildings and indiscriminately murder innocent people in the name of their religion while the genuine Muslims are judged unfairly.'

'For goodness sake girl, calm yourself. Are you all right?'

'Not really, no. It's a sad indictment of our country when a girl can't walk the streets after dark or take a cab without fearing for her safety which happened to me in broad daylight and I was just going about my business. Tell me ma'am, seriously, what are the police doing about the raping of teenagers by Muslim gangs in Bradford, Telford, Rotherham, Luton and now Bingley. I'll tell you what! They do nothing! They are frightened of being accused of being racists and this so called racism is this country's biggest shield for so much that is wrong. Good people and the vast majority are not racist. It's a bloody cop out rather than face true and just punishment. Look at all the knife crimes.' Jade stopped her ranting tirade then there was silence. Julia Deakin had let Jade get it out of her system and, in truth, agreed with her about the state of the nation and the overused racist card.

'I'm so sorry you were attacked Jade and I do understand what you mean. Your dad is of course right. It is our job to protect Britain and it's getting increasingly more difficult. The IRF want Britain to be an Islamic state by 2050 and they even believe they can swing elections to that effect. The monster is at our door with Islamic extremists bullying anyone who speaks out against them and they will not stop until they take over our country. Are you okay to carry on?'

'Yes ma'am. I went to Colliery Terrace, the parental home of Tazi Emir and spoke to a neighbour and more importantly his aunt. She confirmed but without going into detail that he was been funded throughout his senior schooling and university by a Middle Eastern oil company. The details are in my report and personally I think there is more to Mr. Emir than meets the eye and going by what his aunt told me, I believe he's an Islamic extremist.'

'I do think I've had enough for one day now so if it's alright with you, I'm going home.' Julia could sense Jade was in slight shock from her dreadful experience in Bradford and hoped she'd be back to her bouncing best by Monday!

25

The three Bastion agents walked out of Adana Sakirpasa airport and crossed the concourse to the car rental offices and selected, as before, a pickup as it gave them wider options to carry out the work and to transport the kit they planned to use as their destination was ninety three kilometres away from the airport and situated in the industrial port of Mersin.

Their target this time was the factory and offices of Aydin Boat Supplies who manufactured up to twenty five, three metre RIB's a week to sell to anyone who wishes to buy them. Their biggest customer by far was Boats To Freedom who once had warehouses in Normandy and Albania but Bastion's Operation Buttercup had eliminated those warehouses and launch centres and in the short term it would impact on that people smuggling gang until another gang filled that vacuum.

Max had already thought how he might destroy the boat maker's factory but first he would need to get inside it to estimate its size, what material was in there and the optimum placement of explosives.

On the surface Aydin Boat Supplies was trading quite legally but certainly not morally and because their operation had government export approval there shouldn't be the need for any guards at the factory and certainly not armed ones as in the case of the two previous targets that made up the Buttercup trilogy.

The team got to Mersin and found out where the nearest agricultural supplier was so first stop on their shopping list was at Cadena Farm Supplies. They pulled into the car park and Mason ordered five bags of ammonium nitrate fertiliser to form the oxidising element for Max's homemade bombs and stored them in their pickup.

Next on their shopping list was a fifty metre drum of 2.5mm power cable from a local hardware store where they also bought a three pronged grappling iron and a length of rope. Max felt he was now ahead of the game and only needed five ten litre drums of marine fuel oil and two five litre cans of petrol to complete their pyrotechnical requirements.

Max explained to Mason. 'The ammonium nitrate is like the engine behind the explosion but it needs fuel, like any engine, to make it work which is where the marine fuel comes into play and the secret in making it work is in the mixing of an exact ratio which will be calculated by Callum, our explosives guru, just like he was back on our mission to the oil reservoir in South Yemen. Anyway the detonation will be fed through a 2.5 electrical cable which is the basic idea and the fuel oil added to the oxidiser element will make a very nasty bang. We shall use the old fashioned and highly inflammable petrol to accelerate the flames to win the race against the local fire service.'

They saw a gas station up ahead and Mason did the shopping, buying the five petrol cans and filling them at the pump. 'Fuck sake Callum don't crash this mobile bomb or we'll be blown to Timbuktu or Ankara at least.' Callum reassured Max. 'Although it isn't the best cocktail of cargo to carry as long as they are kept separate there won't be a problem but I promise to drive carefully so don't worry.' They pulled into the marina just inside Mersin port and collected the five drums of marine fuel oil they required, after which they drove along the quayside lined with containers and gantry cranes, reminding Max-Catt so much of his Rotterdam mission.

The industrial warehouse buildings were facing them on the other side of the main port road and they soon came across Aydin Boat Manufacturers and Supplies and parked across the far side of the double width supply road that had rail tracks built into it for carrying freight from the docks.

Through high powered binoculars, Max surveyed the building they are hoping to destroy very soon. The windows were high and although there were no guards that he could see, the building could be a blueprint for Fort Knox. 'This is going to need a totally different approach as the reinforced doors and heavy alarms on the access points are going to be our main problems and I can see from here that this little beauty is going to be a hard nut to crack.' Max was really thinking allowed but it prompted a question from Mason.

'If we can't go through the doors without bringing the might of the dock police down on us how are getting into this fortified bugger?'
'Through the roof Mr. Perkins, through the roof! Another concern is the amount of transport police driving around the port almost as if they are expecting trouble. We'll make a note of how often they pass the factory to see whether their patrols are random or scheduled and will do it in shifts.'

'I'll take first watch so you two get some rest in the cab. It'll be dark in three hours and I would think the factory closes at 17:00.'

The two Bastion agents made themselves as comfortable as they could in the cab of the pickup while Max was on the first observation shift. He noticed that lorries were regularly coming and going through the RIB manufacturer's gates and five deliveries or collections were made within a short space of time. At 17:45 the factory workers started drifting out in ones and twos with the volume increasing shortly afterwards to at least fifty or so piling out through the double gates evidently eager to get home from the grind of factory life.

Cars were joining the escaping workers from the staff car park, tooting at their colleagues to get out of their way. The scramble for home was soon over as the employees of Aydin Boat Manufacture and Supplies dispersed. Some got into waiting cars, others walked quickly to catch their public transport but all of them had the same common goal to get home. Max continued his surveillance and was keen to see if there was a night shift or a night watchman service cloaking on but didn't see.

At 20:15 it was getting dark and was time for Max to wake up his team. After a blissful sleep the two climbed out of the pickup and stretched. 'Okay boss is it on for tonight?' Mason enquired.
'Yes and no guards either by the looks which is just as well as we don't have any weapons with us for this job.'
'Were there many patrol cars crossing by?' Callum was keen to know this.'
'There were a few before the factory closed but none since.' Max reassured his men and asked Mason to drive them to the back of the factory to the staff car park. The pickup stopped by the locked double gates and Max hopped out and within half a minute of wiggling with his Chalkies, his all-purpose set of master keys, he'd picked the lock and beckoned the pickup through the gates and secured them behind them.

‘Okay chief are you going to enlighten us with your plan to break in?’

‘We will anchor the grappling hook to the rainwater gutters and hoist up the rope ladder to the eaves. Mason, who is the lightest, will climb up and make the rope ladder more secure by tying it to the lightning conductor mast. Then with the two heavy duty battery drills we purchased, we should be able to easily cut through the insulated plastic coated metal roof. By boring a series of holes in a 0.70m diameter circle, we can push the centre pieces through which will allow a big enough space to lower our homemade explosives down. In addition to the main access hole, we will bore a series of holes in various sections of the roof to enable petrol to be poured in as Callum, our explosives expert, will explain.’

‘We will insert a 2.5mm electric cable into the mixed cocktail of explosive material and attach this to the lowering rope then when we’re ready we’ll attach the cable’s positive and negative leads to the pickup’s 12 volt battery and here’s where it gets technical. There is a difference in electrical potential, commonly known as voltage, and the air ionises the atoms in the atmosphere around the broken connection and will start to carry a current known as an electrical arc. The current will then flow and we will get our spark. Simple!’ Max and Mason looked incredulously at Callum and shook their heads. ‘How do you know all that shit Cal?’

‘It’s my job.’

‘Let’s get cracking then shall we?’ The over keen Mason asked enthusiastically. The three ex-SAS men knew almost instinctively what to do without speaking. Mason took the three pronged grappling hook and threw it to the height of the metal rainwater guttering trough and after three attempts the hook lodged over its target. Mason pulled on it by swinging his full weight off the ground and was satisfied that the hook was secured on the roof so he decided to take the rolled up rope ladder up in his backpack and pulled himself up the grappling rope to the eaves.

The one hook that had gained a purchase moved with his weight so Mason wasted no time in tying the rope ladder securely around the steel brackets that were supporting the gutter. With this done, he climbed on the more substantial ladder and from there he was easily able to climb onto the thirty degree pitch roof and walk with a rope in hand to a chimney like structure. As instructed by Max, he was able to lash the ropes around the solid structure to hold the extra weight of men and materials that would be coming up on the roof next. Then the rope ladder was released from the gutter and transferred to two ropes secured around the chimney-like stack.

'The ascending rope ladder and pulley hoist are in position and ready to heave up the gear.' Mason shouted down the information that Max wanted to hear. In the meantime Callum mixed his explosives, ensuring that he had the exact ratio for an optimum mix. The idea was to cut off the tops of the five litre fuel oil containers and fill them with the fertiliser based mixture and lower it down through a large enough hole in the roof. Mason had already scampered down, collected one of the drills and the jemmy bar as he didn't need instructing again as this independent thinking was a legacy from his SAS days. Max mused. It's damn good working with these no-nonsense professionals again.

Max didn't have time for daydreaming though so he took the second drill up onto the roof. He was pleased where Mason had planned to make the opening as it was near the ridge of the roof and therefore when the bomb was lowered through that hole it would be on to a central floor location. The noise increased dramatically as Mason jemmied the drilled perforated holes that would form an aperture of over half a metre in diameter. The final thrust downwards from Mason's size 10 boot sent the circular piece of metal dropping inside the warehouse. Mason looking into the dark hole. 'I'm through, Max.' But Max couldn't hear him as he was busy drilling scores of smaller holes in the roof to randomly to pour petrol through. Max needed a new drill bit and was on his way to get it and was at the top rope of the ladder when something hard hit him in the back which made Max turn and looked down, Callum, who was about to throw another stone at him, whispered: 'Max we have company, there's a vehicle at the gate and two security guys are opening it. If they come round the back they'll see our pickup and ladder.'

'Okay we'll come down!'

The two security men were inside the gates and rattled hard and repeatedly at the entrance door to the warehouse which remained secure. After checking that door they were much more relaxed and chatted as they walked the perimeter of the building but they would soon get to the end and see the pickup. Max's team had nowhere to go and as the two unsuspecting guards turned the corner they literally didn't know what hit them. Max grabbed the nearest one, banged his head against the brick building twice and dragged him to the floor. Callum dealt with the other with a lightening quick pace that matched his leader. The unsuspecting patrol guards were taped and gagged within under two minutes and put in the back of the pickup.

All the explosive concoction had been mixed by Callum and the tops of the five, ten-litre containers had been cut off, filled up and gently packed down. Two slots were drilled into the them before filling which would have the rope attached through them for hoisting them down through the roof. The assembly line was

Callum on the ground connecting the grappling prong to the looped rope on the container which was then pulled up by Mason who would carry the full container to the hole in the roof which Max was standing over. The grappling iron was then hooked on the loop and the mixture lowered gently down inside the warehouse. This was repeated ten more times within a half hour period and with Mason shining a torch inside the warehouse, Max was able to get swing momentum to direct each container to its own space for an optimum explosion.

They lowered the last container with more care as tied into the knot was the 2.5mm power cable which had an extended tail from the knot that was pressed deep into the mixture. 'Okay Mason, carefully now, we don't want to disturb the electric cable.' They both lowered away very slowly as if it was an unexploded bomb which in fact it was!

With a slight swing motion and a great deal of circumspection, they placed it centrally where they had left an intentional gap and after two attempts it was lowered perfectly into place. The next job was the petrol fuel which was poured randomly through the drilled holes all over the roof area, even down the other side of the roof pitch. The factory that manufactured the RIB's for the illegal channel crossings was well saturated. 'Come on guys, those guards probably have to report in frequently and we don't want any more visitors. Let's get this baby burnt!' Max led the way down from the roof.

They drove the pickup to the bottom of the ladder and Callum exposed the battery compartment and as he had made the explosive cocktail, it was only fitting he should fire the ignition. He split the end of the twin and earth cables with his knife and pared back the inner strands to expose the copper tips of the live and neutral wires and the other end of the cable was already stripped to expose the copper wires which were planted deep in the mixture. The three held their breaths as they waited for the electric arc!

There was a slight hesitancy as a thought hit Callum. Have I got the correct ratio with the mix. There's only one way to find out! Callum, with a lead in each hand, put his live wire to the car battery's neutral wire and his neutral to the batteries live. His answer was an instant massive explosion that ripped through the building. Windows were blown out and flames were fighting for the scraps of reducing oxygen spreading fiery fingers across the drive to the entrance gates. It would be suicidal to drive through that gauntlet of fire so the three men all ducked behind the pickup!

26

Max knew they had to move pretty fast and made the decision to abandon the pickup which was an easy choice. They got the guards out of the back of it and took them with them to the other side of the building that was less effected by the flames and continued mini explosions.

At the front of building they could just about get to the main gate without being roasted. Max put his Chalkies to work on the gate's lock and had it opened in seconds, he needed to, the metal was heating up fast from the spreading flames. The Bastion men taped the two security guards to railings fifty metres away from the burning building and they would soon be noticed. Then the three raiders crossed the wide port road but were held up by a slow passing goods train that shared the port access road. 'Come on guys, let's get to the marina as the first thing the cops will do is cordon off the port entrance and perhaps we should have taken that train out!'

They dropped down onto the lower quayside road that was virtually at sea level and not knowing the layout of the port, they skirted the inner harbour wall until they reached the marina they had previously visited to buy the marine fuel oil. Max selected a pleasure motor yacht that would hopefully be their way out of the port and used his chalkies again to easily open the locked cabin door and luckily there was a spare bunch of keys on a keyring shaped as a blue and white anchor. It's a yachting thing! Max surmised. The Azimut 500 was a slick motor cruiser and the Bastion leader had had experience with this ten metre model when he and Penny took a hired boat around the Greek Islands just before she was tragically murdered.

Max eased the Azimut away slowly and as they reached the harbour exit they saw the orange glow that had replaced the warehouse they had just destroyed, with the sound of the emergency services carrying loudly across the quiet protected waters of the harbour but the state of the water quickly changed as they hit the choppy unpredictable open sea. Max kept three hundred metres from the coastline and looked for a suitable marina or landing stage to get back on terra firma.

Mason shouted over the noise of the fully revved motorboat. 'Max there's a boat speeding up behind us!' By the time the Bastion leader turned to look, a powerful searchlight was upon them followed by an order in Turkish through a loudspeaker to heave to. It was the maritime police wanting to check out who the nighttime cruiser was as they were on full alert after the explosion in the port. 'I assume we are not going to stop eh Maxy?' Callum knew his boss well and braced himself for the full throttle pull away. He wasn't disappointed nor did he have to wait for his answer.

Max turned inwards to get closer to the beach and as the police patrol boat had a deeper draught it would not be able to get in as far as the fleeing Azimut. Well that was Max's plan but it was obvious to the Turks and they knew they have a chase on their hands and responded with their more powerful speed.

Options for Max suddenly went to nil as another Turkish patrol boat came into sight in front of them, obviously called up by the first boat. 'How the fuck are we getting out of this Maxy boy? Another fine mess you've got us in!' Mason was ribbing his boss as he had been in many a close scape with Max-Catt. 'Hold on to your hat Mason and stop your whinging.' The two fast patrol boats had out manoeuvred Max by sheer power and there was only one way to go and that was to the shore.

'I'm going to beach this baby. Let's see how close our friends can get to the shore so both of you hold on tight.' The Azimut screamed with friction s it hit the seabed but its speed kept it careering towards a sandy beach then a crunching halt that threw Mason forward causing him to collide with the cabin door.

'Come on, run to that cover!' Max pointed to a copse of pine trees past the beach. The two following boats had to veer off at the last minute but it was too late for one of them as it grounded twenty metres out from the beach. The searchlights, however, followed the fugitives into the darkness of the trees.

'They will call ground forces for backup and are sure to give them exact GPS coordinates so we can't stay here as it'll be swarming with police in five minutes at the most but hopefully we're outside the initial police cordon.' Max urged his team on.

'You're bleeding Mason, are you okay?' Callum enquired. 'Yeah, I'm fine, the bloody cabin door gave me a sore head but no bother, thanks.'

'We have to keep moving so we'll stay just off the road, I've checked with my GPS which shows that we are parallel and two roads away from the main highway that leads to the airport so we will need to get a flight out before detailed checks are made on all passengers leaving Turkey. They will soon get our identities from the hired pickup but although it will be a burnt out shell by now, their forensics will be able to get the VIN number and trace it to the hire company so I'm hoping we can get a flight out before they can identify us.' The three moved along keeping in the shadows of buildings and, as Max predicted, five minutes later there was the ear-splitting wailing of police cars driving in both directions.

‘Crossing two roads is going to be difficult with all this police activity but we must cross them.’ Max spoke rhetorically. ‘Fuck me, how are we going to cross the roads with police everywhere.’ Mason was getting a tad worried as he knew that the chances of getting on the next flight out was diminishing which was crucial to their escape. The next building they passed had a double unit that appeared to have been turned from retail to an all-night diner with a couple of rooms for rent above the eatery. ‘I could kill for some coffee.’ Mason was having another moan but the other two had the same thought. They were tempted to go in until Max spotted a police patrol vehicle parked outside.

‘Callum that beautiful police car is going to be our exit visa!’ Max had seen a possible way out of their restricted route to the airport. ‘We are going to nick that cop car.’ An easy task as all three were trained in the art of carjacking with Mason opting to do the unlawful business. Minutes later they were all in with Callum driving towards the airport. ‘Callum stick the blue lights on this baby and don’t worry about being done for speeding!’ That brought a collective laugh from the team.

Callum didn’t need encouragement to drive well over the limit in whichever country, but now in a police patrol car with flashing blue lights, he was in his boyhood element and was clocking one hundred and thirty miles per hour. The cautious Mason didn’t say a word in fear of being branded a wuss but Max didn’t mind as they were hardly going to get pulled over for speeding.

'It's ninety three miles to Adana Sakirpasa airport and I reckon we can allow ten minutes drinking up time before the police officers find out their patrol car has been nicked and I think we can add another five minutes to that for their headquarters to put out a call to all vehicles to look for us but we are going to dump this hot potato in seven more minutes and not a minute longer so Callum give that accelerator some more stick and I mean as fast as you can!' Callum drove at the limit until Max barked the order to pull off at the next exit that accessed a service station.

'Callum hide the car in those bushes down that track.' Max pointed and Callum took it down a gravel path that lead to a picnic area well out of view from the road. 'We'll leave it here and they won't notice it until the morning at least.' The team went into diner as they were now desperate for some food and a gallon of coffee. They couldn't help but notice what was on the news, as there were five big screens around the place, which was all about the warehouse explosion and the total destruction of the factory plant. The police confirmed it was arson and sabotage as they had found two unharmed guards tied up well away from the burning building. A burnt out vehicle was to be taken away for forensic examination once the twisted metal had cooled down enough and minutes later a police spokesman reported that two of their patrol boats were in pursuit of an unidentified motor cruiser and that it had beached at high speed to get away from them with what looked like three males running up the beach at Kalim point.

Mason picked a selected car and started the motor all within three minutes. As Max and Callum came out of the diner the car thief called to them.' Over here, hop in.' This time Mason was behind the wheel as, truth be told, his nerves couldn't take another mile of Callum's driving!

27

Mustafa Arslan, a senior officer of the Turkish secret police, was called in to take charge of the explosion incident at the port and believed it could have been an internationally planned terrorist attack. 'I want special agents for the next three days at all air and seaports and all international border crossings. Adana Sakirpasa airport is only ninety three miles away from the attack and that's where I think they'll try and escape so I want to double the police and secret service agents there until I tell you to stand them down. Do you understand Hussain?'

Hussain Balik agreed with an enthusiastic nod and a positive sounding yes!
'Yes Inspector, right away.' Hussain shouted to his second in command. 'Double the officers at Adana airport, half of which to be armed and organise it now!'

Hussain over emphasised his loud instruction for the benefit of Mustafa Arslan as, in truth, he was nervous in Mustafa's company.

The team from Bastion had dumped their transport and took individual taxis to the airport, arriving at different times and had all got all had got through airport security on their own passports. They guessed the sheer number of armed police milling around was not coincidental to the their pyrotechnics performance of last night with people being checked at random and Max realised it was only a matter of time before his team would get picked upon for a more thorough inspection. Their flight was due to board in fifty minutes so they would be called to the gate very soon. Each agent tried to look relaxed and Max prayed there wouldn't be a delay to their Heathrow flight.

'Have we had the forensic report I asked for from the suspect pickup?'
'Yes Mustafa, as you know and as mentioned in the initial report it was burnt out but our forensics team were able to trace it by the vehicle identification number to a local car hire company and they are sending over their CCTV footage which should be with us in the next thirty minutes.'
'Brilliant, send the CCTV over to me immediately you get it. The gang must be using Adana airport to get out of Turkey so distribute their names and faces to all air and seaports as well as all international borders just in case they travel overland. Have we found the stolen patrol car yet?'
'No, it seems to have vanished!'
'Okay, get the pickup hirer's details sent to my phone immediately you get it. Now get me over to Adana airport!' Mustafa screamed the urgency of his demand to the ever nervous Balik who in turn screamed at his subordinate to bring a car and driver round to take them to Adana Sakirpasa airport immediately and should get to the airport within an hour.

At the same time the secret police chief climbed into the car the flight to Heathrow was due to close! It was going to be a very closely run thing for the Bastion team. Too tight to call!

Max was the closest to the gate's passport and boarding card check and as the airline representative scanned the barcoded document, a border security guard stepped forward and demanded Max's passport. He scrutinised it and it wasn't a perfunctory inspection and he pulled Max out of the queue to study him further. He looked at

Max's passport then at him then took another look at Max before finally, after what seemed an age, allowed him to go through the departure gate.

'Wait.' the passport officer called Max back as he exited his kiosk. Max turned, feeling a nervous, sickening sensation in his guts: They've realised I'm in the CCTV from the hire company. Fuck! 'Do you want me?' Max innocently replied.
'I didn't ask you what your business was in Turkey?'
'Golf! I stayed an old colleague who now lives here.'

The chief airport security officer led Mustafa and Malik to his office where the intel on the three Brits had already come through. 'Shit! We received these ID's fifteen minutes ago but they didn't get forwarded to our passport check in time.'

The flight to London had finished boarding and the cabin doors were closed with cross checks completed. All that was left before take-off was for the cabin crew to check that the passengers were buckled up with their armrests down and window blinds open. The pilot made his usual announcements predicting the flight time and the weather in London before asking passengers to pay attention to the safety drill in case of an emergency and the aircraft pushed back as the two cabin crew completed their lifejacket demonstrations.

Back in the security manager's office it was clear that three Brits had hired the vehicle found at the explosion site and were now on a Turkish Airlines flight to London.

'Stop the flight to London Heathrow leaving gate. Now! It must be stopped!'

The safety demonstration had finished and the pilot had been given clearance from air traffic control to taxi his aircraft into its final position in a waiting queue of two. Mustafa Arslan was purple in the face with uncontrolled rage and was still screaming to stop the flight, demanding to be taken onto the airfield by airport security. The observation tower who had contact with the pilot was told to stop the flight and bring it to gate 15. The control tower knew the safety rules and certainly couldn't allow the flight to be abandoned at this late stage as the aircraft in front of the London flight had just taken off. The Turkish Airlines pilot had already taxied on to the vacated slot and was next for take-off. The pilot was still oblivious that his flight had been requested to be aborted and that the airport was in a security crisis! The intelligence boss, Mustapha Arslan, Malikwas screaming at the control tower to abort the London flight and armed police were demanding access onto the runway on the orders from their boss, Arslan, who had a given up with the control tower and took matters into his own hands. His threats and seniority had the effect he demanded and the runway vehicle gates were reluctantly opened.

Max couldn't believe what he was seeing, police cars with blue lights flashing were screeching through the airside gates that accessed the runway in a race with his flight.

The convoy of three secret police vehicles were not letting up as Arslan wanted the three foreigners to stand trial for a serious incursion on Turkish home soil. Mustapha was manic and led the convoy to cut off the plane and physically make the pilot abort his take off which was a highly dangerous manoeuvre. Arslan in the lead car was speeding at forty-five degrees towards the runway and it was now the power of the aircraft against the position of the pursuing police vehicles.

In fairness to the pilot there was no possible way he could deviate from his take-off path, not at this late stage, even if he wanted to but he couldn't believe his eyes. He and all the passengers were straining to see the action on their left side as the second car in the convoy turned towards the aircraft but because of the vehicles speed and its acute angle it flipped over several times. The passengers on the port side of the plane screamed at what they were witnessing, the sparks flying from the vehicle rolling along the runway. Mason was the only one of the team seated on the left side of the aircraft and knew immediately who the convoy was after. Shit happens when you take on the SAS Perkins mused as he was still getting used to the fact he was now working for Bastion but still felt himself very much to be an SAS blade. The plane lifted smoothly at two hundred and twenty miles per hour leaving the runway in turmoil and an apoplectic Mustafa Arsla!

The three Bastion agents had missed being captured by the skin of their teeth and, with renewed confidence, they moved closer together and ordered a bottle of champagne. 'Here's to the success of Operation Buttercup.' The three ex-SAS men had two flutes of bubbly each and were all feeling pretty good with another successful operation under their belts and they relaxed in the safety of international airspace.

28

09:30 Saturday, Bradford.

Saturday morning at 09:30, the river mole Severn aka Tazi Emir walked out from the Bradford rail station into bright Yorkshire sunshine, not a usual experience in those northern parts, a he had arranged to meet up with the hired assassin. Tazi Emir arrived at the mosque and looked forward to seeing the five other rivers spies and Brad Zimmermann, globally dubbed Phonoi after the Greek spirit of murder and killing.

Mousa Alami took morning prayers earlier that Saturday morning in light of the emergency meeting called by the IRF leader, Kamal Hafeez, and saw Sani Yosef who also attended the prayers. 'Ah Sani I'm glad you have come today and remember what we discussed at our last little chat? If you're serious about helping the progress and furthering of the Islamic cause in the UK then you will meet our southern leader of the IRF. He will be arriving anytime now and I'll introduce you to him before he starts an important meeting with our brothers. Do you still want to meet him Sani?'

'Most definitely Mousa. I will help all I can to fight for the cause of Islamic values.'

'Good, go to the canteen and have some tea, wait there and I'll bring our leader to you there when he arrives.'

'Yes, I'll do just that Mousa, thanks.'

Mousa introduced Dani, alias Sani Yosef, to Kamal in the canteen and they shook hands. Kamal held his face close to Dani's in a momentary cold stare which dis-

played all of Hafeez's natural suspicious disposition. 'Always good to meet a new recruit who has potential but you understand we will have to make many security checks on you.'
Dani perceived an air of uncertainty about the IRF boss and he could feel himself getting an unavoidable cold sweat that he couldn't fight. Then fear came over him as he thought they were sure to check him for a device before discussing the plans of the IRF. 'Excuse me gentlemen but before we continue I must have a pee!

Inside the cubicle he moved fast as he had a hunch the minders might just need a pee as well! He wasn't naive enough to throw his phone out of the window so instead he wrapped it in toilet paper and flushed it down the toilet but to his horror it didn't flushed away, it was staring at him from under the water. There was a bang on the door and a loud voice asked 'Have you finished yet, the boss is getting inpatient.'
'Uh...yeah just a moment.' Dani pulled his sleeve up and put his hand into the bowl pushing it up the bend with his fingers. He flushed again with a big wad of toilet paper and a final finger push. The phone was now on its way to the sewage works somewhere in Bradford.

'Come on. Now!' Dani dried himself with toilet tissue then opened the cubicle door with as much composure as he muster. 'Sorry, too much curry last night.' The big minder escorted Dani back to his boss while the other inspected the vacated toilet. 'I haven't got all day. Now we are going to a private office to ask you a few questions.' Hafeez wasn't renowned for his patience and Mousa led the group along the corridor to his study.

Okay Sani, first let me have your phone. I always start with checking that! Nothing personal you understand?' Kamal held out his hand to receive his request. 'I don't have one at the moment. Actually I can't afford one, I sold mine two weeks ago to pay my bedsit rent.'

'Sani, search our friend and Ahmed you go and check the toilet again and look for any hiding places. Even the area outside the window in case it was thrown out. You do understand why we need a thorough check?'
'I understand sir.'

Ahmed returned with a shake of the head that sufficed. 'Well it looks like you're clean Sani! So welcome to our organisation. Your English is exceptional so we'll start you with some small tasks and promote you accordingly but until we are totally satisfied with our checks you will not be allowed into meetings of strategic importance. Our checks will be over within a week and I must say that if you are not who you say you are then you will wish you hadn't even heard of the IRF. For now Sani take my blessing and I do hope you'll be doing our expanding Jihad against the infidels in this corrupt country.'

Kamal Hafeez settled behind his desk facing out to eighteen chairs that were in rows of six, the front row being reserved for the revered six river spies. They had just settled down when a well-built guy, who could easily have been a body builder or personal trainer or both, stepped through the door. He didn't smile and looked pretty menacing as he stood at the back of the room. 'You must be Phonoi?'
'Yeah, are you Hafeez, Kamal Hafeez?'
'That's me, I have a meeting now,' At that moment Mousa walked into the room. 'Ah Mousa will you take Phonoi into the canteen for some tea or perhaps coffee as he's American.'
'I'll give you thirty minutes and if you are not in the canteen by then I'm leaving and going back to the States. I don't do waiting!' The anger in the IRF boss

was evident as he fought to control his temper but Hafeez was desperate for Phonoi's services. 'It won't be more than thirty minutes.' Phonoi didn't answer and turned on his heel to follow Mousa to the canteen. Hafeez went back to his desk and called the meeting to order.

'You are all here today my brothers to be updated with all things IRF. You all know we have lost an important safe house in Shelly Street in London. I have come from the IRF central committee and it has been agreed that after the closing down of our explosives lab and factory at Bushy Road in Watford we are going to change our attack strategy. Instead of bomb planting and the destruction of iconic UK sites, we are going to take our jihad to the heart of British public security and are going to target on duty police. We will start in London and will strike at the British system by throwing London into chaos that will eventually have serious ramifications.

The majority of you in this room do not know the six brothers sat in the front row as you would only know them by their river code name. You rivers must, from the start of the police culling, be extra vigilant in your observational roles as to whatever the UK secret services are doing and if they get any leads about our operations we need to know immediately. Severn is at Bastion, Clyde is in the Home Office and Avon is working for M15 and they should be first to know if the intelligence services have found out about our plans by using the drop off method of communication only.'

The attendees filed out of the room except for the six river agents. Hafeez waited for the last of the group to leave and faced the undercover agents. 'Are any of you under suspicion in your respective organisations?' They all answered with a confident no apart from Severn aka Tazi who explained his situation!

29

Max had decided to drive to his family home, Brandscombe Manor, for two reasons, first to see his parents and siblings who were all home for the weekend and the second was to collect some personal effects from his lodge that included part of his reserve stash of Lochavennie malt whisky.

Max met up with his family in the drawing room where the news was still broadcasting about the destruction of three bases that were used by the human smugglers and it was being reported that the way the factories were destroyed looked like the work of the British SAS which the UK government had strongly denied.

Max could see from the look his father Christopher threw at his second son, Archie, that he knew Max was somehow involved. 'Max these raids on warehouses have all the hallmarks of the SAS, the sought of capers you got up to when you were in that mob. Are you sure you had nothing to do with them?'

Christopher was toying with his son and Max knew that from experience. 'You know I can't comment on such sensitive stuff.'

'The French government are going bonkers and have called in the British ambassador but apart from that it's a damn good show whoever carried the raids out. It certainly won't stop the Channel crossings forever but it's bound to set them back for months. By the way do you know your brother has an announcement to make at dinner tonight.'

'Is he still seeing the lady he met at the Young Farmers Association dance? Holly Saunders? Her brother runs Oak Tree Farm near here.'

'Yes he's bringing Holly tonight.'

'That'll be good to meet her properly, a nice country-fied lady, just what Archie needs. Now I must dash I have some reports to type up for my new boss, Julia Deakin. I'll write them up it in my lodge. Is it Aperitifs in the drawing at 19:00 and dinner at 19:30 and is it black tie or are you making it a white tie event as we have a formal announcement?' Max enquired with his mother.

'Don't be sarcastic Maximus, I want white tie tonight as I feel this is going to be a life changing announcement and the men shall wear white and that's final.' The matriarch had spoken.

'Is Pippa still with the older guy, the Harley Street consultant dermatologist?'

'No she moved on from him two months ago which shows that you don't visit us as much as you should.' Virgina got the final dig into Max who couldn't really make excuses about his workload and missions.

Max was ready for dinner and walked to the manor, arriving a few minutes after 19:00. He was the last to arrive but hid in the conversation of dear Mrs Cooper, Max's second mother and midwife when he was born twenty-six years ago.

Pippa came to Max first. 'little brother Maximus, where have you been? It must be all of two months. Did you have anything to do with what's on all the news about a squad of our SAS boys blowing up a series of buildings across Europe?'

'Hi Pips, please don't start, I've had the family inquisitors grilling me about that already. Anyway what's this I hear that you have yet another new beau? What happened to the sports doctor?'

'That bastard! He was shagging a nurse and his receptionist at the same time as seeing me. The funny thing was his sister told me what was going on. Apparently the two women had a punch up in his Harley Street consulting rooms which spilled out onto the pavement. I didn't need that in my life!'

The drawing room emptied as the dining room filled up as a Mrs. Cooper dinner was about to be served. It was good to see at last that Mrs. Cooper had an assistant to wait and carry. Christopher said grace and welcomed all the diners to the Brandscombe Manor estate.

It was time for the announcement which turned out, by prior agreement, to be a double celebration. Archie announced the wedding day for him and Holly Saunders for the 19th of July and then Rory, Max's best friend and old school chum, announced his and Jenny's wedding day for the 18th of June. Max of course had already been asked to be best man by Rory so it was a great dinner that finished with an overspill of happiness and the delight on Virginia's face was tangible which spread amongst the family. Max took time to chat with his sibling's fiancee before finding Jenny and Rory to hug them both and exuding genuine pleasure that at last they had named the day. Two weddings to attend in four weeks and the first one just seven weeks away.

Next day Max needed to leave early as he had so much on at Bastion but first he had to go to his Thames view apartment to drop off some personal belongings. He felt relaxed in the security of the whole block and that the penthouse was additionally secured by an alarm system that would alert Bastion and the local police if it were activated also the security of a gated entry into the grounds and very secure access into the building plus his front door had a ten point bolt locking mechanism if a would be intruder ever got that far!

30

Kamal Hafeez hurried into the canteen with just a minute to spare before Phonoi's self-declared deadline to leave as the IRF leader sensed the hitman wasn't bluffing. Bini Akrami, Hafeez's number two, scurried behind his boss into the room. 'You left it a bit tight and I was just drinking up to leave.' Phonoi glared at his would-be paymaster but Hafeez held his temper for the second time within the last hour as he wasn't used to being spoken to like that and he had murdered the powerful Khan to replace him due to his intolerance.

'The amount for taking out Max-Catt is half a million US dollars in cash but if I fail there is no charge and these are my terms as we agreed on the phone so get the money ready as I will not fail. Now what information do you have for me about my target and do you have his home address?'

'We have done better than that. One of my undercover agents has not only found out his address but he got into Max-Catt's apartment and made copies of the gate, building and apartment keys.' Hafeez passed the keys over to the hired killer. While he was weighing up Phonoi, a thought occurred to Hafeez and he deliberated: What if I offer this marksman another job to take out British police officers as part of our new attack plan. Just the first day perhaps which will ensure we hit hard at the start with some guaranteed hits!

'What would you say Brad to another big pay out for say three hours work if you hit a certain target? I promise you it'll be target practice for you, shooting fish in a barrel comes to mind but unlike a payment per shot, as you advertise your services, if you hit ten targets in a three hour stint we'll pay you two million dollars!'

'Yeah I can do that but I want to see the plan before I commit myself. I always do my own planning as I trust no one as I find third party involvement usually ends in a big fuck up and I don't do fuck ups!

'That's no problem so come to my next meeting that's about to start.' Hafeez led Phonoi to Mousa's study where a selected team were waiting for their leader to explain the new attack strategy.

'Excuse me Kamal I need a piss. I won't be long.' Hafeez's second in command, Bini Akram, turned towards the main mosque toilets and coming out was Dani Quibi alias Sani Yousef. The two passed and Akram turned and gave a second glance then continued into the mens room thinking: Where have I seen that bloke before. It wasn't here at the mosque so where the hell was it? Akram was pissing when it struck him who the passing guy was. Yes, of course! He was the dude at the safe house, that's it! He escaped after we dipped his arm in burning oil! Of course that's him, what the fuck is he doing in an IRF friendly mosque.....

That was the last thought Bini Akram had that day or any other day for that matter. He was dead! Dani Quibi withdrew his knife from between the pissing victims shoulder blades and left him in his own pool of blood. Dani cleaned his knife and dragged the body into a cubicle and sat the corpse on the pan, leaning him against the partition. Dani locked the door and climbed over the top but dropped back down quickly as somebody was having a piss but was facing away, looking down at his flow.

The pissing guy took ages to finish and then meticulously washed his hands several times. Dani was sweating with nervous tension. Come on for fuck sake, just go! I need to get some critical intel back to Bastion and I have no phone. Dani was already under suspicion from Hafeez over his missing mobile that was ironically lost down the same toilet as the dead dude was now sitting on.

Dani gingerly popped his head over the door and as it was all clear he quickly heaved himself up and over the partition onto the floor. He noticed a smear of blood he'd missed and wiped it away with a couple of hand tissues, which might just give him a few more minutes to get away, and slipped out of the main mosque entrance where piles of worshippers shoes were parked.

'I know that guy.' Severn pointed towards Dani as he was leaving the mosque. 'He worked for MI6 when I worked there. He was a double agent for them based in Aden and his code name was ZX3 and was dubbed a hero for it. Hafeez caught him once but he escaped in a refuse truck so what the fuck is he doing here, he must be spying again for MI6 or perhaps Bastion. I'm going to see where he's going as this isn't right. You come with me Kamal and you, Akrami, go to Hafeez and tell him he may have had a spy in the mosque. Tell him we are going to follow him and stop him in case he heard what was said in the meeting!'

Dani got a cab to Bradford station followed by Emir and Malik who held back to allow Dani to buy his ticket. They assumed he was going to London's King's Cross station so they took a guess on buying two single tickets there. Their guess was correct when they saw Dani waiting on platform twelve for the London train while still keeping a good distance from him.

Dani Quibi recalled his escape from the boiling cooking oil in the back of a refuse collecting vehicle with all the skin and some flesh dripping off his right arm. And the scars of a ten hour skin grafting operation would never let him forget it either. He figured he had little choice in killing Akram once he'd recognised him in the toilet.

Back at the mosque the team had gathered with Phonoi as the guest. 'We have, over the last three months, purchased and modified two sightseeing buses and have just received our London sightseeing permit. Our company will be called Met-Hoppers which is the name on the license. Now we will go on a short five minute journey to a warehouse where you will see the special alterations we have made to the bus. It has already been sign written and we have three allocated routes that covers all the iconic buildings throughout the city where there will be lots of police standing around keeping the peace or so they think!'

At the spacious warehouse the sheeting was removed from a gleaming new bus with the red, yellow and black livery of the Met-Hopper bus company with messages blazed on both sides and each end which read Hop on Hop off at your favourite London stop.

Inside the bus were brand new headphones with recordings synced with information about the places of interest along the route. The party of seven followed Hafeez onto the bus and upstairs to the open top floor where the IRF leader went to the front. 'This is where it gets very interesting.' Kamal turned two recessed hidden bolts, one in one direction the other in the opposite direction. 'Now watch.' He lifted an upholstered metal sheet revealing a concealed compartment the width of the bus end to end.

‘Okay everybody except Phonoi go down, half of you go on one side of the bus and the other half of you go the other side. I want you all to look for any movement on the sides of the bus.’ The selected team did what they were asked. Hafeez passed Phonoi a telescopic rifle with a suppressor fitted. ‘Here take this and climb in, crawl to any end of the bus and tell me when your face is a third of a metre from the end.’

‘What’s a fucking third of a metre, speak in US measurement.’

‘Okay say, um, two feet then’

‘Okay I’m at the end, it’s bloody cramped in here and I just banged my head as there’s only three feet of head room.’

‘Right feel into the front and side corner about a foot up where you’ll feel a button, then press it.’ Incredibly a 150mm square opening appeared and Phonoi could see three of the team scouring the side of the bus. ‘Bring the rifle into position as if you are going to shoot one of the team but don’t push the nose of the silencer more than…urm, two inches outside,’ there was a slight pause. ‘have you done that yet?’

‘Yeah!’

‘Can you get them in your sights?’

‘Yeah!’

‘Good, now change sides. It’s going to be tight but you should be able to make it, then do the same as you did on the other side and let me know when you are two feet from the other end.’

‘Okay I’m there.’

‘Press the button, it’s at the same location but now it’s on your left side. Press it and it will open like the other side did. Do the same and sight the team on that side of the bus but make sure you don’t protrude the nose of the silencer more than two inches outside.’

‘Yeah done that. What now?’

‘You can come out.’

Hafeez asked both teams. 'Did you see anything obvious?'
All but one said they hadn't, one said he thought he saw something move but couldn't swear to it. 'The apertures that opened on the sides are in an area that has special 3D vinyl surrounds. It's very clever providing a gun barrel doesn't stick out more than five centimetres or two inches in US measures it's difficult to notice and the gun barrel blends in with the 3D image.'

Akrami came into the warehouse. 'Mr. Hafeez can I see you privately? It's urgent!'
'Yes, come into the office.'
'Well what is so urgent Akrami?'
'Tazi Emir asked me to tell you that he is sure there has been an undercover spy at Halifax Road. Tazi recognised him as Dani Quibi, an MI6 agent, who may be working for Bastion and saw him several times at MI6 headquarters when Tazi worked there and is now worried he may have overheard our meeting this morning about changing our attack tactics. Tazi Emir and Kamal Malik followed Quibi from the mosque and they believe they should bring him down but are awaiting your instruction. Can you ring Tazi now?'
Hafeez was already dialling: 'Severn eliminate the spy! Where are you?'
'We are in the next carriage to the target, on a direct train to King's Cross. We'll deal with him in London as the train is full. By the way, I don't think he has a phone as he hasn't used one for the last hour.'
'Okay make sure he's taken out before he can make contact with anyone or buy a new phone. Keep me posted as there is so much at stake.'

The Bradford train pulled into King's Cross station at 16:05. Doors banged and suitcases thumped and scraped along the platform on their four little wheels.

Some passengers scurried quickly trying to pass the slower ditherers and regular commuters who were in less of a hurry. Tazi and Kamal Malik were trying not to lose sight of Dani Quibi who was obviously in the scurrying category. Moving at the same rapid pace as Dani, the two pursuers followed him along the platform as far as the automatic ticket barriers which was when Dani, who was on his guard anyway, recognised Tazi Emir as their eyes transfixed on one another. Fuck, that's Tazi Emir from MI6. He has to be a double agent, working for Bastion and the IRF! They must have followed me from the Halifax Road mosque. I've got to get a message to Joe Carmichael or Max-Catt!

Dani's mind was thumping. He had to get away! He turned away from the queue waiting to insert their tickets in the automatic barriers otherwise he'd be trapped. Turning from the crowded ticket barrier he ran past a railway official and grabbed his pen from his top pocket as he sped past. The race was on as the two behind him started their chase as they were as desperate as Dani. He jumped down onto the tracks hoping they wouldn't be stupid enough to follow but they did and were only thirty metres behind him. Commuters were watching them, horrified of the consequences. Dani crossed the four electrified tracks and eventually came to the side end of the station to what look like a spare rolling stock, siding. He jumped down onto an expanse of gravel and ran twenty paces before climbing a massive coil of heavy duty cable on a wooden drum. From that gained height Dani jumped and almost cleared the spiked metal fence but his trousers got caught and tore from his shin to his foot which restricted his intended leap making him fall awkwardly but thankfully his cotton trousers gave way to the fence and he was now falling free to the ground.

Unfortunately he fell on his side rather than landing on his feet which bruised his hip and shoulder but adrenalin kept his flight to a maximum. The road sign Dani passed told him he was in York Road which ran parallel with the stations tracks. Although he fell badly at the fence he'd actually gained some distance on his chasers. A First City hotel further ahead on his left gave Dani the thought that that might be his best option so he ran into the hotel looking for a toilet. Time was against decency to look for a mens room so he ran into the ladies toilet instead, hoping he'd lost his pursuers but he hadn't! They followed him into the hotel and as there was no one on the Reception desk at that time, they searched around the ground floor area and eventually came to the ladies toilet and went straight in.

Dani had already scribbled out a note on the toilet roll:
THIS IS AN EMERGENCY, IT'S NOT A JOKE. LIVES ARE AT STAKE. CALL MI6 AND ASK FOR MR JOSEPH CARMICHAEL AND READ HIM WHAT IS BELOW:
THERE ARE SIX INFILTRATORS IN SIX SECRET INTELLIGENCE SERVICES ACTING AS DOUBLE AGENTS FOR THE IRF. THEY USE BRITISH RIVERS AS CODE NAMES IN CORRESPONDENCE. I'VE HEARD SEVERN AND TRENT MENTIONED AND THERE IS ALSO A HIRED KILLER FROM THE US CALLED FONNAY OR SOMETHING SIMILAR. THE IRF ARE PLANNING A NEW METHOD OF ATTACK AGAINST LONDON THAT IS IMMINENT. I AM UNDER ATTACK NOW.

There was a hard knocking on the door which Dani didn't answer. He stuck his toilet roll note to the door with chewed gum, hoping it would stick and that someone with the necessary acumen would hand the note in.

'If you are a female speak now or we break in.' Nothing! Tazi got astride Kamal Malik's shoulders and quietly walked towards the door and from his elevated position he peered over the top of the cubicle door.

Looking down into the toilet he could see Dani had his back pressed against the door with both feet placed against the pan making a strong brace, determined not to let his attackers in but they didn't need to get in as Tazi used his Bastion issued Smith and Wesson with an attached silencer to put a single 9mm bullet into the top of Dani's head which he didn't expect nor did he feel it! The two IRF men wanted to search Dani's pockets to see if he had a phone on his but Dani was lodged solid against the door so the two IRF men deliberating and calmly walked out of the hotel and went on their respective ways. Tazi went straight to his drop off newsagents and placed his message in a magazine and took it to the coordinator at the counter who would arrange the for the pickup courier to collect and deliver it.

Marked urgent it read: Suspect eliminated. Didn't have a phone. Believe no compromise has occurred.

Back home now, mission accomplished.

Severn!

31

A knock on Julia Deakin's door could only be the expected Max-Catt. 'Come in. Did you have a good weekend?'

'Indeed, two weddings announced, a venison and apricot pie, a whole bottle of Lochavennie consumed and I saw my parents. Yes a brilliant two days, thanks. What about yourself?'

Not as satisfying as yours by comparison but I did go out on a date. My old uni friend has been on to me for ages to go on a date so she threw a dinner party and guess what? Of course it was a matchmaking event. Me and the mystery chap were literally thrown together and it wasn't declared prior to the date trap invitation. Anyway as it turns out he's a decent chap and a military man. He's a captain in the First Rifles based at Beachley.'

'Good God, what's his name?'

'Gordon Long, why?'

'That's my old regiment, in fact my old battalion. I was based at Beachley. I know Gordon he was a first lieutenant in A company and commanded three platoon. What a bloody small world! Did he get his leg over?' Max froze! The thought of Gordon made him forget who he was talking with. 'I beg your pardon, what did you just say Maximus?'

'Oh sorry, it's an old battalion joke when a soldier meets a special lady, but I should have said it to the soldier not to the lady. I've been out of the mob for too long, sorry.'

‘No you haven’t and yes he did. We stayed together the whole weekend, it was bloody marvellous.’ The surprised stare changed in an instant from Julia to Max!

‘I think we have a serious problem Julia! Jade Jackson used great initiative and went to Tazi Emir’s parents address in Bradford to find out more about him and guess what, he has ties with a mosque there we have had under scrutiny. We needed some proof of our suspicions about that place and have, as you know, put a man, Dani Quibi, on the inside who is acting as a good muslim.. Worryingly I’ve not heard from him for several days and he’s a damn good and loyal guy and was instrumental in getting my imprisoned SAS team out of Aden.’

‘The other worry, well for me anyway, is my apartment has been entered by an uninvited guest. I used the old trick of pinning a light cotton line across my bedroom door which I’ve done since my tour of Afghanistan and the personal threats that followed.’

‘Anyway, to my horror, the cotton was broken although nothing was stolen apart from a photo of me. I do have a few unhappy terrorists after me swearing revenge but that goes with my territory I suppose. A legacy from Afghanistan and Winchester which is part of the job I signed up for but still this is a bit close to home, don’t you think.’
‘Bloody hell Max. Do you want to come back to your quarters here?’
‘Nah, thanks anyway Julia. I think I can look after myself which I have done since my schooldays.’
‘Okay, now I want chapter and verse of the missions in France, Albania and Turkey.’ Max explained his recent mission including finally getting out of a Turkish airport with his team by the skin of their teeth.

Max then had to dash and excused himself from Julia while asking her that if MI6 called with news of Dani to let him know immediately.

Max grabbed some lunch and asked Tazi to see him in his office at 14:30. 'Okay Tazi, you do realise you are still on my probation watch and I can send you back to MI6 whenever I choose. What you did and what you didn't do in Shelly Street was nothing short of dereliction of duty, a sackable offence in fact so why should I keep you in the Bastion team. We are the elite in Britain's security and you are far below our expectation level. What do you say about that?'

'I killed to save Maclean's life didn't I?'

'Bad decision and according to Maclean the man was in the gutter dying anyway when you shot him twice unnecessarily in cold blood. Look I'm not a saint, you can't be when you have to make instant decisions and there's always collateral damage in our line of work which is accepted but you had time to make the right call and you didn't.'

'Until I'm satisfied with you I want your Smith and Wesson and any ammunition you are holding and I want to see your weapon log when you bring me your gun. From this afternoon you will be in an unclassified office until further notice. Now go and fetch me your handgun.'

Tazi didn't like being put in his place and made a vow to get Max-Catt if Phonoi failed but with the Yank's global reputation he doubted if he'd get the chance. Emir slunk off boiling inside and returned immediately to Max with his gun, twenty-four rounds of 9mm ammunition and his weapon log.

Tazi was then dismissed to report to an unclassified administration office. Max checked the weapon which was pristine and well oiled, as indeed it should be. Tazi's weapon log showed twenty-five rounds of ammunition signed out on the 18th of April and it was now the 24th. There was no bullet in the gun's chamber so one round was missing and unaccounted for. Max pondered this: I'll not press him on the missing cartridge just yet.

Then Max went to speak to Jade to debrief her properly about her trip north and to tell her she was to be included in the next operational mission. Jade covered everything while Max made notes, he mentally acknowledged he was very proud of her actions!

32

Kamal Hafeez took Phonoi back to Mousa's office. 'Well Phonoi can you handle the tour bus operation? Remember you must take out a minimum of ten coppers, or no pay-out and it must be on the same day. We need to make an initial impact. Well do we have a deal or not?'

'You have a deal but I must see ten or I want a retainer.'

'You'll see more than ten, that's a promise. There is a recess that has a slide cover that will be your sealed chemical toilet…'

'How long will I be in there for?' Zimmermann interrupted. 'Could be six hours, depending on your performance with your rifle.'

'That won't be an issue. I didn't get my nickname for nothing.'

'Yeah sure, anyway with you sealed away, the bus will drive to Belvedere Road which is route one Stop 1. There we will take on passengers in the normal way and the tourists will be given headphones and unless it's raining we will fill up the top deck of the bus first. Ahmed will have an earpiece if you need to speak with him in an emergency. The tourists nearest to your unit won't hear the muffled shots from the soundproofed unit as shown in the practice firing session and with the raised 3D vinyl place around the firing apertures your gun barrel will not be seen providing, as I have said, you don't protrude the nose of the silencer out more than five cen…oops sorry, two inches.'

'We start tomorrow morning and there are between 1,500 and 2,000 coppers on duty in central London so you'll have plenty of targets to choose from. After each killing there will be chaos and devastation in the bus's wake as it leaves the scene looking every part to be innocent.'

The driver has practiced the route several times and he will keep driving normally after you make each kill and will simply drive to the next stop. I want double figures and you must indicate to Ahmed when you have reached your target kills of ten. He will then discharge the passengers at their requested stops but not take any more on, saying that the bus has finished for the day.'

'The idea is that if the bus is searched at a roadblock or cordon there will be genuine tourists from many countries onboard and this will satisfy the police. We have all bases covered and the driver is connected on a three way communication system so will know to slow down when approaching the targets so I think we are all set. All I have to do now is to advise Transport for London that we will start our service tomorrow.'

Hafeez then gave Brad Zimmermann Max-Catt's address which had been given to him by river agent Severn, Tazi Emir. 'Here are the keys to the gate, the block and the special security key to the penthouse. They may take some waggling as they were copied from a mould and be careful as we have made several attempts to rid ourselves of Max-Catt only to finish up losing some experienced hitmen. He is ex-SAS and is deadly as well as brave. I know your reputation goes before you but he's good!'

The yank tossed the keys up and down in his palm and just smirked disdainfully at Hafeez.

Brad Zimmermann took the Tube to Kew Gardens and then took a taxi to Strand-on-the-Green, just a couple of miles away. His first impression of the area was one of affluence with the south facing line of apartments overlooking the Thames. The trained marksman walked the area making mental notes as was his modus operandi and this meticulous preparation before a killing made him the best.

He was now in the building and had a thought: I should try the buzzer first to see if anyone is home in Penthouse 3.

He got through the gate and building easily enough and was keen to test the key in the ten-point locking system. It took some gentle wiggling before the key turned three times in the lock and with the slightest of pushes the door opened and Brad Zimmermann was in Max's apartment.

After checking every room, Brad left the penthouse and walked to the front of the block that overlooked the Thames. The angle was too great from the nearside of the Thames but he saw some buildings that were higher on the other side of the river and estimated that from the roof of two of the tall buildings he would have a clear sight across the river and into Max's apartment. His favoured Tikka T3X Tact A1 rifle was long range so he decided to check out the high buildings.

He went into one of the building unchallenged and took the lift to the fifth floor and found the stairs which led to the roof which had a had a good view of west London and a clear view across the river, almost opposite Thames Mews. He went to the riverside edge of the flat roof and crouched behind three giant air-conditioning units with their propellers turning naturally in the wind.

From the cover of these quiet fans he laid down on the decking and simulated firing a rifle at Max's large panoramic window. Through binoculars, Phonoi picked out a bowl of fruit and pretended to pull the T3X's trigger. If he did decide to use the the roof he would wear a white smock and carry a parcel that would get his Tika T3X into the building without it being noticed.

The balance was swinging towards the roof and he would make his mind by the following day.

33

It was just like any other day, tourists coming in and going out of the First City Hotel in Kings Cross in London apart from one exception, there were double the amount of people checking in for that time of year.

A flustered cleaner came from the bar area trying to get the attention of any of the Reception staff but was not having much luck so, Pam Jones, the cleaner jockeyed her way to the front of the check in queue.

'Please can I have a word, one of the toilet….'

'Go away, cleaners are not supposed to be in Reception, can't you see I'm with a guest and we're flat out. I've not even had a chance to drink my coffee.' The abrupt receptionist apologised to the couple she was checking in while simultaneously waving Pam Jones away with her hand as if she was just an irritating fly. 'Arrogant bitch.' Pam muttered under her breath but as luck would have it she saw one of the housekeeping staff who she knew.

'Carol can I have a quick word! I can't get into one of the cubicles in the ladies toilet in the lounge bar. Do you know where Tom the handyman is? I tried to get Reception to call him but I got brushed away by that arrogant cow.' Pam Jones pointed to the rude receptionist.

'I have Tom's number so I'll call him for you Pam. Shall I tell him to meet you at the entrance to the bar?'

'Yeah, thanks Carol. The thing is I can't sign off the toilets until I've cleaned all of them and number three is locked which it has been all the while I've been cleaning all the toilet for the last half hour and if I don't sign that toilet off I'll get in serious trouble!' Carol acknowledged Pam Jones' concern with an understanding nod.

Tom the caretaker-handyman came straight away following Carol's request. 'Pam is it you who needs my muscle getting into a loo?'
'Hi Tom, thanks for coming so quick. I'm all behind as it is. Number three cubicle is locked and it has been for a good half an hour. I've tapped on the door several times but there's no answer and I just hope it isn't a spaced out druggie!'

'Come on let's go and have a look.' Tom pushed the door on cubicle three but there was no give so he put a bit more shoulder into a second attempt and that time there was a slight budging! 'That's strange, it's definitely not a jammed lock and the indicator is showing engaged.'

Tom went into the next cubicle and stood on the toilet pan and heaved himself up to peer over the partition into number 3. 'Oh my God, oh my God! There's a body in there! That's what's preventing the door from opening and there's blood from a head wound by the looks! Stay here why I tell Reception and close off the toilets!'

The handyman rang the assistant manager. 'We have a dead body in cubicle 3 and by the hole in the top of his head I'd say it was foul play? Get the police immediately and I've asked Pam Jones from cleaning to close the ladies toilet and stay by the entrance to prevent anyone going in there.'

The police arrived within ten minutes and across the entrance to the ladies toilets was placed 'Police crime scene-do not cross this line!' The body of Dani Quibi was placed on a plastic sheet in the washroom area for the forensic pathologist to inspect. The cause of death was obvious to any onlooker and the pathologist gave the time of death as between 16:00 and 17:30 the previous afternoon, just after the cleaning was signed off by Pam Jones. A uniformed constable found the note on toilet paper on the washroom floor and handed it to a detective. It was a third of the scribbled message with the remaining two thirds of the note still stuck to the toilet door which was removed by an inspector who bagged it as evidence to eventually be forwarded to Joe Carmichael at MI6.

A photo of the victim and a copy of the scribbled note was sent by police courier Miss Julia Deakin who immediately called Max to her office.

'Look at these, they have just arrived from Joe Carmichael at MI6.' Max took the folder that Julia slid across her desk towards him. 'Christ that's Dani Quibi, oh no, no!'

'You obviously know the dead man. Was he a friend?

'He saved four of my SAS team, that's who he is! My God, Dani! He was working undercover at the suspect mosque in Bradford so they must have discovered him which is why I've had no communication from him for a few days.

Max read the note for Joe Carmichael's attention out loud. There are six infiltrators in six of our secret intelligence services. 'That must include Bastion and our infiltrator is pointing strongly towards Tazi Emir with his coincidental connection with Bradford and the Halifax Road mosque so we were right to suspend him from field activities.' Max continued reading: They use British rivers as code names, Severn and Trent were mentioned. 'Do you know Julia, I heard a couple of rivers mentioned either in passing or on a document somewhere but I'm damned if I can recall where or when but one was definitely Severn as I remember not being able to make head or tail of it.' Max continued reading the last piece of the message. There is also a hired killer from the US called Fonnay or something like that and the IRF are planning a new method of attack in London which is imminent. I have to finish now, they are trying to break in.....

'A hitman? I wonder what or who the target is but it sounds serious for the IRF to bring in a special professional. Very ominous indeed.'

There's a different style of attack coming imminently to London so we have to be on our toes Julia.'

'I agree Max, I wonder should we arrest Tazi?'

'Not yet, we don't have any actual proof he's involved but, by golly, we'll be watching him closely from now on and I'll get Callum or Mason to put him under surveillance. Now the next worry is what is the new imminent IRF attack in London and I suspect that Dani must have been getting close to their plans before he was uncovered,' Max's phone rang, interrupting his conversation with Julia, which he normally would have ignored but the ringtone was personalised for Joe Carmichael. 'Excuse me Julia, it's Joe Carmichael MI6.'

Max and Joe discussed the tragic murder of Dani and both were clearly upset over the loss of a true brave friend.

'Please let me know when his funeral is although I doubt it will be soon as the coroner's office will need to investigate it thoroughly owing to the circumstances in which he was killed.' Joe didn't say anymore, he couldn't.

'Sorry about that Julia, Dani meant so much to me and was like a brother to Joe. He will be sorely missed.'

'I understand Maximus but unfortunately death goes with the Bastion territory and is always just one step behind us.

'Just one thing, Julia, Joe said Dani was killed adjacent to King's Cross Station and must have got there from the Bradford to London train. Do me a favour and get one of our snoop departments to get the names of the passengers on all the King's Cross to Bradford trains starting from say from 13:00 on Saturday through to 17:00. Let's see if that throws up a certain Tazi Emir by any chance which would certainly put him in the frame. Emir worked for MI6 when Dani started there so I bet he recognised him at the mosque. I can't wait to get the forensic's ballistic report on the bullet that killed Dani as one of Tazi's is unaccounted for according to his firearm log. I fancy the net is closing in on Tazi Emir who probably has the code name of Severn.'
'I'll instruct that order now.' Julia was already ringing the snoops as Max left her office.

He was still churning over ideas when a knock on his office door startled Max. It was Jade Jackson. 'Ah come in Jade, I wanted to see you but you evidently want something so you go first.'
'Tazi is acting very strange and is asking me if I know why he's been suspended from field duties and had you said anything to me about him. Of course I wouldn't divulge anything to him as I don't trust him.'
'Good, I'm almost certain Tazi is an undercover agent for the IRF and he can inflict untold damage to our organisation so I want to try a plan and I need your to help me with it!'
'Anything Max. What is it?'
'Get in discussion with him about the new intel that's just come in about the IRF and our planned raid on the Halifax Road mosque which should get him interested. I'll give you a top secret folder for you to leave on the top of your bag and like any Magpie or rat, he'll see the bait. Have a friendly chat with Tazi and say that you want to get a coffee and a sandwich and could he keep

an eye on your bag and he's bound to look into it in your absence.'

'He must be desperate for any information and will think he's hit the jackpot with that folder and will want to warn his IRF handlers immediately.'

'I intend to follow his every move after he reads the memo and need to see how he dispatches his information to the IRF but he will know how effective our listening and intel department works so I doubt he'll make contact by phone so if it's by courier we shall have a team of two motorbike riders follow the rider. Then, the sting!'

34

There was raised tension at Rorke Street in Limehouse, the new IRF south headquarters, higher than on most normal days which emanated mostly from Kamal Hafeez as he raged that an infidel enemy had infiltrated the sanctum of the IRF communications hub in Bradford. 'What the fuck is going on at Halifax Road? I turn my back for a few hours to prepare, organise and almost guarantee a hit at the heart of Britain and I get news that we have an infidel spy amongst us! My beloved deputy and trusted friend Bini Akrami was found dead in our own fucking toilet at Halifax Road. Fortunately I've had a message from our river agent Severn that he and Trent were going to deal with him. I blame you Mousa for this breach, it was on your recommendation that I interview Sani Yosef for my staff. He had special talents you said, a brilliant prospect you said, never missed prayers you said! Now he's murdered my deputy and run away and I just hope Severn got to him before the bastard got back to Bastion.

There was a waiting message for Hafeez delivered by the drop off courier which negated Hafeez's stress momentarily which read: The man I followed from the mosque is Dani Quibi, he must be an infiltrator as I recognised him from my employment at MI6. He was an undercover field agent used by MI6 in South Yemen. Staff at Vauxhall Cross refer to him as a hero. In my opinion he was co-opted by Bastion to go undercover at the mosque. Anyway I can now report I have killed Dani Quibi and am positive it was before he had a chance to report anything to Bastion. He didn't have a phone on him or used one during the time Trent and I started following him from the mosque. On a different point, I am still suspended from field duties at Bastion stemming from Shelly Street and believe I'm under suspicion! Severn.

'Thank goodness we have some people with brains in our organisation. That man you recommended Mousa was a spy from Bastion.'

'Yes Kamal, I'm sorry. I can see I was careless in my choice of recommendation.'

'Anyway it looks like the problem has been averted and the infidel spy killed in the process so no real harm done I suppose. Now we have things to do as tomorrow we make our first planned attack on the Metropolitan police. I need to see Phonoi so has he arrived here yet?'

'Yes he's waiting for you.'

'Send him to me then get a train back to Bradford.'

'Phonoi are you ready for tomorrow morning? The special bus left Bradford this morning and will already be in our industrial unit at Isleworth and it is planned to leave there at 08:30. Will you take a taxi to the warehouse or shall I pick you up from your hotel? I am going there to see the bus team off and get you settled into your compartment.'

'Yeah, pick me up at my hotel, I'm staying at The Rose hotel in Brentford tonight and I'll be outside tomorrow morning at 07:00 so don't be late!' The lack of respect for Hafeez was evident from Phonoi but the IRF southern leader wasn't bothered as long as the assassin did his job for the cause tomorrow. 'Alright and in the meantime I'll get a drop off courier message to Severn.'

Brad Zimmermann left Limehouse for his west London hotel and had a few drinks in the bar before doing what he always did before a hit which was to take his rifle apart and oil every moving part then reassemble it and through the fine net curtains he practiced shooting pedestrians by lining his magnified sights up to get the crosshairs on the head of a selected target. He breathed out and moved his rifle at the pace of the walker and then a click followed by the pretend putt-putt noise that the silencer would make.

Wednesday morning was a bright sunny Spring day with the sun beaming through the Rose hotel's breakfast room window into the eyes of Phonoi. He moved to the other side of the table as the glare was no more than an irritant but it was distracting his concentration while he was going over the plan for that day's turkey shoot. Brad Zimmermann had his holdall by the table and had already checked out.

'Hi Brad, are you ready to get very rich?' There was no reply from the sullen Brad Zimmermann and Kamal Hafeez got the message. The two walked into the hangar-like warehouse to see the bus they had last seen in Bradford which was still gleaming with the striking red and yellow colours on the black livery. Hafeez led Phonoi over to a group of three men who made up the team.

'Okay, this is the day we get revenge for all our martyrs that died trying to bring the UK government down. We failed in our attempts to destroy the Houses of Parliament in Westminster and failed to attack the planned Luton shopping centre because of Bastion and their so-called elite agent Max-Catt but, my brothers, today we hit at the very heart of London's security system and will cause chaos throughout the Metropolitan police and the government.'

'Our audacious attack will have the government shuddering and their COBRA committee in turmoil. Now put your earpieces in and Ahmed you will be crucial to coordinate the operations between our driver Abdullah and Phonoi. Now talk to each other as you have a three way system so each will hear the conversation of the others. Right Abdullah speak with Phonoi.'

'Phonoi, can you hear me?'

'Yes.' That was all Brad Zimmermann could muster.

'Okay Ahmed now you speak to Abdullah.'

'Do you hear me Abdullah?'

'Yes Ahmed, loud and clear.'

'Good, now Phonoi we shall seal you into your compartment.' There was no reply from the man who only speaks when he thinks it's necessary to do so but he did follow Kamal Hafeez up the stairs to the front of the bus

The cleverly concealed release bolts allowed the front upholstered sheet to be removed allowing Brad Zimmermann to enter the secret compartment with his now fully assembled Fold AR-15 rifle and sports bag with refreshments and rounds of ammunition. Phonoi was ready and was sealed into the soundproof claustrophobic chamber. Hafeez asked for Ahmed's earpiece and spoke to the hitman. 'Can you hear me Phonoi?'

'Yep.'

'Try the auto opening flap on both sides.'

'First one, left side is fine,' There was half a minutes pause, the time taken for Zimmermann to twist around and get to the right side. 'Yeah, all good on the right side.'

'I'll be watching on TV and I expect 10 kills, nothing less! Abdullah take the bus to the Belvedere Road bus stop Good hunting.' The bus left for its first stop.

35

Friday 08:00

Callum Maclean, Mason Perkins and Jade Jackson sat in an interview room at 08:00 waiting for Max-Catt to arrive. The sun was beaming through the small high windows catching the sparkle in Jade's excited eye and the solar warmth was a blessing after five days of continuous bad weather. The sun was not the only thing shining as Jade had already spoken to Max about a possible way to entrap Tazi Emir, the ostracised field agent they didn't trust.

'Good morning team and what a lovely day. Sadly I have to confirm that we have a traitor in our midst!' Max explained all the latest developments concerning Tazi Emir, the death of Dani, the man who had made Max and his SAS team's escape from Aden possible and also touched on Jade's visit to Bradford and her intel.

'With Jade's help we will entrap Tazir and bring him to justice and we have a plan.'

'You two fine fellows are going to follow Tazi everywhere he goes and your surveillance and pursuit skills will be tested with this one so we will set the trap at lunchtime today. Callum and Mason go to the makeup and disguise department and get some realistic following gear. Tazi must be using a courier service and it's probably by motorbike I would think.'

'Okay folks let's set the trap. Here's the file Jade so leave it on the top of your bag and as I said to you earlier watch Tazi and make conversation with him then ask him to watch your bag while you get yourself some food and a coffee. The rest is out of our control until he takes the bait but once he reads the contents he'll need to warn the IRF of the raid. We will intercept the courier and see what warning Tazi has sent, well that's the theory. Good luck.' Max then went to Julia to explain the plan.

'I think that's a smart move Max, that should draw him out and get us the proof we need. Bastion has sweeping powers but we are not above British law although, reading some of your mission reports over the last year, I wouldn't say you are actually law abiding but internal affairs need to be more circumspect which I'm sure you'll agree?'
'Of course Julia, one must not upset the wokey civil servants must one.'
'Now you are piss taking Maximus which doesn't become you.' They both caught each other's expression and grinned which said more than any words could but Max knew what his boss was alluding to and realised he would need proof to take any action against Tazi Emir.

Jade Jackson was in an unused room that had a view across the corridor to the main unclassified material filing offices for intel that came into Bastion but was deemed not sensitive or would pose a risk if it leaked. This intel came into Bastion from the four other UK secret service organisations each day and was vetted by a skilled team to sort and place into the classified category or not. Tazi, until proven otherwise, was in that department where he could do no damage.

Jade waited until Tazi and a few others left the unclassified office to go for lunch in the canteen which was one floor down. Jade held back until another group from another department went down as well and then fell in with them as part of that group.

'Hey Tazi where have you been hiding.' Jade pretended she didn't know he was doing the most unimportant job in Bastion. 'Hello Jade I've been dropped from field duties.'

'That doesn't seem at all fair to me Tazi, you had such good results in all your exams when we passed out from our final exams. Let's have a little catch up but first would you keep an eye on my bag while I get some lunch and coffee?'

'Sure.' Jade placed her bag, not too obviously, on a chair one way from Tazi so he couldn't reach it from his current seating position.

Jade headed for the self-service queue and it wasn't long before the river spy rat sniffed out the inviting bait, the brown folder with top secret stamped on it. He slid stealthily to the next chair and, with a quick hand movement, the folder was on Tazi's lap below the table where he photoed the contents and then quickly pushed the folder back to where it was.

'Thanks Tazi, may I join you?'

'Yes but unfortunately I have to get back so I'm taking my food with me and I'll see you around Jade.' Tazi didn't want to take chances and now was his opportunity to see what the contents of the top secret folder were and he knew exactly what next port of call was but so did Jade!

When Tazi got back to his office he opened his phone to read the contents of the top secret file that he had copied.

His worst fear was there before his eyes. Shit, they know about the Halifax Road mosque and they are going to raid it imminently but there's no mention of me. I've got to get a courier message to Bradford as soon as possible.

'Excuse me Colin, I have a migraine which is killing me with the bright sunshine and lights so can I take the afternoon off? I want to get to a dark room, preferably my bedroom would be good.'
'Sure Tazi, we are up to date with our in-trays and I won't put it down as a holiday as I can see you are concerned.'
'Thanks Colin. I'll get off then and will see you on Monday. Have a good weekend.'

Tazi Emir came out of his office and Jade watched him descend two floors to the underground car park. Not wanting to lose him, she ran down the stairs to the car park and watched Tazi drive out, then quickly running to her car, Jade followed the exiting suspect. She was four cars behind Tazi's blue Toyota and provided she didn't get held up at any traffic lights, she was a healthy distance away to follow him. They went through Uxbridge and turned onto the Harrow Road and she watched as Tazi turned into a side street and parked up. Jade was about to follow him into the street when she noticed him getting out of his car so she instinctively swung round to her right and parked across the road.

She didn't have full eyes on him until he passed a parked lorry and was then walking in her direction but turned sharply into a newsagents on the corner of the junction that split the street where he had parked and the Harrow Road where Jade was parked on double yellows. After putting on her hazard lights she followed him into the shop.

Jade, in full disguise, pretended to be looking for something on the shelves while keeping an eye on Tazi who was poring over a magazine which he then closed and took two other magazines to the counter presumably to buy in full view of Jade. Then something strange happened. He placed the two magazines on the counter and paid the vendor with a ten pound note but only took one of the magazines away with him and then the shopkeeper put the other magazine under his counter. That's odd paying for two magazines but only taking one. This must be a message collecting point for the IRF.

It was quick decision time for Jade Jackson. Did she follow Tazi or wait for a courier who might collect the other magazine. She returned to her Fiat 500 and called Max on a secure encrypted line. 'Max your trap worked, Tazi is off work. I followed him to a newsagent on the Harrow Road in Uxbridge which I believe is a message hub for the river agents to contact the IRF. I was in disguise so I followed him into the shop where I saw him mulling over magazines. All this could have been innocuous but he picked up two glossies and paid for them but left one of them on the counter after which the shopkeeper placed it underneath the counter. I let Tazi leave thinking it would be better to watch the newsagent to see if someone collects a possible message. What do you want me to do Max?'

'I want you to keep your phone on Jade! I've been trying to contact you all bloody morning. There's been a terrorist attack in central London this morning. I've sent Callum and Mason to Westminster and it's pandemonium there! We have a much bigger problem now as ten coppers are dead, shot by a sniper in central London! Jade composed herself and prepared her explanation!

36

FIVE HOURS EARLIER

The morning was bright sunshine with a slight nip in the Spring air but the days were edging ever closer to May and the blossom on the trees were defying the previous cold snap brought in from the northeast by Artic winds. That morning had a late Spring feel to it and people were shedding their winter garments.

Tourists were busy chatting excitedly in the yellow route queue at bus stop number one on Belvedere Road. Orientals in large groups were sporting top of the range photographic equipment around their necks and everyone seemed to have a cell phone on a stick hoping to get a selfie in front of Big Ben or one of the many iconic buildings in the famous city.

When the bright gleaming Met-Hopper tour bus came in to view the anticipating passengers didn't know it was its maiden journey. The bus had a team of two, the driver and the friendly money collector and most of the tourists purchased the twenty four hour day pass to hop on and hop off the bus as they wished. As the chatting tourists climbed aboard they each collected their earphones from Ahmed and most passengers, owing to the sunny day, chose the open top upstairs. Ahmed checked that everybody was sitting down and gave the nod to Abdullah to take the bus away.

The headphones went from the entry music to a welcome message in a choice of six languages that the individual tourists preselected once they had plugged into the facility with the narrative synched to each point of interest on the yellow route.

The bus moved slowly away into London's heavy traffic and left the South Bank by crossing the Thames towards Covent Garden and the Royal Opera House. Ahmed had been instructed by Kamal Afeez not to start the shooting until the third stop.

The tour bus moved on to Ludgate and St. Paul's cathedral and at the second stop some tourists got off and new ones got on so the bus was nearly full on the top deck obviously due to the glorious weather.

Ahmed spoke into the penny sized microphone on his sleeve. 'Very interesting building on the right.' The driver was also privy to this message and slowed the bus down. Phonoi was lying on his left side so twisted his body in the claustrophobic compartment. He felt in the dark for the recessed slider to open the concealed flap and immediately identified his targets. Two police officers were talking to each other as they walked across a grassed area near a full sized statue. 'This is the third time this week I've got the cathedral beat, It's as boring as…..' 'Shaun what the….' Three things then happened simultaneously. A women dropped her shopping bag and screamed at the entangled dead bodies of Shaun and his colleague, the small unnoticeable flap closed and the yellow and red gleaming bus went through the green traffic lights and on to Queen Victoria Street, stop number four, where more people boarded the Met Hopper tourist bus.

All the seated tourist had headphones bar none and were totally oblivious to the two executions now well back in their wake. Ahmed suspended further instructions to Phonoi for two reasons, no targets and to get a good distance away from the scene of the first shootings.

The information coming through the headphones was holding the attention of the global band of tourists who were listening in their different language options and moving their heads from right to left as each place of interest was pointed out to them.

The next passengers to alight from the deadly bus was at stop number six where Ahmed spotted another police officer but thought the angle would be, in his estimation, too difficult when there would be other better options along the route. So on they went picking up and dropping off passengers and it wasn't until stop number nine that Ahmed got excited and pretended to tidy the piles of plastic bags that held the red headphones to disguise that he was talking into the microphone on his sleeve.

'Interesting building on the right.' The ninth stop was Westminster Bridge and when the flap slid open Phonoi could see three police officers, two together with one speaking into his radio and the other with his arms folded and the third was away from the pair and crouching into a car window to a driver who was in a queue of stopped cars at the southern end of the bridge. No one in the trio of police expected what happened next! Phut, one down, phut, two down.

Phonoi lined up the side-on profile of the helpful lawman's temple. Phut, three down, shutter closed. The bus was still stationary but about to move off with the traffic light changing to green at the end of the bridge. It was over so quick as a few passers-by rushed to aid of the fallen policemen but most of them sensibly ran for any cover that they could find. Then sirens could be heard with police cars racing to the scene and the pandemonium was compounded by motorists rubber necking at the passing police cars.

Abdullah, the driver, once more left behind a lethal wake of misery. The operations room's phones were jammed at the Metropolitan police headquarters as other organisations called to get any detailed information. The anti-terrorism office, MI5 and Bastion were now on the highest terrorist alert.

At Buckingham Palace Phonoi got the 'Interesting building' message and manoeuvred himself in to position. There were, as expected, large crowds outside the palace with plenty of yellow high vis targets everywhere. Phut, the first officer was somewhere at the feet of the crowd and out of sight until the crowd cleared an area around him.

Phut phut! Bullets whistled into the chests of two more targets. Screaming and chaos was everywhere as the crowd dispersed in panic which prevented the tour bus from returning up the Mall. This time the Met Hopper passengers saw the adjacent slaughter but were totally unaware that the executioner was in their tour bus.

Abdullah put his foot down scattering the flow of people in his path which worked like Moses parting the sea.

Police and ambulances arrived at the scene as well as unmarked blue flashing vehicles, all heading towards the King's palace and the mayhem there.

The glossy red and yellow bus was again stopped but this time it was in a traffic jam caused by a recently constructed roadblock across the Mall.

The police were checking all vehicles leaving the palace area and Ahmed greeted the two plain clothed officers as they boarded the bus. All the passengers were asked to show their ID's and were asked to stand away from their seats as the police checked for weapons. The police did the same on the top deck but were satisfied that the bus had no involvement in the murders of their colleagues and allowed it to go once they had inspected the licences and permits required for tour bus operators. Then the bus dropped quite a few scared passengers off at stop number eighteen in the Haymarket but no one got on.

Ahmed two police motor bikes on the right side of the wide road and spoke softly into his sleeve-mic. 'Interesting building coming up on your right.' The sniper twisted and positioned himself by the right side aperture and looked out of his peephole. Two more quiet phuts from his Fold AR-15 rifle and the two motorbike biker officers collided into each other before being thrown off their bikes with only one visible as the big 650cc BMW bike covered him.

The bus moved sharply on, having slowed down for the hitman's benefit which was unnecessary as Brad Zimmermann's speciality was moving targets and he was globally renowned for it. Now it was time to stop the killing as he had reached his quota of ten strikes as confirmed by Ahmed and Abdullah the driver. At stop number nineteen, the penultimate stop of the tour, Ahmed asked everybody to leave the bus because stop number twenty at Westminster bridge was closed off as a crime scene.

With the devil's work done, they returned to the Isleworth commercial park and once inside the temporary garage the bus stopped for the last time that day. Kamal Hafeez was there to greet them: 'I have seen the television coverage and you have been on all the news stations since 10:00 this morning.'

Hafeez slapped Brad Zimmermann on the back.

'I don't need your accolade, just give me my two million dollars and I'll get back to my hotel.' Such a friendly arsehole. Hafeez thought sarcastically. 'Here you are, in two bundles of a million each.' Phonoi turned on his heels and left Hafeez shaking his head but he was fully aware and now had it proven that Phonoi was the right man to get Max-Catt!

37

FIVE HOURS LATER (PRESENT TIME)

Jade Jackson apologised. 'Sorry Max, I had to turn my phone off, I was on close surveillance watching Tazi and couldn't afford to attract attention to myself.' Jade explained all the events of the morning up to Tazi leaving the newsagents.

'Bloody hell Jade, I should have known you had a good reason. You did the right thing and I'm coming to like you, I'm certain too that a courier is going to visit the newsagent very soon and if he turns up before I get there follow him if you can keep up with what is sure to be a motorbike.'

I've thought of that and have a tracker that I'll stick on his bike when he's in the shop doing the pickup.'

'Bloody well done Jade. I didn't think about doing that but be careful though as he'll probably be armed.'

'Yes sir, I will but be as quick as you can please!' Max didn't answer as he was on his way to Uxbridge with a magnetic blue flashing light stuck on his Porsche.

Thirty minutes passed before a smooth looking machine pulled up almost outside the shop which looked like a very rapid bike. The guy didn't remove his helmet which was a sure sign that the rider wasn't going to be hanging around but Jade was already preparing. As the biker went into the shop she pretended to be just walking by but as she passed the bike she stooped and deftly placed a magnetic transmitter on to the underside of the chassis frame and then nonchalantly walked on.

‘Hi Max, he’s just literally gone up the road.’

‘Jump in Jade.’ The two Bastion agents had started the chase with Jade navigating, guided by a bleeping red dot on her phone. ‘Good God, what’s been happening in central London?’

‘I’ve got our other two agents at the Met’s mobile control room, although the attacks started at St. Paul’s and then the shooting spree moved on to Westminster bridge, Buckingham Palace and then at the Haymarket where two motorbike patrol riders were shot. It appears that this spate of attacks has stopped or at least paused but whether temporarily or not we have no idea but I suppose we’ll know soon enough!

‘We are gaining on our quarry and according to my receiver we are now only half a mile back from the biker.’

‘It looks like he’s heading for the M1 motorway which would be the route he’d take if, as we suspect, he’s going to the Bradford mosque. I don’t know whether to stick on my blue magnetic light and pull him over or just nudge him off the road.’

This decision wasn’t necessary as events dictated. They could now see the biker turning into a petrol station to obviously fill up with petrol before his assumed journey north. ‘If he doesn’t go into the loo I’ll um….let’s say interview him on the forecourt here.

Again this decision was made for Max as the courier paid for his fuel and sweets and was heading for the toilets as Max-Catt was entering the shop in anticipation. The biker had to go through the faff of dropping his weatherproof over trousers that didn’t have a fly in them and just when he had dropped these around his knees Max pounced. He dragged the startled guy to the wall, pressing his Glock 19 deep into the neck of the pathetically frightened man with his over-trousers around his knees begging not to be shot and offering Max all his money. 'Take my wallet, my cards and watch, anything but don't shoot me please.'

'Have a quick piss, pull your trousers up and don't forget to wash your hands. Move!' Max kept his gun handy in his pocket and when the pisser had washed his trembling hands, Max gave him further instructions. 'Okay pal, walk to your bike, don't try to run or deviate from my instructions. After you. Right sunshine, walk your machine over to the rubbish bins but don't start it up.' The courier hadn't lost his anxiety and kept looking suspiciously at Max and Jade who had now joined them at the bins.

'Okay Postman Pat, you and I need a chat so give me the message you have in your pocket and if you say you haven't got it I'll search you and you really will not like that because every piece of your clothing I take off will be put in those bins over there. Are we understood?'
'I don't have no letter.'
'Tut tut, such bad grammar. Okay take both pairs of your trousers off or I'll take them off for you!'
'Stop, let me explain.'
'Too late for that pal. You have two seconds to get both pairs of your trousers off. 1….2.' Max made two quick moves and the biker was flat on his back. Max put his foot on the man's chest while roughly cutting his trousers right through the zip area and the belt with his SAS issued knife. The man screamed as his clothes fell from his body. A do-gooder came across from the pumps and inquired what was going on. Max turned to face him but continued to keep his foot on the chest of the squirming biker.

Max didn't say a word and just gave the do-gooder a cold stare as his body builders physic replaced any requirement of words. 'I…erm, just wondered if anyone

needed help?' Still no words as the stare had the last say and the man turned and scurried away without another glance. The trousers were off. 'Stay there. Jade watch him a moment.' Max went over to the bin and threw the two, almost in half, pairs of trousers into the recycling bin. 'Okay my friend give me your dispatch envelope. Please!'
'I've just come to fill my bike up, I don't have anything. Honest!'
'1....2.' Max pulled the guy up and removed his jacket but the man pulled back in a token of weak defence and got a slap across the face for his protestation. The leather jacket, like the trousers was sliced parallel to the zip-line as the sharp knife found no resistance from the black leather and Jade assisted by pulling the coat off. 'Search the pockets Jade.' It was one of those jackets that had too many zip pockets. After a thorough search with no luck Max asked again. 'Give me the envelope or the note. 1...2. Okay turn your head Jade this may be ugly.' With one swish of his Special Forces knife, the guy's black Calvin Klein boxer shorts flapped in two parts. The man was screaming which produced another slap from Max and was told to shut it. The biker was down to his shredded undies and shirt. He'd had enough.

Pointing to one of his leather boots. 'It's in there.' The almost naked courier was shivering with the cold. 'Jade take his jacket to the rubbish. I do like to keep my promises...um that's a point I don't even know your name yet and you have already shown me your dick. How rude of me.' Max looked at the courier's credit card. 'oh it's Mohammad Feisi. Where are my manners? So Mohammad all that just for nothing apart from losing your clothes. You guys never learn do you?'

‘Look in that boot Jade.’ Max pointed to the furthest flung leather boot and stuffed down it was a crumpled brown envelope.

Max read the typed note:

*Bastion are aware of the Halifax Road mosque.

*A raid on HRM is imminent.

*Possibility they know we have six undercover agents with river codenames.

*I am under suspicion and working hard to reverse that.

*Recommendation clear all IRF personnel out of HRM now along with coms equipment and revert to common prayer only!

Severn

‘Bloody hells bells this note tells us most of what we have been suspecting for so long.’

Max-Catt phoned his pal in Scotland Yard, Detective Chief Superintendent Timothy Barlow. Max explained the message and that he wanted his DCS pal to come and arrest Mohammad and hold him for at least three days on suspected terrorist charges and that he mustn’t make contact with the IRF. Barlow of course agreed and sent a local car to the garage but Barlow had a crisis on his hands. ‘We have had probably the worst attack on our police ever! There was carnage today all over central London and we have two of your men helping.’

‘I know Tim and I do believe the IRF are behind the attack on your guys. This bozo I’ve got with me is in that organisation and he’s their courier between Bradford and London.’

‘After their failed attack on the Houses of Parliament I’d bet any money the attack on the police is down to them.’

‘Okay Max, if there’s a connection then it may help our inquiries because up to now we have jack shit!’

38

Halifax Road was buzzing with high fives everywhere, an atmosphere not seen in that mosque before.

This was replicated in 723 Rorke Street in Limehouse in East London, the southern headquarters of the IRF as their new plan to terrorise London had been a complete success with the murder of ten police officers. It wasn't all a bed of roses though as Kamal Hafeez's second-in-command had been murdered by an infidel spy at the Bradford mosque but Hafeez had been assured by Emir that the spy had been killed before he had the chance to report to Bastion.

The IRF's central committee based in Afghanistan was delighted with the global news of the shooting and chaos in central London especially with the road network in London being closed to all but emergency services and the Tube and train networks cancelled bringing London to a standstill, an outcome that was far better than Hafeez had thought possible.

'We must go again with another tour bus attack once more in London before we move the bus operation to Manchester.' High octane greed had overwhelmed Hafeez's usual careful approach to attacks and he wanted more of the same.

'I'm hoping we can persuade Phonoi to stay on a week longer which shouldn't be difficult as he's obviously driven by money so we will dangle the cash carrot in front of him. Fetch him to me Hussain.' Hussain Badir was Hafeez's new deputy and had been appointed to that position in recognition of his input with the tour bus attack. Badir found Phonoi drinking coffee in the kitchen where he was ready to start his precise preparation for the assassination of Max-Catt when Hafeez's messenger arrived and out of interest rather than demand, he went.

'Brad come in. I have another job for you this Sunday which you can do before you set about killing Max Catt.' Brad Zimmermann looked suspiciously at his generous paymaster. 'What is it and how much?'

'Another tour bus shooting extravaganza! That's what! In London again but on our purple route and just six police infidels this time as it's essential that we get the bus away to Manchester as quickly as possible afterwards which would culminate in a profitable week's work in anyone's book. Well are you on for Sunday?'

There was no answer. Brad Zimmermann went back to his hotel for his preplanning on the demise of the Bastion agent without speaking another word to Hafeez but he was considering the extra job on Sunday.

Hafeez had another concern growing: 'I'm worried that our dispatch rider has gone missing. He hasn't called in and he's always reliable. Our message hub in Uxbridge contacted us and said he had received a message from Severn and that he had given it to Mohammad Feisi who left for Bradford but never arrived!'

'Thames, who is working for GCHQ in Cheltenham, has reported heavy chatter coming in and out of Bastion since Fridays attacks but we are not any getting messages through from any of the river agents. Where is our courier? Has he been caught?' Hafeez asked that rhetorical question that nobody could answer.

'I hope any fallout from Shelly Street and Severn being watched doesn't impact on our other river agents. I need contact with Severn and quickly.'

Badir could see his boss was very perturbed by the unknown which he had no control over and that was his problem!

39

Cautiously Max went into his penthouse apartment with considerable stealth, fully aware that dangerous people were out to get him for big bucks so he moved through each room with his Glock 19 primed and ready. He cleared each room and then checked the fine thread across his bedroom door which hadn't been broken and allowed him a relaxed calm from his anxiety. He turned on the lights and flicked off his pencil torch and collected from his bedroom his Chalkies, a set of incredible skeleton keys that had never failed to open any secure double locking device.

Max put on a disguise of a dark auburn wig, black rimmed glasses and a matching auburn beard and collected a few items that he needed for his night excursion and placed them in his backpack. Then the Bastion agent was ready to leave his penthouse so he secured a rope to his Juliet balcony and slid down it to the small forecourt that belonged to the ground floor apartment. He skipped over the metre high brick wall into the landscaped gardens, passing a fountain and flower borders enroute then climbed the rear wall that was unlit and unwatched by security cameras. Max was on a night mission that only he knew about! He took a taxi to an address just off the Oxford Road and got out half a mile from his destination and walked purposely to Waterloo Terrace which looked a decent area with well cared for houses with many with floral hanging baskets showing off their Spring flowers.

Bastion Human Resources had confirmed that Tazi Emir lived as a lodger of a Mrs. Granger. Max approached the lit bay window of the living room where a lady in her late fifties was watching television. Although he couldn't see the television directly, it was the coloured flashes reflecting off Mrs. Grangers glasses which confirmed this. A light from an upstairs window suggested that Tazi was in his first floor accommodation but what Max didn't know was if the double agent occupied the whole of the first floor or if Mrs. Granger had her bedroom upstairs as Max's intel only stated that two people shared the house.

Max approached the door and opened it with his Chalkies and saw the stairs facing him. Max could see a pinch of light emanating from the living room and heard the loud noise of the television that the landlady was watching, who was perhaps a little deaf. 'Is that you, Tazi love?' A lady's voice came from the living room which made Max-Catt freeze on the third stair.

He gave a muffled reply. 'Yeah, it's me Joyce.'

'Okay love, night night .' Mrs. Granger lived a lonely life and had never married but had two sons who lived away and didn't much care for her so to say she was vulnerable was an obvious understatement. She badly wanted company and has fallen for the chatroom charm of Tazi and before long he had moved in as her lodger. She had even stopped eating pork in support of Tazi's Islamic religion but denied this to anyone she discussed Tazi with.

Max heard no more from the landlady and stealthily made his way up the stairs, moving along the landing to the front bedroom after having checked out the bathroom and the middle and rear bedrooms while screwing the silencer on to his Glock. Max concluded that the biggest room to the front of the house was Tazi's living area and as he pressed his ear to the door he heard that the television was on but much more quietly than his landlady's. Max turned the door handle very slowly, then with the slightest of pressure inwards, the door was now ajar.

Then with the speed of an athlete Max was in the room with the lamp in the corner illuminating the scene. Stealth was over. The shocked look on Tazi's face was one of incredulity. 'Who the fuck are you?' Max acted instinctively and answered with his Glock 19 by waving the extended barrel in the direction of the back wall.'

In a soft Irish accent Max ordered. 'Sit down and don't speak again or I'll shoot your fucking left kneecap through.' Tazi Emir didn't argue with the red headed Irishman with a menacing tone in his voice.

Tazi was desperate to know who this intruder was but common sense prevailed. *This nutter sounds as if he means what he says.* Tazi reasoned. Max removed a roll of tape from his backpack and secured the now silent Tazi. Max then looked around the room and picked up Tazi's phone off the coffee table.

'Are there things on here you don't want to share?' Tazi threw Max a suspicious glare.
'Who the hell are you, look I'm quite well off and I'll give you a grand, my Rolex and all my credits cards and you can max them out.'
'Will you save me the bother of searching your digs for money or will you tell me where it is?'
'You'll let me go if I give you everything I have right?'
'We'll see. Where is it?'

Underneath that coffee table.' Emir pointed to the centre of the room and to Max's delight he found nearly forty grand in cash which he stuffed into his backpack and took Tazi's Rolex too. 'I know about you and the five other rivers agents who are planted within the British secret intelligence services and I know your code name is Severn. I work in GCHQ in one of the listening rooms and we have had a bug in the Halifax Road mosque in Bradford which was planted by a Bastion undercover agent called Dani Quibi. We also know you attacked central London with a sniper called Fanay or Fanoy or something like that.' Tazi Emir's throat had completely dried out and he couldn't swallow nor take in what he had just heard. 'As I was saying, I know everything but it's your lucky day pal! The government pension is shit for the work we do so therefore this is how I supplement it. Call it a perk of the listening job.'

'You are going to send a message via your newsagent friend tonight! Yes I know all about your message centre at the Harrow Road newsagent and this is the message you are going to dispatch and you'll sign your name at the bottom. I have your driving licence here so make sure your signature is a good likeness. I've already killed a colleague who knew the contents of the mosque recordings so you see Tazi I'm not impartial to the odd bit of foul play to get a financial reward and I do hope you believe me!'

'Here's the message you will be sending and I'm going to follow you into the shop where you will place the message in one of two magazines you pick up. Then you will take them both to the counter and leave the one with the message in it on the counter like you always do. Got it?

The bogus red haired Irishman passed a note to Emir: To Mousa Alami. A man who works at GCHQ in Cheltenham is holding me hostage. He wants two million pounds for my freedom. He also knows about the other five river agents and will reveal them to the police unless the cash is not left in locker box 214 ay King's

Cross Station at exactly 12:00 sharp tomorrow. The locker door will be open so place the money in it and spin the combination dial. If this is not done he will be hand over me to MI5 and the other five rivers will exposed. He assures me he's not interested in blowing the whistle as he wants only to retire a rich man and go back to Dublin. Please do it! If not for me, do it for the security of our undercover agents. He tells me also he has access to a listening bug at Halifax Road and he will give me the recordings once he picks up the money. You need to act fast as he assures me there will be no time extension.

Severn.

'Now sign it!' Tazi had no choice as the Glock once more was the persuading element in the room. 'Come on as your message centre closes at 23:00 so we have forty-five minutes. You will….' There was a tap on the door followed by an offer. 'Tazi would you like to share my bed tonight? It is Friday!' Max raised the handgun to Tazi's temple and shook his head at him. 'Sorry Joyce, I have a migraine.'

'Oh dear, I was so much looking forward to it. It's been five days since we had some rumpy-pumpy.' It was clear that Tazi Emir was very embarrassed about having sex with his fifty nine year old landlady. Then it all went quiet as Mrs. Granger went to her bedroom.

'As I was saying, you are going to drive us in your car. Come on move!' Max had already picked up the car keys to Tazi's VW golf and cut Tazi's tape. The VW was parked a few cars down from the house and Tazi knew a short cut to the Harrow Road message hub so they got there in no time. As instructed, Tazi Emir went into the shop and sauntered to the periodicals, picking up two and placing the message in one. He paid the shopkeeper and left the message enclosed in the magazine on the counter which was duly placed under the counter by the shop owner. The red-headed Irishman looked on but was looking for any signal from Tazi to the shopkeeper. 'Thank you, I'll see you soon.' Then the double agent left the shop followed discreetly by red beard.

It was clear that Max-Catt had made a substantial breakthrough in unearthing the six planted river spies and actually holding one was going to hopefully exploit further dividends. He must keep Tazi Emir out of circulation and there was only one safe place where he would not be found which was his lodge at Brandscombe manor which was where they were now going but not that Tazi Emir was aware of it. 'Okay Tazi or do you prefer me calling you Severn? No matter, pull over into that lay-by and stop the engine.'
'What are you going to do to me?'
'Nothing if you behave yourself. Now squeeze into the boot.' Max blindfolded and taped his hands and legs together, closed the car boot and drove to Brandscombe.

Memories came flooding back to the time Max had transported the body of Connolly, his beloved wife's murdered, and had been stopped by traffic cops but lived to tell the tale but he certainly didn't want a reoccurrence of that unbelievable nightmare.

Max unlocked the lodge door and closed all the curtains. He could see the twinkling lights from several of the rooms up at the manor and the silhouettes of the majestic Cedar trees slowly moving in the night breeze.

Once in his lodge's soundproof basement room, Max removed Tazi Emir's blindfold which made the captive's eyes squint after so much darkness. Max tied Emir to a chair, filled up the rabbit drinkers and showed his captive how to drink from them when Max left him.

Two litres should suffice before he returned. 'I'm going away to collect the money and you should have enough water but you'll have to piss yourself.' Max left in the VW and headed back to London. He parked up in one of few areas that wasn't residents parking only but it did mean that he had a mile to walk back to his Chiswick apartment. It was getting on for 01:30 by the time he got to the rear wall of his apartment block and reversed his earlier exit then slept in his secret bedroom!

40

Frustration was probably the wrong adjective, it was closer to exasperation being felt that Saturday morning by Kamal Hafeez but on the big plus side he had planned and succeeded in inflicting by far the worst atrocity ever encountered in peacetime against Britain's police force with ten policemen killed within a two hour attack. Moreover, he was about to give the green light for a second raid that day and should have already got started as he was due to pick up Brad Zimmermann at 07:30 from his hotel who had called Hafeez to confirm that he would take the extra job but all this had to be postponed.

Hafeez called Phonoi and told him to stay in his hotel and await further instructions as there had been complications which didn't go down at all well with the impatient, aggressive sniper. Hafeez then called the Isleworth warehouse where the sightseeing bus was ready to start another death tour and told the team there to stand down but to stay at the warehouse and be at a state of readiness to go.

The complication that postponed the second attack on London was profound and disturbing and Hafeez had received the dire information from the Bradford mosque at 03:45 that morning. Mousa Alami had sent a courier to the IRF southern headquarters stating that an infidel was aware of the IRF's six river agents and also that the IRF had carried out the London attacks.

Hafeez called for his new deputy, Hussain Badir. 'Hussain we have a major problem!' Hafeez explained the content of the courier's dispatch. 'What are we going to do, we have spent years cultivating these men from boys, educating them, getting them into top British intelligence services jobs and all this will be wasted if we can't stop our river agents being identified. We will just have to pay the money, you must realise that!'

'I do, but two million pounds sterling! We will find this man and dispose of him once we get our ransom back. I will take the money to King's Cross myself and we can't set a trap as he's bound to have an accomplice who will blow the whistle on our rivers. The positive side to this is at least we are still in partial control as this guy just wants the money to retire so he couldn't very well then tell his employers who we are.'

'I agree and that's our saving grace but we can't take that risk. Do you want me to come with you as it's a load of money in cash to carry across London?'

'That might be a good idea Hussain and bring a gun with you just in case.' Hafeez sent a courier message to Phonoi and the Isleworth warehouse telling them both to stay put until he got back from a trip to King's Cross station. He collected the money from the IRF safe deposit box in Hatton Garden and, accompanied by Hussain, left for the station. The two went through the barrier and found the banks of lockers as directed by a station worker. There were five banks of twenty lockers and number 214 was in the second bank. They placed the bag of money in the locker and spun the combination dial to lock it.

As they walked out of the station Hafeez was raging. 'I'll personally torture this fucking infidel myself, as God is my witness.' Hussain thought it better to let his boss calm down before speaking, a definite good call at the moment!

Max, still looking like the red headed Irishman, went to box 214 and removed the packet and after a peep inside the bag and a quick assessment of the amount he briskly walked off with two million pounds under his arm. Although pleased with this result, Max still had plenty on his mind and a lot to do!

The IRF leader and his deputy took the Tube back to Rorke Street in Limehouse and, over tea, discussed the dilemma they were in. 'We have an important river agent, Tazi Emir, taken hostage and his captor is aware that we have five other undercover agents in essential roles within the British secret services and we have no idea who the blackmailer is or where he is. He is holding all the cards at the moment and two million pounds of IRF funds so we have to wait for him to make the next move and just hope he doesn't expose the other rivers as that would set the IRF back many years.'

'I think the guy who's holding Tazi will demand more money for each of our river agents unless we can get to him first. Hang on, the message Tazi sent says his captor works in the listening room at GCHQ in Cheltenham which is where Borak our river agent Thames is! He has given us important intel and has saved many of our brothers from being arrested with his tipoffs in advance of raids. He is friendly with a communications secretary if I remember rightly who would surely know who is in the listening room and who was missing yesterday and today so once we know who he is we'll send a team to bring him to us and that can't come soon enough!'

Hafeez called for a messenger to go to the Harrow Road newsagent with a message for Thames. Thames please find out if a male was missing yesterday and today from the listening room at GCHQ. You should be able to whittle the names down then get back to me with the name as quick as you can. Much depends on it including your own cover. I'll keep a courier bike on standby at Uxbridge!

'It's too late to send the bus out now so I'll stand the crew and Phonoi down for the night and we'll go again tomorrow. The route I've planned will duplicate our previous successes and we will start at stop one at Hyde Park, stop two Kensington Palace, stop three Notting Hill, stop four Marble Arch, stop five Oxford Street and stop six Piccadilly Circus. We are on the brink of greatness which will elevate the IRF as the most successful radical Islamist group ever assembled. Allah Akbar!'

'Do you think Severn will give out any more information to his captor?'

'No, his kidnapper is just a government dude using the information to get very rich quick and would not be interested in taking on too much trouble as he's already poked the bear. No he'll be off to a Caribbean island if we let him but I do relish the opportunity to stop him and retrieve the IRF's money and make him rue the day he stole from us. No, my real worry is not an inexperienced opportunist, it's the whereabouts of our senior courier that worries me although he's loyal to the cause and I doubt if he'll crack under questioning. It's just the uncertainty of it that's a niggle so can you find out if we've heard about Tazi yet?' Hussain checked with Halifax Road but Mousa Alami hadn't heard anything or received any messages. The deputy then rang Isleworth and stood them down for the night but told them to be at the warehouse the next day and to be ready to drive out at 08:15. He then called Brad Zimmermann and said that Hafeez would collect him from his hotel at 07:30 sharp. The sharp bit pissed off Phonoi as there was not a wide margin between Brad being angered!

All seemed set for the Tour of Death to take to the road on the following Monday morning!

41

Max got back to his lodge at 14:10 and, as he suspected, the smell of ammonia confirmed that Tazi Emir had pissed himself and probably more than once and judging by the vile smell, he had had at least one crap in his pants! Max had been on several battle fronts and had even sat in his own excretion but that didn't prepare him for this. It made Max heave several times and Tazi was still five metres away from him. 'Where the fuck have you been, I've bloody shit myself.'

'Oh so that's the smell, I'd never have guessed.' Max put a hankie around his face and took an industrial breathing mask from his workbench drawer. The rabbit drinkers had obviously worked as there was only a quarter left in the second bottle.

Max sprayed the room with lavender air freshener making it slightly more tolerable. 'Your voice has changed, where is your Irish accent. I know that voice.....' A stunned face developed as the wig and beard came off and the spectacles were removed.

'Fucking hell, Max-Catt? What the hell do you think you're doing. Have you gone mad, I'll report you to Bastion and Julia Deakin will know of this immediately. You have kidnapped me, threatened me by holding a gun to my head and made me sign a document under duress. Release me immediately. Is my VW here and, by the way, where is here?'

'Just save your breath for your answers and don't lie as some answers I already know,' Max walked to his tool cabinet and brought out a pair of small bolt croppers. 'These little beauties have been nicknamed by me as the persuaders'. Let me tell you a true story. About eighteen months back an IRF brother of yours wouldn't give me the address of one of your safe houses in Luton. I ask a question and gave him thirty seconds to consider answering but he was a brave lad and didn't see the sense in telling the truth until he had lost his index finger, his middle finger and even his resilient stubborn thumb before he eventually told me the truth. I checked it out that he was not lying and he wasn't so I released him so remember that there's no extension to the 30 seconds. I want the names of the five other undercover river agents. I obviously know you are Severn as you admitted that much at your digs and by the way, you weird fucker, how can you shag your old landlady who must be at least forty years older than you. Still I suppose it's one up from a goat! Now where was I? Yes, the other agent's full names and what service they are they working in?' 30, 29.... Thick mucus saliva was propelled at Max from close range which covered most of his face. After wiping his face, Max continued the countdown. '2, 1.'.... snip! One of Tazi's index fingers was severed at the proximal interphalangeal or second joint in layman's terms and his scream was worse than a piglet squealing for its life.

The half digit dropped onto plastic sheeting then the dripping, that sounded like rain, picked up its pace.

'Give me the five names and their places of work?' This time Max moved from the range of the spitting captive. '30, 29, 28....4, 3, 2, 1.'..... Snip! The thick middle finger, pruned down to the second joint, dropped onto the plastic to join the index digit and the dripping from the two fingers was almost rhythmical with a crimson pool gathering on the plastic sheeting. Max took a picture and showed it to Tazi who winced and looked away but still continued sniffling.

'The names Tazi, the names! This really is deja vu for me as it only seems like yesterday that I did this before to one of your lot. Anyway 30, 29, 28....4, 3, 2, 1...... Snip! The thumb was at least twice as resistant as the fingers but even with extra pressure from the massive hands of Max it still didn't quite severe and was determined to hold on with its last sinew swinging in midair away from its hand. It looked untidy so Max fetched a pair of scissors and neatly cut it through, allowing it to fall to join the two severed fingers as the screams from Emir hit a new level. The finger percussion orchestra had got three chords of drips going on. 'Well done, you've equalled the another terrorist's record of two fingers and a thumb and apart from not being able to pick your nose you should still manage to pick up things but if you lose another it's going to be bloody difficult. Okay now let me tell you that we have two more to go on your left hand and another five on your right. Then we'll start on your toes. You terrorists don't have the monopoly of dishing out pain you know! Come to think of it, I've never got as far as feet before. Now the names and workplaces of the five if you please. 30, 29, 28,...4, 3, 2, 1...'

Stop. Okay, okay no more, for fuck sake you infidel bastard. If I give you the names will you let me go free? I mean free! I can't go back to the IRF after I give you the names of my brother as they'll cut my fucking head off and send it to my father so I'll have to go to my aunties in Pakistan.'

'Well that depends, so come on the names and places.' 'You know my name is Severn and where I work then there is Trent whose name is Kamal Malik and he's in the Foreign Office, then Clyde is Mohammad Mohammad at the Home Office, Thames is Borak and he's in GCHQ, Avon is Faraz who's at MI5 and Wye is Akrami who works for the National Counter Terrorism Office. I feel like shit, I'm in great pain and I've betrayed my brothers so I am cursed until I die.'

'You don't only feel like shit, I can assure you, you smell like it.'

'Can I have some pain killers?' Max made up an aspirin solution in water and Tazi drank it straight down. 'If your pain persists after this stuff, I'll give you a shot of morphine. Now I want to know about the attack on London and quick!'

Max lifted the blood congealed bolt croppers gesticulating another round of pruning which made Tazi Emir wince at the thought of more excruciating. 'I don't know the details but I know it's a different style of attack from our usual ones and it's on a need to know basis. I know they have brought a man in from the US to kill you who is an ex-US navy seal called Phonoi I think and he's said to be the best hitman in the world who guarantees completion of his contracts. You're fucked Max-Catt, he'll get you!'

There was a hint of pleasure in Tazi's voice in spite of his pain. Max thought Emir was speaking the truth but needed to double check. 'I don't believe you! You murdered a very brave man when you shot Dani Quibi and I have just received confirmation from our forensics department that it was your Bastion issued Smith and Wesson gun that killed him. Also we intercepted the message you sent from the Harrow Road newsagent where you confirmed that you had killed our brave man. Yes we know about your boss called Hafeez but we would like to know where he is. So if you tell me more about the attack on central London and the safe house Hafeez is hiding in I'll let you go. It's that simple,' Max moved back behind Tazir Emir. '30, 29, 28….4, 3, 2, 1….'

'I don't know.' And with that Emir started to genuinely cry.'

‘Shut the snivelling. You scum kill innocent people including children, you have no morals, you hide behind a blind faith of extremism and terror and you give good Muslims a bad name yet you can’t take it when pain is inflicted upon you. You're kind sicken me to the stomach but for what it’s worth I believe you have told me all that you know.’ Max collected up the severed digits and flushed then down the toilet before dressing Tazi Emir’s hand and giving him a shot of morphine. Max put the plastic floor cover in a bag after pouring the pooled blood down the sin then he cut the tapes of his captors ankles and hands and told him to get into the passenger seat of his own VW.

Max locked his lodge door and put the key in his secret hiding hole and returned to drive Tazi to Croydon police station to be held there until Barlow sent for him. Max got into the VW but there was no Emir as he’d done a runner! Max rushed back into his lodge and picked up one of his three hunting rifles, fixing his SAS night sight to it and then went hunting for his escapee.

Max thought that in fairness to Tazi Emir, he could not be blamed for taking the opportunity to run as he thought Max was going to finish him off in a dark lane somewhere anyway and had nothing to lose. Max had a great advantage over Tazi in that he knew the terrain, the fenced perimeter fence of the estate and, of course, the help of the infrared night sights. The quarry had no idea where he was, where he was heading and which direction was best to take. Max was a keen stalker and had been trained to an elite level by the SAS mountain and jungle training. Max was soon closing in on his man who was going in an unintentional circle and Max’s keen ears soon picked up the noise of breaking dried twigs fifty or so metres to his right.

Max edged towards the noise and saw a shape who he thought must be Emir and he mustn't let him escape. Max knew, whether by luck or chance, that Emir was getting close to a road and the sound of sporadic traffic passing. Max lifted his rifle to use the sight, spanning an arc in the direction of the noise. He could see the manor's perimeter fence as it formed a straight lined horizon that stood out from the shrubs and trees. Then there was movement, it was a man running towards the lights of passing vehicles and the fence. Max knew that once Tazi was on the road he'd stop an oncoming car and say that he'd been attacked. Then he'd be gone so he mustn't be allowed to climb the fence but Tazi had already got to it and Max was still sixty metres away, Tazi threw himself as high as he could at the fence, clinging to the top with his good right hand. Max had only one choice and that was that Emir had to be taken out and quick.

Max-Catt was probably in the top ten marksmen in the UK but this wasn't a clean shot as trees, bushes and shrubbery gave his target good cover and Max only had another couple of seconds at most so he zoomed in his sight and aimed at Emir who was straddling the top of the fence and was about to drop on to the road. A quick breath out and phut phut, two silenced shots found Max's target! Max ran quickly to the sprawled lifeless body entangled on the barbed wire fence which was snagging Tazi's clothes in too many places to disentangle so Max ran back to the lodge for his wire cutters and military body bag. After several minutes of snipping at the wire fence, he was able to pull Tazi's body back on to the estate side of it then Max placed Emir in the bag and zipped it up.

He heaved the bagged corpse over his shoulder and placed it in the boot of the body's own VW. It's probably for the best, this scum would have got legal aid, a human rights lawyer and the support of do-gooders even though he had bad intentions towards the UK so fuck him, bloody terrorist! This is revenge for you Dani Quibi! Max got quite upset thinking about Dani but anger stopped him dwelling on the sad loss.

Max then drove the VW to the garage at his lodge at Brandscombe manor then jogged along the main road for about two miles before calling a taxi. 'That was quick.' Max had only waited five minutes before a cab arrived. 'I had just finished a fare and was on my way back to Croydon. Where to guv'nor?'

'The Bell and Crown in Chiswick please.'

Max's Porsche was still at his designated parking spot at his Chiswick apartment which was part of his alibi should he be questioned about the death of Tazi. He had worn his red headed Irishman's disguise since leaving his lodge and calmly walked through the gates to the building. Back in his penthouse he placed his wig, beard and black rimmed glasses back in his hidden bedroom.

42

The Bastion leader's head was spinning with ideas. He had gathered some groundbreaking intel in the last couple of days but knew from snippets of collated information that another callous terrorist attack on was imminent. He placed two phones on a table, one belonging to the courier and the other to the late Tazi Emir.

Max-Catt was now thoroughly trained in opening mobile phones and bypassing passwords so he downloaded the courier's phone first. The contacts looked useful so he scrolled down and found some names and numbers of particular interest. Then he read the messages which referred to maealim almadina several times but most of the others were innocuous but he would keep his memory stick close for a more thorough scrutiny.

He did the same to Emir's phone but unlike the courier's it had more content and a vast contact list. Max went in to the messages: Sani Yosef is a spy. His real name is Dani Quibi who prayed at HRM. The Halifax Road mosque Max concluded.

Then the same words as in the courier's message in a sentence that must refer to the central London shootings: We have confirmation from KH that maealim almadina is on for Friday morning. The message had been received the previous Wednesday.

Then an unopened message of that morning. Maealim almadina is changed from today and postponed until

Monday morning. Please confirm receipt of this message. KH.
This excited Max: If maealim almadina is connected to the atrocities yesterday it could mean there'll be another attack on Monday and if those words refer to the same it could be the codename for the operation! Max deliberated in his mind that if his hunch was correct Bastion had little time to prepare for the next attack so he decided to call his field agents back to the fortress.

Max called both Mason Perkins and Callum Maclean to instruct them to come to his office
'Who's calling?'
'It's me, Max. Be at my office in half an hour or as quick as you can. Where are you? I'm in bed and was asleep.' 'Get a cab now!'
Max now looked like Max again as he strolled through the building to the lift and descended to the basement garage and drove his Porsche out of his designated parking bay.

He had been at his desk for five minutes when Mason arrived. 'What the hell is this all about Max?'
'I hope it's worthwhile Mason, I really do. Fancy a coffee?' Max and Mason were discussing the central London atrocities when Jade and Callum walked in together as they'd met in the lift a fraction past 23:15. 'Thanks all for coming so promptly and I'm sorry for spoiling your Sunday night but this is really important. Jade and I set a trap for Tazi Emir as we had suspicions about him and especially you Callum after the debacle of Shelly Street. Well he took the bait we set which was to let him find a message bluffing that we knew about six undercover double agents with river code names who all worked in the secret services. He in turn wrote a message and had it dispatched to an obvious message hub on the Harrow Road which is not far from here.'

Jade took it upon herself to follow Tazi to the message centre and to put a tracker on a motorcycle courier's bike. I joined up with Jade and we followed the tracker and, long story short, Detective Chief Superintendent Tim Barlow arrested him. I have the courier's phone and have downloaded information from it which indicates there's going to be another terror incident after the IRF's success on Friday. Although it's in code I believe the second attack will be tomorrow morning so we have a long night ahead of us guys and firstly we are going to the projector room to watch Friday's CCTV footage that I've received from Tim Barlow. As of this moment the police do not know how or where the marksman was able to shoot so many officers without being detected.

Max prepared the projector while Mason attended to the lights. The footage had been joined into one continuous recording with a facility to allow freeze framing and magnification up to times fifty. 'Before I roll the film please be very attentive to every detail of the attacks and particularly any unusual movements of motorbikes with perhaps pillions or anybody running from the scenes.'
'Callum and Mason, you two have field experience and SAS training and we don't have much time. Lights, Mason. The first killings were the two officers walking towards St. Paul's Cathedral near the Lord Benjamin statue when they were gunned down. Notice there are people about but not as many in the ensuing footage and there is no panic with the crowd which you would expect if they saw a man with a sniper rifle which tells me he's hidden.'

The film rolled on to the second, third and fourth attacks before Jade spoke. 'Max what I've noticed is that the distance between St Paul's to Westminster should take a motorbike five minutes even allowing for traffic lights so let's double that and say ten minutes tops but the times of the shootings are forty minutes between the first one and Westminster. Do you think he was lying low or even that it was perhaps timed shootings from a high building at each attack?'

'That's an excellent point Jade. Please write these ideas down and any others you have and we'll go over them. Half an hour later the film finished and they all went back to Max's office to discuss and analyse what they had watched and their notes and queries. Max had a thought. 'Excuse me guys, I need to make a call.'

'Hello, is that the Crown pathology service.'

'Yes, I'm the night receptionist.'

'Good, may I speak to the duty pathologist please?'

'Who's calling?'

'Max-Catt from Bastion.'

'Where's Bastion?'

'What the hell lady, is this twenty questions just put me through this is urgent.'

'There's no nee….' Max broke in!

'Just tell your pathologist Bastion is on the line and needs to speak with him. Now!'

'Hello Professor Clarke here, sorry Amanda is new here and doesn't know who Bastion is and she said you got shirty with her but anyway what can I do for Bastion, I know we have to jump if you bods need anything.'

'For a start, you can stop being flippant. You know what happened to ten brave police officers on Friday, well I'm trying to prevent a similar occurrence and you should have asked me for a passcode before giving out information.'

'Sorry, I'd better check, just a moment.' The Professor went away. For fucks sake come on man. Max thought frustratingly. 'Are you still there?'

'Yes, for fucks sake what are you doing? Don't you know what fucking urgent means?'

'No need to lose your temper Mr…um,' Max broke in again. 'Listen pal if you don't get what I want in ten seconds flat I'm going come down to your laboratory and give you a backhander, now have I got clearance, yes or no?'

The three field agents pissing themselves but were trying hard not to let Max see the amusement they were getting from their boss who was losing it with bureaucracy.

'Yes, you had the right passcode now what do you want after all that threatening behaviour, I'm going to report you for this.'

'You can tell the fucking Pope in the Vatican for all I care now get me the ten angles of penetration that killed the officers in central London on Friday morning. Don't say another word but I expect those details to be sent to me by email within the next five minutes and if you don't pal I'll come and get them personally and it won't be a pretty experience and you won't ever forget my name again that I promise you.'

Before the jesting had stopped, Max's computer pinged three or four times with emails coming in one after the other from the Crown pathology services, four of the little beauties with diagrams. There was a pause and the pinging started again, this time five more emails came through. 'This is going to take some reading but I hope it will be worth all the shit I just had to put up with. Okay let's get down to it. We shall divide these results between us. What I want is the angle that the bullets entered the victims bodies. I expect and am hoping the ranges to be within one degree of each other unless the shooter is moving up and down to different height levels.' Four heads were down poring over the pathologist findings and after twenty minutes Jade had, in her opinion anyway, completed her task. 'Max the ones I had came out at an average of 5.3 degrees of the line of fire.' Max came up with his two at an average of 5.4, Mason's two were 5.2 and Callum, who had three to do, gave his average of 5.3.metres 'Good all very similar, now if I remember my Pythagorean theorem to find the length of a missing side of a triangle and in our case we have the angle running out at around ten degrees. In brief, the height of a given object is determined by calculating the distance from the object which we don't know but we do know the angle of elevation is ten degrees or very close. The tangent of the angle refers to the object height so if I divide the distance from the object the height is obtained,'

Max scribbled his remembered formula down. 'As we know angle we should be able to get the height from which the projectiles were fired,' Max scribbled as he worked out his formula, speaking as he calculated. 'We don't know the distance the rifle was fired from but a sniper worth his salt wouldn't be closer than a hundred metres so let's opt for that distance as a base line marked D for distance. Tan A over Tan B - Tan A with the distance at say 100 metres then the unknown distance, let's say 50 metres and then calculate that.' Max finished the sum and got his estimation. 'Okay this is what I have got.

'We know the angle is ten degrees, I've estimated the distance being at 100 metres which would be the preferred distance for accuracy and escape. I've ruled out that the shots were fired from a building as the attacks were fluid across central London so he, she or they were on the move. My calculations are based upon taking the 5.3 degree line D to 100 metres and I estimate the height of the sniper to be between 3 and 3.5 metres so that would rule out a motorbike or a car but it could be a high vehicle like a double decker bus or something of that height.' They watched the video again on Max's computer but again found nothing suspicious!

43

Max returned to the information he retrieved from the courier's and Tazi's phone. 'I got this intel from the phone taken from the courier that Jade and I stopped,' Max wrote down on his information board maealim almadina. 'Does this mean anything to you guys. The context is a definite reference to the attack and they have mentioned it in an attack for tomorrow, hence the importance of our emergency meeting on a Sunday night.'

'I've seen those words, I know I have. It'll come to me, it won't beat me.' Jade was racking her brain to remember.

'The other piece of intel gleaned from the phone and Dani's desperate message is that a globally recognised sniper has been contracted to carry out hits for the IRF with me being one of his targets apparently. Anyway, I think he might be our cop killer.'

'Max, I have it, maealim almadina means sightseeing in Arabic. I used to work in a travel agents as a Saturday job and in my summer holidays and I even got my ABTA qualifications.'

'That's it, that's it!' Max squeezed Jade who thought he'd lost it for the second time in an hour. Come on you lot bring your pads, we're going back to the cine room.' He played through the first hit and there it was, a gleaming sightseeing bus called Met Hopper with a red, yellow and black livery.

They went to the next shooting footage and there it was again and was present at all the attacks. 'That's it guys, that's our common denominator at the shootings!'

Well done all of you. Who's up for a pizza.' A unanimous yes came back but it was too late, all the takeaways were closed as it was 01:45. 'Probably for the best as we've got work to do and an early start tomorrow. I want you all back in here at 06:00 when we'll work out our strategy.

Max thought. The strange thing is that the bus looked to be full of tourists unless they were all IRF sympathisers acting as extras in a propaganda movie for the IRF's cause. 'Okay off you all go and thanks guys, you have been brilliant.' Max was putting the classified stuff he had received into his safe when he noticed Jade hadn't left. 'Hey Jade, did you want something?'

'Yes Max, do you have a spare bedroom I could use tonight as I live quite a way from here and I don't particularly want to disturb my parents at this hour and it would be helpful to get back here for the early start in the morning too. I hope you don't mind me asking and it's not an issue if it's inconvenient as I know you have just moved in.'

'Not at all, glad to oblige. I think I have a spare toothbrush as well at no extra charge, come on let's go!'

Max drove his Porsche 911 into the car parking bay for apartment number eighty seven. 'This is us, my parking bay is handy for the lifts which are just over there.'

'It all smells very new and I love the lighting and it's only the garage.' They went up the four floors to the top penthouse level and Max opened the front door allowing Jade to pass him and enter first. She walked into the lounge and made straight for the patio door that led onto a balcony which had a set of all-weather table and chairs.

'Wow look at the lights of London and the moon on the river. This is a superb place Max.'

'Yes, it took some finding I can tell you and I love the walks along the Thames path, the easy parking and the twenty minutes drive to work. It's all good and I'm glad you approve.'

'Who wouldn't.'

'I'm going to have a Lochavennie as a nightcap so will you join me out here on the balcony?'

'Yes, well I say yes but what is Lochawhatsit?'

'Lochavennie and it's my favourite malt whiskey by a country mile.' Max poured two reasonable measures from his decanter and passed one to Jade. 'Cheers Max.'

'Cheers and here's to success tomorrow!'

'I'll drink to that! By the way that was some breakthrough we made earlier.'

'An all round team effort and we'll need the same tomorrow and it was so lucky you remembered your days in your travel job. Anyway, we only have a few hours so we'd better get some sleep.'

'Sure, but can I have a shower first as I feel grubby and it's been a long day.'

'Sure but you will have to use mine as I'm having a steam shower fitted in the guest bedroom but no bother though.'

'I have to send some messages to my parents and a friend I was going to see for Sunday lunch so I'll be ten minutes so you crack on Max.'

'OK I'll nip in the shower first then.'

Max set his alarm for 05:00 then threw off his clothes and jumped in his shower, enjoying the steam and heat. Max hadn't really stopped since before Operation Buttercup and all the fire practice although arson would more accurately describe it.

Max jumped out of his skin. The shower door opened and in got the naked Jade Jackson. 'What the…' Jade put her finger to his lips but didn't speak and the next five minutes were insane. It was the most spontaneous sex he'd ever encountered, thrusting almost with animalistic tendencies. Still nothing was said. He left the shower stunned but incredibly sated. Jade then showered as if nothing had happened. He got into his bed knowing Jade would have to pass him to go to her bedroom and he knew it wasn't a fantasising dream as he could hear her still showering. What rationale can be given for a twenty-two year old beauty with a gorgeous body and a quick thinking mind to do what she had just done? Max pondered the thought.

The ensuite door opened. 'Mr. Hainsworth-Catt, I make no apologies as what I did may be tantamount to male abuse, I don't know!' Jade looked as if she was part of the new penthouse set up as she had borrowed one of Max's towelling dressing gowns that swamped her and wrapped around her almost twice and only showed her ankles.

'Would you mind if I shared your bed for a couple of hours at least. It's not as if we have to break any ice is it sir?' She waited for permission that came in an instant and still Max hadn't spoken to his guest since finishing his whisky, he just pointed to the other side of his bed. He was in a state of strange perplexity as Jade hopped in as if she had done it many time before almost as a wife would.

Max fumbled for the alarm in the dark, dropping his phone in the process before eventually finding it under the bed to silence it. He still wasn't convinced he hadn't dreamt what had happened just a few hours earlier.

He turned to the other side of the bed but it was empty but reality walked through the door and he knew that smell of fresh morning coffee couldn't be simulated in a dream, the powerful smell was for real. Jade walked in as if she had done it a thousand times before

'Coffee sir, just how you like it.' Max put the bedside light on and accepted the coffee from across the bed. 'Well wasn't that something last night? You'll not believe me after my attack on you but I haven't had sex for eighteen months. Again you won't believe me after my impromptu performance but it's true, God's honour.'

'To say I didn't need something like that Jade would be a lie and I won't be pressing charges for you taking advantages of me.'

'What's so funny Max-Catt?'

'Nothing Jade. Come on Miss, we've got to leave in ten minutes so I'll have a quick shave while you finish your coffee.'

'Better not, I'll take my coffee into the lounge and put my face on in there. I washed while you were sleeping and incidentally, you nearly got some more this morning!'

44

Sunday morning was cloudy and the high pressure that came in was funnelled by the fickle jet steam from the south, weakened as it headed north. There was quite low cloud that particular morning but it wasn't raining. The wind had freshened from the northeast that gave a three degree colder feel to the actual temperature. Brad Zimmermann, who lived and worked out of the warm sunny climes of San Diego in California was waiting outside his hotel, blowing warm air into his hands and feeling the capricious nature of the British weather.

Kamal Hafeez tooted as he arrived on the other side of the road and Brad, holding his large holdall, jogged across to him and got into the passenger seat of the car, still confused on which side to get in. No good morning was offered. 'Where the fuck have you been? It's bloody freezing.' Phonoi was holding his open hands over the dashboard heat vents and the rest of the journey was muted. They pulled into the Isleworth warehouse where the Met-Hopper was fuelled up and ready to go and Hafeez called the tour bus crew together, Ahmed the ticket man, Abdullah the driver and Phonoi the assassin.

'Okay before we go over the attack today, I have some disturbing news. For three days now we have lost contact with Severn who has been kidnapped and in addition to this our courier has disappeared without a trace along with his motorcycle. We don't know if this a coincidence or something much more sinister and if the infidels have the courier I doubt that he will betray us but they may get intel from his cell phone which is the unknown factor!'

'However operation maealim almadina will recommence this morning so Ahmed you will be coordinating through the three-way interconnecting transmitters and receivers. Abdullah you did a good job slowing down at target sites and Phonoi completed the coup de grâce. We take on passengers again as that saved us when we were searched by police on the first attack. We will stop at Hyde Park, Kensington Gardens, Notting Hill, Marble Arch, Oxford Street and Piccadilly Circus where all passengers will disembark and you will then return here.' The red and yellow bus trundled out of the double gates onto the highway and headed for Hyde Park Stop 1. Abdullah had worked in central London for Transport for London and knew all of the area well and short cuts when and if required but the coordinator, Ahmed, was the helmsman who would be searching out targets and selecting ones suitable for a clear as possible shot although the final decision on any target was with the marksman.

Ahmed opened the well disguised compartment and Brad Zimmermann climbed in and prepared for his morning's work. Inside his shooting hide was complete darkness accept for small shafts of light coming from the air vents. His torch gave him enough light to reload or move to the other side and he was all set. Abdullah pulled up at the first stop and as usual an early bird queue of eleven passengers had already formed who paid Ahmed in return for their ticket and headphones. Like most tour buses and of course subject to the fickle English weather, most passengers wanted to go up to the open top floor and those eleven were no acceptation. On the bus's last outing nobody had any inclination that somebody was shooting from just in front of them in the padded chamber!

45

Max and Jade were first into the office to discuss their plan for the expected IRF's Operation maealim almadina and Jade made coffee for two without asking her unexpected lover. 'At least we don't have an elephant joining us for coffee Max but I just want to say that you must know you are a massive turn on to women but if you don't I'm telling you now. God you have the handsomest of faces and a body most girls would die for. I got the hots for you more or less the first day I joined but understand this that I'm no bunny boiler so don't think I'm going to stalk you or give you any grief. I've had a few boyfriends who, to be frank, were below any intelligent conversation and I'm not saying if you ever fancy a quickie and I've not found a decent fellah, then give me a call but I do promise that it will not impact on my work.'

For the second time in the last four hours Max was gobsmacked by his young attractive field agent. 'I don't think I can follow that Jade and I'm still coming to terms with the steamy skirmish in my shower. It's still unreal so let's forget it as lust does have a lot to answer for in the complex workings of the human mind.'

Mason joined Max and Jade for coffee which they had all finished by the time Callum bowled up. 'Sorry Max, the first gatehouse wouldn't let me in because of everything that was going on last night I hadn't changed my passcode. The guard on the gate called his boss who came from the second checkpoint who knew me and overrode the security to allow me through both gates.'

The complete field team collected their weapons and grenades, giving them a routine check before they left and Callum was the first to break the concentrated silence. 'Sorry I forgot to say that I looked up contract killers for hire on a secure website on the dark web which of course wasn't secure to the Bastion geeks in our IT and AI departments who got me access. I have found the sniper that is over here to get you Max and who is most likely the killer behind the IRF shootings. Dani thought he heard the name Fanay but it was actually spelt Phonoi. He is in the top three contract killers in the world and was dubbed Phonoi after the Greek spirit *killing and murder!* He got the nickname for his history of killing successes and apparently he's never failed to deliver a contract. His real name is Brad Zimmermann and he lives in San Diego, California. That's who's after you Max so you had best be ready.'

The team left for Central London and hoped for a quick sighting before more carnage ensued.

The crowds in the hot spots of London were starting to buzz which brought the heavier traffic that was now the norm in any city centre at any time of the day and even most of the night. Max searched for a non-red line where they could park and chose an area outside the Park Lane hotel which didn't restrict the drop off or pick up routines of the hotel as it was tucked away from the entrance. However, it wasn't long before a jobsworth strolled purposefully up to the driver's side of their vehicle and gave a hard tap on the sports car's window. 'Excuse me sir, please move off the hotel premises at once unless you are a guest in the Park Lane.' The looking-down-his-nose doorman had an air of arrogance. 'We are British secret intelligence officers and are looking for a defecting Chinese agent who we believe is checking into this hotel. Now go away or I'll have you arrested under the 2000 Terrorism act.' Max showed his ID and it was the crown heading that put the wind up the uniformed doorman who moved away much less assertively.

Max called Tim Barlow and explained where he had parked and within five minutes a dark blue Jaguar pulled in behind Max. The jobsworth doorman duly marched towards the Jag but before he had chance of even an utterance Barlow flashed his warrant card with another crown on it and a glaring Detective Chief Superintendent Barlow printed across it so the doorman gave up.

Max left his car and climbed into the Jag. "Well Max what's this exciting news you have since we last met?' Max explained his team's late night think-tank meeting. 'I used my own sniper experience for optimum firing distances and used calculations based upon the pathology data that gave us the angle of bullet penetration and of course Pythagoras's formula and taking the average over the ten slain officers we came up with an average trajectory height of 7.5 degrees.

'From this and the distance based on a hundred metres we were able to estimate the shots were fired from a height of between 3 and 3.5 metres so that rules out a high building and is too low for a bike or car. Then one of my agents understood what the words maealim al-madina meant which is sightseeing in Arabic. Then we revisited the CCTV you sent me and there it was, the same sightseeing bus at every shooting. It is yellow and red with Met-Hopper written on all sides with black livery and here's a picture,' Max handed Tim an enlarged shot of the side view of the killer bus.

‘I have two agents at Westminster Bridge so may I suggest you put your armed response teams on alert throughout central London as we suspect an attack is imminent according to our intel but it is understood that the people on the bus are probably innocent tourists and are there to distract any boarding investigation so your armed officer’s must err on the side of caution.’

‘Please advise all your units to be on the lookout for the red and yellow Met Hopper and call me as soon as they see it!’
‘Of course Max and bloody good detective work!’ Barlow left to join his armed units with renewed vigour.

Max’s phone vibrated. ‘Yeah?’
‘The Met Hopper has been spotted, it’s heading towards Hyde Park and we have two unmarked vehicles following it.’ DCS Barlow had given Max what he had been waiting for since early that morning. ‘That’s good news Tim. We are on our way.’ Max got Jade to call Mason and Callum to tell them to head for Hyde Park Corner as the Met Hopper had been spotted. Max went as fast as he could but was governed by heavy traffic that was adding to his frustration. Where are they going to attack first? Max thought.

In Max’s car, he and Jade got to where he had arranged to meet Tim Barlow and with a quick flash of his headlights pulled in behind him. Max left Jade and ran to Tim’s Jaguar and got in. ‘The tour bus is over there and it’s taking on passengers.’ The DCS pointed across the road towards the tour bus and it was definitely the same one that was on the CCTV at all the shootings. ‘Tim there must be twenty or more passengers onboard with another six now getting on so I’m going to get on it with Jade .as tourists but we will have to be quick so can you get someone to take my car.’ Max didn’t wait for a reply as he didn’t need to as Bastion overrode every other security service but out of respect for Tim, who Max had joined forces with many times with the wiry head of Scotland Yard, he asked him. 'Come on Jade, you and me are a couple so get your bag, take your high heels off and hold my hand.'

They ran through three lanes of horn blasting traffic as they slalomed in and out and got to the red and yellow bus just as the last person was paying. Max stepped aboard followed by Jade and got a disgruntled stare from Ahmed indicating that he wasn't pleased with the late arrivals but, short of throwing them off, he had no choice but to take their thirty quid each for a day ticket. As the bus pulled away Ahmed followed the last two onto the top deck and Max noticed his ear receiver and cuff transmitter as he'd done too much spy work not to notice the obvious.

Max nudged Jade and she lifted one side of her head set so she could hear him. 'Look at the guy who gave us the headphones, he's got an earpiece receiver and cuff transmitter.' Jade nonchalantly turned in Ahmed's direction and gave Max a thumbs up to confirm she had seen the discreet communication gear.

Max sent Jade a message: I think the man with the transmitter is the observer and he must be linked to the driver and the shooter. There are only two people downstairs so it can't be them so one of the tourists up here must be Phonoi but how did he fire without other passengers witnessing it last Friday?

The bus turned the corner at Hyde Park and Ahmed spoke into his cuff as the bus slowed for a few seconds and pulled away again. Nothing! Then Max's phone vibrated, it was Tim Barlow. 'Max, for fuck sake didn't you see the two officers on horseback standing at the corner of Hyde Park's western end gate, they have both been shot! Nobody saw where the shots came from so do something Max or we'll have a repetition of last week's slaughter.'

Max stood and turned pretending to do what other tourists had been doing, taking pictures. There in the wake of the Met Hopper stood a group of people with an out of control riderless horse bolting up the road causing traffic to stop in the crazed equine's path. How could it be from this bus? Max thoughts were at bursting point. Tim's call came immediately after the cuff call from the ticket seller so he's bloody coordinating the shooting!

Another nudge to Jade as Max lent across and whispered. 'There's been another shooting and the ticket seller must be the coordinator. I've got to take him out and then the driver so cover me and get your gun primed.' Max stood and called Ahmed over and with lightning quick actions Max had an arm around his throat and heavy compression on Ahmed's carotid artery restricting the flow of blood producing cerebral hypoxia which rendered him unconscious then Max quickly took his reinforced tape and secured Ahmed to a seat. Max tried to calm the now hysterical passengers but they were panicking so he flashed his ID and shouted: 'We are MI5 so keep calm as we have the situation under control.' Max couldn't stop one man running down the stairs so he had to let him go. 'Everybody listen to me. The bus is going to stop any moment now and when it does I want you to stay your seats. My partner has a gun and she will protect you and you can't leave the bus as there might be a terrorist amongst you and the one that ran away may have been one of the terrorists.' Max was interrupted by a woman. 'Nah he's not a terrorist, he's my chicken shit of a husband, he left me and fled the bus.' Max hid a veiled smile but was pleased that the escapee wasn't dangerous. 'Anyway as I was saying, please stay calm, it's all under control and I'm going to stop the bus. Jade will check you all for firearms as a matter of safety but don't be alarmed as we are in control and she will prevent anyone from going downstairs until we've ascertained your identities.

Max went down to the lower deck and moved to the front of the bus. Abdullah turned and was surprised to see someone other than Ahmed standing close to him. The driver was shocked further when the cold end of a fitted silencer was pushed into his neck. 'Stop the bus now and pull over there.' At that moment Abdullah couldn't compute what was happening but an encouraging press into his cheek with Max's gun soon cleared the mist of perplexity for him as he stopped the bus too quickly and without using a signal which brought a continued blast from a black cab as it nearly ploughed into the back end of the bus.

Two unmarked police cars pulled up in front of the now stationary bus and Tim Barlow was first out followed by two armed officers with automatic weapons. Tim Barlow saw Max by the driver and by the time the police chief entered the bus, Max had already taped the driver's wrists. 'Good work Max, we'll take it from here and I know you'll want to interview him later.'

'Tim, Jade is watching over another terrorist on the top deck and I haven't released any of the passengers yet as some might well be involved. Unless the man that did a runner was the marksman who got off the bus but I doubt it as a woman said it was her husband who had a yellow streak but you might like to interview her first as she could be his cover.

'The ticket seller is taped up and he spoke into his cuff just before you told me of the shootings so he must have coordinated the targets to the sniper and driver. I've not seen any suspicious looking tourists so I'll need to interview him and the driver later.'

Tim Barlow took the names, identities and country of residence from each of the remaining tourists and warned the coward's wife that he would need to interview her husband by 18:00 or he would be arrested. Once all the details were taken the frightened passengers were released back onto the streets of London.

The two taped men were taken away by armed police to be interviewed by DCS Tim Barlow and the bus was taken to the police vehicle compound for a thorough forensic inspection and Max asked if he could have the results of the suspect bus as soon as they had finished searching it.

46

Max was relieved that the Met Hopper terrorists were in custody and pleased his calculations were spot on but he was still baffled by the absence of the shooter which made no sense to him. He had temporarily forgotten about Tazi Emir who was still in a body bag back at his lodge's garage on the Brandscombe estate.

That changed his plan which was to take action at the Halifax Road mosque in Bradford but now he had macabre work to do first. As he drove in his Porsche to the family estate his mind flashed back to the last body he had taken and dumped away from his lodge. Then it was the killer of his beautiful wife, Penny, Patrick Joseph Connolly who was body-bagged and dumped on waste ground in Luton but not before a Porsche enthusiast traffic cop pulled him over and even sat at the wheel of his favourite car not knowing that a stiff was laid out across the back bucket seats a few centimetres behind him. Considering the brushes with death Max had experienced in his military and anti-terrorist skirmishes, the time with that police officer was his most scariest moment.

These thoughts ate up the miles to Brandscombe and he was soon driving through the big double gates. He called at the manor unannounced and had a late afternoon tea and scones with Christopher and Virginia, his parents. 'It's only a flying visit as I have some concentrated studying to complete in my lodge by tomorrow which is of vital importance so I can't be disturbed.'

Max left his Porsche by the manor intentionally and walked over to his lodge. 'Hi Rory are you at your apartment tonight?'
'Hello Max, bloody hell, Jenny and I were only saying yesterday we've got to meet up with you to discuss our wedding details as you are my best man.'
'Of course, perhaps we can sort a weekend out at Brandscombe in a week or two's time but in the meantime I need a favour. Can you pick me up on the corner of Oxford Road and Waterloo Terrace at 23:00 tonight then take me back to Brandscombe. Say no if it's not convenient and I'll understand if you can't at such short notice?'
'Good job you phoned when you did as I have just downed a pint and am watching the Quins playing Leicester. I would have had at least four pints by the end of the game as Monday is my day for watching recorded weekend sport accompanied by a few beers but I'll be there at eleven mate. See you later.' Then Rory was gone, evidently wanting to get back to the rugby match.

Max discounted the idea of having a swift Lochavennie as he had an important job to do that night and didn't want a fuddled brain. He waited until 21:30 before opening the lodge garage door and reversing the VW out with a boot full of terrorist. He placed a set of his false Velcro number plates over the originals and drove to Church Road in Isleworth next to the London Apprentice pub.

He had checked the Thames tidal tables and noted that it would be high tide in forty five minutes. The Bastion man was in his auburn wig, beard and glasses worn as an added precaution as he reversed down the slipway used for launching small craft into the Thames. Max dragged the body bag from the boot and laid it flat between the car and the rising river. The disposal could only possibly be seen from the other bank however it was a dark moonless night and the shadowy manoeuvre couldn't be witnessed and to add to that the rain that had promised all day started.

Rigor mortis sets into a human body between six and eight hours after death and a corpse stays stiff for a further twelve hours. Over twenty four hours had elapsed since his death and Tazi's body had returned to its limp state, making it easier to manoeuvre it to the water's edge with Max pulling the corpse of the terrorist spy into the rising tide. Max had to wade into the river up to his knees to enable an untangled launch and the powerful current then took control taking the body. The corpse spun around in a pirouette movement and paused as it faced Max giving him a final grotesque sickly grin before another swirl of water erupted and Tazi Emir was gone, swallowed up by the greedy current.

Max drove back up the slipway just in time as the rising water was lapping at the VW's tyres on the vanishing slipway. He stopped by a park, climbed the fence and dropped onto the grass just as all the evidence went up in a petrol fuelled bonfire that comprised of the body bag, Tazi's passport, credit cards, driving licence and lastly the rubber gloves that Max wore whilst in the VW. Max didn't wait for the ashes to blow away as he had a rendezvous to keep. He returned the VW to Waterloo Terrace, Tazi's address, and parked it in more or less the same spot from where it had been and took off the false Velcro plates.

Rory was already waiting for Max in his BMW and as Max climbed in he jokingly said 'home James.'

'What's all this about Maxy lad?'

'I can't say or I'll have to kill you Rory and we don't want that with your big day just around the corner.'

Once they had reached the approach to Croydon, Max opened the car window and threw the VW keys as far as he could towards a hedgerow. 'What are you doing Max, what was that you threw out?'
'Same as before Rory, think of your wedding!' Rory smiled and just shook his head. 'I've not been able to keep up with your antics since you used to abscond from our house room at school and climb back in by a rope ladder. What are you like Max-Catt?' They both chuckled at their shared past memories.

'Stop just before this junction and I'll walk from there which is all part of my intriguing operation. Thanks so much Rory and we'll make up for your lost beers in a week or two. I'll let you know and bring Jenny of course. Bye mate.'
'See you Mr. Bond!' Max laughed as he walked on the lane to the main gates of Brandscombe manor carrying in his backpack his auburn disguise and false number plates. He had intentionally left the light on and curtains closed at his lodge to give the impression that he was home working with his Porsche parked by the manor as an alibi should he get investigated but he didn't think anything would come of it. The average time period for a body to be washed up or caught somewhere between Gravesend and the Thames barrier takes nearly three weeks.

Max had more pressing things to organise than to worry about a detective's questioning that would only amount to peripheral inquiries at any rate. What else would they be as Max would not implicate his fellow Bastion agents or DCS Barlow. It would remain his and Tazi's secret! He lit his fire, showered and changed his uncomfortable sodden trousers, socks and shoes in exchange for his comfy heavy towelling bath robe then he slumped into his wrap around leather chair, pulling the silver tray towards him that held the dark amber Malt decanter and two lead crystal glasses with one soon to be in use.

47

Brad Zimmermann or Phonoi looked at his watch. It was 01:35 on Tuesday morning and he was stiff with cramp, cold and in total darkness. He knew the bus had been raided when he peeped out of one of the shooting holes to see why the bus had stopped and his answer came in the form of seeing armed police running around the Met Hopper. He had worked out the bus had been impounded by the police and nothing was said on the three way communication system. He also guessed that the police would strip the bus down soon so he waited until the early hours of Tuesday morning before he thought it safe to make his move. Phonoi turned the releasing knobs which activated the release of the soundproof panel and gently lowered the upholstered metal sheet that formed the sealed compartment. He crept out onto the top deck but kept low, almost crawling along the gangway, between the rows of seats and dared to take a quick peep over the side of the bus to see if anybody was about and found that he was in a hangar like workshop where there were other vehicles.

Zimmermann moved slowly down the steps of the bus with his rifle over his shoulder and his Smith and Wesson gun with attached suppressor in his hand and ready to fire. The hitman was about to step off the bus when he heard footsteps so he crouched between the front and second row of seats and peeped over the top of them to see where the walker was going and if he was armed. Unfortunately for him he came towards the tour bus and was armed. He stood about five paces from the bus with his automatic rifle slung over his shoulder sucking on his vaping device that billowed a significant cloud around him. After his third puff he shot forward, his rifle making a loud clatter as he fell to the floor and became Phonoi's thirteenth police victim in just four days

Zimmermann left the bus and rolled the hapless guard's body over with his foot whose vacant expression confirmed his mortal demise but as the garage workshop was dimly lit, Zimmerman needed to make sure. It appeared there was only one guard on duty so his route to exit the building was clear.

The television news was the same on every channel including the global stations. 'Two more policemen shot dead in London bringing the total to twelve since Friday. Arrests have been made and a sightseeing tour bus has been removed to a police motor vehicle forensic garage for inspection. The Metropolitan police have issued a statement warning the public as they believe the gunman responsible for the shootings is not believed to be among the arrests.' Brad Zimmermann spoke to the television as if it was someone in his hotel room: 'You've got your calculations wrong, it's not twelve dead policeman, it's thirteen now.' The contract killer had been given a number to text if he wanted to get a message to Hafeez and got a text reply within five minutes of the outgoing request: I am to take you to KH. Be ready by 08:00 this morning.

The chauffeur arrived five minutes early and didn't speak as Phonoi slipped into the back of the car. Two streets away the driver passed Zimmerman a blindfold. 'Put this on as we are going to our headquarters. It's nothing personal, everybody gets a blindfold. I have to stop the car if it's removed so I have to watch you from the rear view mirror so please keep it on.' Phonoi was guided to Hafeez's office where the IRF boss was waiting for his visitor. 'That puts your tally to thirteen then. We'll pay you an extra million for those three coppers but don't expect the full amount we agreed upon.'

Phonoi's face gave his response to Hafeez's offer but he couldn't argue with the two payments he'd earned in a few hours of what really was target practice him. 'Yeah, I'm not happy with losing the other million but I do understand although it was no fault of yours that the London police pounced on your bus. Anyway I want the million you owe me and I'll be off to sort out the big target of Max-Catt. I've done my preparations and your man Severn, or whatever his name is, did a good job getting me into his apartment.'

'Yeah, unfortunately Severn is missing and so is our courier which is worrying me big time. I don't think either will grass us but it's the not knowing that's eating into me. It's a pity our maealim almadina operation was exposed as another twelve infidels in little over four hours on the road would have created incredible havoc throughout the city and even their parliament and we'd have ground London to a halt!'

'What the fuck is maealim almadina when it's at home?'

'It means sightseeing in Arabic.' Hafeez answered in a matter-of-fact tone, annoyed that it had come to a premature end.

'Do you think the UK secret service know about you lot seeing that they knew about the bus and you have two guys missing. Is it even safe here?' Zimmermann was thinking about his own safety and of course his two million payout for dispatching Max Catt, Bastion's elite agent.

'Yeah we are safe here!

So here's your million and that puts us up to date and you'll get your final two when you get our nemesis, Max-Catt!'

48

The mood in Tim Barlow's office was a bittersweet combination. He was so sad to lose two more officers but delighted they had taken the death-bus off the road. He knew it was down to Max-Catt, and his grasp of mathematical logic, who had calculated the angle of the shootings thereby discounting that they were from a motorcycle that opposed the consensus from the investigators unanimous belief. The DCS was impressed how Max had worked out the height of the trajectory at around three metres that put buses and lorries in the frame. Then looking for a vehicle that was at all the shootings taken from the available footage which was damn good investigative work that probably saved more of his colleagues lives. Tim Barlow was thinking all this on his way over to the Met's forensic garage where he had arranged to meet with Max-Catt to discuss the still at large marksman.

'Max you beat me to it, anything new since we last spoke?'

'Unfortunately yes, an ambulance has just taken away the armed night guard who was watching over the tour bus and I'm saddened that you have now lost thirteen of your officers in three days. I'm so sorry for your colleagues Tim, it's a terrible tragedy. Your pathologist has just left with his body and he was a young cop as well. It doesn't need an expert to declare the cause of death, it was a 9mm bullet. On a more positive note, we now know where the marksman fired his lethal shots from so come with me and I'll show you.' Max led Tim Barlow and Jade up to the top deck of the bus where the front an upholstered padded metal sheet had been removed allowing the DCS to pop his head in. 'Bloody hell, our suspect couldn't have suffered from claustrophobia for sure.' Max crawled in and asked Tim's assistant to replace the panel. Inside Max crawled to one end and with the aid of his torch, he found the levers that slid the fire hole cover open to see for himself. As he squeezed into position on the righthand side, he saw something reflect his torch beam which was a spent cartridge case. Max put it in his pocket and climbed back into the daylight and the welcome sweet air. Max tossed the cartridge to Tim who would pass it on with other evidence that was stacking against Brad Zimmermann. 'It was a well thought out attack on the UK, our government and the heart of civil security, the police force!' Max would have been impressed if it hadn't been so cowardly and vile.

'Come on Jade, we have to get back to Bastion so please contact Callum and Mason and ask them to be in my office within half an hour.'

'Thanks for getting here early as we have a lot to get through Three topics, well two that really concern you three directly,' Max sat opposite his field team of three. 'Firstly we know the IRF was behind the police killings in central London. The police guard at the police forensics garage took the tally of police officers to thirteen which must be the biggest loss any force has recorded. Thankfully we have the bus from which the shootings occurred and we had intel from Dani Quibi that an ex-US Navy seal globally known as Phonoi was here in the UK. He is one of the best marksman in the world who sells his skills as a contract killer. Not only is he top of his profession but he also charges mega bucks for his service and he always gives a guarantee of satisfaction once he accepts a contract. We don't know what his passport name is as he goes on the dark web as Phonoi which is a Greek mythology spirit. Dani thought his recruitment by the IRF was to kill me so I suppose I should be honoured having such a big name after me,' Max-Catt gave a smiling wink at his three agents. 'Anyway he's over here and in hiding and I know someone has been in my apartment on the pretence of a technical problem from the council over a trumped up structural defect or something like that. That could well have been Phonoi sussing out my abode and I think he was given the Met Hopper shooting job as a bonus and it just happened to be planned while he was in the UK but that's just my theory. Why I need to tell you this is that he might involve you to get to me which is my concern.'

'However the two issues that involve you directly are to locate the five remaining river spies. We know who the sixth one is, our own Tazi Emir who has gone missing. The Uxbridge police have come back to me and confirmed he's not at his digs but his car is still parked outside it. The police have interviewed a Mrs. Granger who said she hadn't seen him since last Friday night and it looks like he's done a runner back to the IRF most probably….' Jade interjected. 'Why didn't he take his car then Max.' That temporarily threw Max until he gathered his composure.

'A good point, perhaps he felt it safer by public transport. Who knows!' The answer seemed to satisfy the inquisitive Jade Jackson. 'As I was saying until Miss Marple interrupted me, the river agents must be rounded up.

Max knew the names of the river agents which he had got from Tazi. 'We know through Jade's initiative when she followed Tazi Emir to the Harrow Road newsagent that it's a message hub between the IRF leaders or cell managers to the river agents who work in or around London. Jade and I intercepted a courier and gained good intel and we devised a plan to trick Tazi Emir into sending a message to the IRF. He took the bait which proved his guilt beyond doubt so now the next plan is to draw out the other rivers.'

'We are going to send a message to all the river agents via the newsagent acting as a new courier. Severn we know is Tazi Emir and he's fled somewhere and the other five are Wye, Clyde, Thames, Avon and Trent. We will deliver five separate messages addressed to their river names sent from KH which are the initials that I took off the courier's phone. The messages will be delivered by Jade who knows how to pass over the messages. Jade you will wear leathers and keep your helmet on and visor down. Do exactly what you saw Tazi do when you followed him. Are you okay with that?'

'Yeah of course! When do I do it?'

'Here are the five messages.' Max handed the five notes that all read: Urgent emergency meeting. Be at the bandstand nearest the Peter Pan statue in Kensington Gardens at 17:00 sharp this evening. Don't be late. Make sure you are not followed. We have had to abandon Operation maealim almadina. KH

The four of us will be armed this evening and will enter individually at the Coalbrookdale gate at 16:00 five minutes apart. I will go in first with Jade second, then Mason and then at 16:15 Callum and make for the wooded area where you can observe the gate.'

'Once we have that mission out of the way, we are heading to Bradford for a raid on a mosque that is up to no good but first things first. Now get some rest, but no drinking as we have an important mission ahead of us. Jade get fitted out with leathers and a helmet and take the messages for the rivers by 13:30 so you'd better get your skates on! I'll see you all at Kensington Gardens later this afternoon.' Max left his field agents in his office as he was in a hurry to see his boss, Julia Deakin.

He hadn't reported in or submitted any operational reports for a week and was well overdue. 'Ah Max-Catt, I believe you owe me an explanation. I've had no reports on you and your team's absence and where is Tazi Emir? I asked for him to see me but he's missing. Did you have anything to do with his disappearance?'

Julia gave a sideways look at Max that was edged with suspicion. 'First, sorry for not being around but you know I was heavily involved with the shootings in central London and other side issues developed but you'll have chapter and verse in a few days. I'm hopefully going to bring you some good news soon regarding the IRF and the capture of a sightseeing bus that was at the heart of the London shootings so I'm asking for your patience for a little longer as I have to leave with my team to go to Kensington Gardens and then a trip to Bradford. Will you give me that time please Julia as it's essential.'

'Of course but I want a detailed report on my desk by close of play on Friday. You might have zero status outside Max-Catt but not in here with me. Now go and do what you do best!' A wry smile was worn by Max as he turned and left Miss Deakin's office. I wonder if she's as kinky as her predecessor, the incorrigible Miss Cordelia Fernsby who went badly rogue. Max increased his smile at the thought.

49

The atmosphere was not good, in fact it was full of tension in the IRF's headquarters at Rock Street in Limehouse. The IRF central committee based in Afghanistan had been informed that their investment of the River programme over the last fifteen years was in danger of collapsing as was the maealim almadina operation although that did achieve a better result than expected on the first tour bus operation which pleased the IRF's founding fathers.

Kamal Hafeez felt he was taking the rap for others making mistakes in the field who failed him and discussed as much with Hussain Badir. 'It's not my fault Hussain is it and I can't see any other way but to get our river agents out now but the central committee are telling us to hold our nerve and leave them in place to see if they have been exposed. The committee don't give a monkey's cuss for our rivers, it's the undercover positions they hold and they want us to try and salvage fifteen years of their investment. They see the river agents as commodities or shares that produce dividends.'

'You know the central committee always want somebody's head and from what you've just told me it seems like they're after yours as they have to justify their investments.' Although Hussain Badir was being pragmatic it wasn't what Hafeez wanted to hear.

'I'm just glad they don't know our headquarters address here. Anyway Hussain please message the five rivers to meet you meet you and bring them to Limehouse be-

fore they're arrested and if you're asked about it you could say you used your own initiative without my knowledge. You'd do that for me wouldn't you?'
'With respect Kamal piss off! Do it yourself if you want them back. You want me to go against what the central committee have ordered but I'd wait until they give us the green light.'
'Yeah of course you are right.'

Chiswick was as busy as always and as Brad Zimmermann walked along the high road he wondered: How many coffee and phone shops does a town the size of Chiswick need. Along with arty-farty bistros making up the proportion of shops.

Phonoi had already waited twenty impatient minutes to be served while listening to an assistant explaining a phone plan that a would be customer obviously couldn't afford, given the shocked face she pulled when the monthly plan was presented to her. The contract killer's patience was at breaking point when a spotty kid asked him what he wanted. When he said he just wanted to buy a phone with a loaded roaming data SIM or a Pay-As-You-Go plan as the Brits liked to call it, this was dismissed by the spotty kid who insisted that it would work out a lot cheaper with the free iPhone that came with their special plan. 'Look just shut the fuck up, I've just listened to your colleague go through twenty minutes of bullshit. Just give me what I asked for. Got it dude!' Spotty yielded, of course he did, looking at the giant Yank who had a very mean look!

The assistant scurried off and returned with an opened phone box. 'I tested this one and inserted a SIM and it's ready to use. There is ten pounds of credit on it so would you like a top-up?'
'Yeah give me another fifty dollars, no I mean pounds worth of credit.'

Brad Zimmermann wanted out of the crowded phone shop so he took a taxi to Strand on the Green, ominously to where Max-Catt lived. He was there to make a final decision on how he was going to hunt down his contracted target. He guessed correctly that Max would not be home on a mid-week early afternoon so he pressed the buzzer for Penthouse 3 and gave it another buzz just to make sure. He had carried out his due diligence on his target and was impressed by his target's military and civil achievements and allowed himself to mentally show respect from one US special forces man to a world famous SAS man, although the SAS would argue that the United States navy seals were not equal to the best elite soldiers in the world but of course the US navy seals would argue differently.

Phonoi had the keys duplicated by Tazi Emir so easily accessed Max's luxury home and filmed a video of all the rooms, the access points and the direct lines to the other side of the river. After ten minutes Zimmermann had completed the apartment check and now wanted to check out the view from the roof of the building that he'd checked out earlier.

Phonoi knew his way into the pharmaceutical warehouse and he confidently walked past the receptionist and took the lift to the top floor to the caretakers store and then climbed the ladder to the roof, repeating what he had done the week before . At the very same air-conditioning unit he took out his rifle and brought Penthouse 3 into view.

Phonoi identified two possible opportunities but both might present problems. Although his rifle was powerful enough to penetrate the tempered glass of the large framed patio windows, the line of fire was at a two or three degree angle from the roof so there was a fifteen percent chance of deflection.

Then the hunted would become the hunter with odds moving to a fifty-fifty gamble. Brad Zimmermann only worked on a 98% plus chance of success so the windy roof that was his favoured choice of attack was discounted as his professionalism to a clinical standard was the deciding element. The assassination would not be from the elevated position and the Yank knew he had made the right choice by adhering to his self-imposed standard of success which had kept him at the top of his profession where he intended to stay for a few more years. He confidently reversed his footsteps out of the commercial building and took a taxi back to his hotel to think again: I'll get this right and when I've completed a plan to my exacting standards you are as good as gone Mr. Max-Catt and I'll be returning to the States a truly rich dude. Brad Zimmermann nodded to himself in the back of the taxi and would scrutinise his options carefully.

Notwithstanding the financial blackmail he was bound to get from an angry Kamal Hafeez, Phonoi would not be pressurised into rushing and possibly botching a contract for anybody. His name and reputation was paramount to him and will remain so. As got out of the cab at his hotel, Zimmermann's mind was flirting with new ideas for Max's assassination and one idea in particular involved kidnap which kept pushing itself to the forefront of his mind so much so that the cabbie had to shout at him three times to pay him but Zimmermann was miles away, hatching a plan that put the odds at his favoured rate of 98% plus.

50

Jade confidently brought her 350cc Kawasaki bike to a halt and parked it where the courier had stood his and walked into the Harrow Road News shop at 13:35, five minutes outside Max's request time but it was not her fault as the man in the motorcycle hire shop took ages over the paperwork. However, she didn't waste any time while she was waiting as she got herself fitted out with leathers and a helmet in the same hire shop.

She walked into the newsagent and copied what she'd seen Tazi Emir do and placed five messages into a magazine then she picked up another magazine and took them both to the counter to pay for them and then left the shop leaving the magazine that had the messages in it on the counter.

The smiling shopkeeper picked up the magazine and placed it underneath the counter as part of a well-used routine. Jade had carried out the first part of the set up and then returned the motorbike, leathers and helmet to the hire shop and took the Tube to High Street Kensington station and walked to the Coalbrookedale gate to enter Kensington Gardens where she was to rendezvous with her two colleagues and her lover boss.

She mused as she entered the gates: I wonder if I play my cards right I might get a repeat performance with Maximus! Jade Jackson knew she had an almost schoolgirl crush on Max but realised now was not the time to pursue it. She saw Max walking nonchalantly through a thicket of trees. I mustn't wave, I must act like a real spy! She giggled at her silly thought as she approached the trees. Max decided that they would pretend to be a couple which of course excited Jade. They held hands and sat on the nearest bench overlooking the Coalbrookedale ornate gate that bears the royal coat of arms.

Jade cozied up to her boss which was outside the expectations of acting. 'Stop it Jade, that's not funny.' Jade moved back to a polite distance. Who's trying to be funny, I'm deadly serious Maxy-me-lad. Jade gave one of her naughty smiles. 'Oh sorry Max, I thought it would look more authentic if anyone was watching.' Max shook his head but he did like his young intuitive field agent.

Callum entered the park and saw them on the bench but continued walking past and the couple realised he intentionally did that to let them know he'd arrived. He then went to the cover of some trees and waited but stayed within sight of the bench where one of the couple was flirting.

Mason had swapped times with Callum as he had an urgent call that he had to deal with so after he arrived he and Callum moved through the shrubbery towards the Peter Pan statue. The couple, much to the delight of Miss Jackson, walked hand in hand and as they neared the statue Jade stepped in front of her boss and snogged him, catching him totally unawares and he had to go through with the half charade because to hesitate or pull away would have looked suspicious. 'Stop it Jade, just behave.' Max hissed his rebuff through clenched teeth while retaining a false beaming smile. Jade had caught Max off guard but he couldn't prevent it and she knew it.

The five river agents had arrived individually with Severn being the only one missing as he was heading swiftly towards the Thames flood barrier.

Max had gone over the plan several times. He would approach the group while his three agents took up positions with their weapons at the ready. Max walked towards the unsuspecting spies and stopped in front of them and spoke calmly: 'Gentlemen if any of you move a muscle from your present position you will be shot. I have guns pointing at you and anyone who moves without my say so will have at least one bullet to cope with!'

The shocked faces of each of the five registered that they had been tricked and were now in danger. 'You are being watched by armed agents who are highly trained in the art of marksmanship so save your lives by not fidgeting. Do you understand?'

Max realised that a problem he had was that these extremists were converted and brainwashed and that to die for the cause would make them martyr. In short, the five were an unknown quantity. Max beckoned to his team to join him. 'Tape these five stagnant rivers up by the wrists'. Max had pre-arranged for the Bastion ten seater people carrier to meet him at the park and it was now waiting at the Coalbrookedale gate.

The five river agents were held in separate rooms at Bastion and Max began his questioning of each of them. 'I want you to tell me your real name, your river codename and which government department you work for as well as your address where you are living.'

Of course there was silence as all those young men were Islamic extremists and were so brainwashed that they were willing to die for their cause which Max knew.

‘Look, I’m not going to waste my time or yours. I have the other four to interrogate and I only have an hour as I need to leave for the Halifax Road Mosque and arrest Mousa Alami.’ Max went to his briefcase. ‘Do you know what this is?’ No answer of course. Max then pulled out a phial and showed the taped prisoner the printed name on the small label. ‘If you can’t read it, I’ll oblige you as it reads Ophiophagus Hannah!

51

The black skull and crossbones on a white background was displayed ominously on a brown bottle and was exasperatingly indicated by Max-Catt. 'See this?' Max stabbed his finger at the symbolic Jolly Roger. 'It's the international symbol of death or deadly poison and this particular poison is the venom from the Ophiophagus Hannah or more commonly known as the King Cobra which is one of the world's deadliest snakes and a bite from one of these beauties will kill you in about thirteen minutes depending on your body mass. An eight year old boy in Thailand died within eight minutes and seeing as you are just a scrawny little fucker I'd put your demise at around ten minutes give or take. The venom has a murine lipid droplet of 50 value of 0.025 mg/kg SC but I don't expect you to know that as I didn't until I asked a herpetologist who are the professionals in venomics but put in a nutshell, it kills pretty damn quick. Symptoms are severe pain at the time of the bite, then nausea followed by vomiting and a rapid heart rate eventually leading to a heart attack and collapse of the nervous system. Not nice!'

'Tape his ankles Jade and secure his arms to the chair. Then I want you to leave as I wouldn't subject a lady to watch excruciating pain on a fellow human.' Jade didn't speak and left as requested to join her colleagues next door.

Max didn't bother giving further warnings as he guessed it would achieve no results so he pushed a hypodermic needle into the phial and extracted ten millilitres of the deadly venom. The facial expression on the secured river agent quickly changed from arrogance to panic as Max moved towards his restricted captive and rolled up his sleeve, rubbed it with moistened cotton wool and tapped his arm to find a good vein before preparing to inject to which the terrorist spy backed away from as much as he was able to.

The syringe went in without any resistance as hypodermics do and the eyes of Max's victim bulged and he let out a muffled cry. Max matter-of-factly replaced the medical kit back into its bag and, like all good medics, he disposed of the needle in its special sleeve. 'I can't remember if I told you or not that you will die if you don't get the antidote within, say, five minutes and that's all the time you have to answer my questions and twenty percent of that time has already expired so you have four minutes to decide your fate.' Max sat by the desk and pretended to read a blank sheet of paper.

Six minutes had passed and the man was mumbling religious phrases or prayers with the usual bowing then two minutes later he fell into a coma. Max called Callum in. 'Get a wheelchair and lock him in a holding cell downstairs but leave his gag on.' Callum took the dribbling, incoherent captive away.

'Right you next.' Max then went to the interview room next door and picked his next interviewee and escorted him next door and repeated exactly the same patter and advice about the highly toxic snake venom of the King Cobra and how his pal had decided to die a martyr and that his young life was in his own hands.

Another brave martyr got taken away by Callum in a wheelchair in full view of the third man and the procedure continued. The third chap seemed more nervous and asked what had happened to his colleague? 'Let me explain about the King Cobra first.' Max went through the now well-rehearsed explanation of how the venom hits with deadly potency and told him how his pals had died for not telling him what he wanted to know in the ten minutes or so they had left after being jab with the killer serum.

'I don't believe you, you're bluffing.'

'Callum take this fool down to the cell and show him the bodies.' Callum encouraged the third captive by pushing him along in the direction of the lift and down to the basement cell. Callum Maclean didn't open the cell but pointed to the two bodies on the polished concrete floor. 'My God!' The third man gasped and was then turned to the interview room where Max was waiting for him.

'Did you see your pals? Two good young martyrs but will anyone from your fanatical organisation come and put flowers on their graves. I doubt that which is how much they care about the likes of you and your colleagues that they regard as their cannon fodder. I expect we will have all five of you in the basement cell within the hour!' Max rolled up number three's sleeve. 'You will not feel this but remember you have only five minutes or thereabouts to receive the antidote. After that it's goodnight Vienna. You'll start feeling drowsy after two minutes and after that your nervous system will deteriorate and then, before I can say bish-bosh, you'll be on a cold concrete floor along with the others like cold sardines.

'I didn't say this to your pals but I know you are all educated lads and you must know science over fiction! How the fuck are you going to enjoy paradise with so many virgins which is your supposed gift for martyrdom? You'd have better luck finding a virgin in Caroline Street in Cardiff on a Friday night. It's total bollocks. Just think about it! Your choice pal!' Number three was feeling queasy after three minutes, light-headed and sleepy, but he shook himself to stop falling into a coma and gave three desperate nods.' Max quickly gave him an another jab which brought him back to cohesion. 'Okay, okay! I don't want to die with no respect. My name is Borak, I'm an assistant in checking through information collated about China and I have worked at GCHQ in Cheltenham for over a year. I rent a bedsit in Brentford and my river code-name is Thames.'

'That's good and very sensible. Now who are your friends, including the dead ones?'

There was hesitation from Thames but his capitulation had gone too far so he thought he might as well collect any cooperation bonus on offer. 'There's me at GCHQ, Kamal Malik, known as Trent, in the Foreign Office, Mohammad, known as Clyde, in the Home Office, Faraz, known as Avon, in MI5 and Mohammad, known as Wye, in the anti-terrorism office. We don't know where Severn is as he's vanished but his name was Tazi Emir and he was at MI6 which is where he identified Sani Yosef as Dani Quibi who also worked for MI6 who transferred to Bastion! We think you are holding him somewhere. Is that so?'

'I ask the questions you traitorous scum. Britain gave you and your family refuge, citizenship and British passports and yet you hate us. If you don't like how we democratically do things here which allows pond life like you to have a voice, why don't you fuck off to a country that has extreme views and treats women as second rate? Why do you think so many of your lot risk their lives trying to get in as refugees when most are illegal, economic migrant males of working age? Ask yourself that.' Max was getting angry which was something he didn't want to do so he called the team in and told them to bring in the other two.

‘Okay Mason and Callum take this filth to the holding cell and give him and the fourth one water but no food.’

‘What with the two dead’uns?’

‘Yes Mason, in with the dead’uns and when you have locked them up, join Jade and me in my office.’ As Max and Jade got to Max’s office, an out of breath Bastion junior ran up to them. ‘Mr. Hainsworth-Catt, Miss Deakin wants you to phone her the minute I found you as apparently your phone is turned off.’

‘Okay thanks for the message, I’ll phone her now.’ Max had forgotten to turn his phone back on after the interrogations. ‘Julia, sorry I had my phone off as I always do when I’m interrogating.’

‘I was informed by security that there are two bodies locked in a cell and the keys are missing. Did you kill them here in the fortress?’

‘They are not dead so please bear with me Julia and all will be explained but I’m in the middle of something important. You did give me until close of play on Friday and it’s only Tuesday.’

‘Okay Maximus, carry on and it’s a good job I trust you.

I’ve had the prime minister on the phone demanding answers to the central London shootings as the government is under pressure for results and the Home Office and the metropolitan police are taking a bashing as well. Ok I’ll leave you to it but when you get any snippet of success please let me know.’

‘Thanks Julia, I certainly will.’

Max waited for Mason and Callum to return to his office. Callum spoke in a shocked voice. ‘Those two stiffs in the cell have come to life, they are groggy and unaware of their surroundings but are alive. How’s that? Mason and I thought you’d done ‘em good and proper.’

‘Yeah, well I let everyone think that as part of the plan and really didn’t have time to explain it to you guys and

I always keep my little interrogation trick up my sleeve which I learnt it from a CIA agent in my SAS days.'

'I pretend to inject a lethal dose of King Cobra venom which genuinely usually kills within ten or so minutes and I get our props department print up a fake phial of Ophiophagus-Hannah which is the Latin name for the deadly shit but the phial really contains Rohypnol or as it's known on the street as *Roofy* or as the press like to call it "*the date-rape drug*". Both serums have the same ten minute knockout but the latter isn't of course permanent sleep! Anyway folks, it worked on number three or as I can now call him Borak or Thames. He was planted in CGHQ by the IRF and it was their sponsors who financed all six of the river spies. Well done team and I applaud you resoundingly!' The team were proud of their participation in the trickery used to capture a gang that could have done double the damage that *The Cambridge Spy Ring* of Anthony Blunt, Guy Burgess, Kim Philby and Donald Maclean ever did in passing secrets to the Russians in the early fifties.

'Good evening Tim, can you get five of the six river-spies collected from Bastion where we are holding them but I will not be here when you call as my team and I will be on another operation, this time in Yorkshire. I have written out and also have a long recording of an inter… let's say interview that bangs the spies to rights! I will get our communications team to advise the relevant organisations who the rivers were working for and I'll have to sort all the bloody paperwork out when I return. Again Tim, I must say how sorry I am for your brave officers who were slaughtered in London in cold blood.'

'Thanks Max, bloody good work on the spies and thank you for your condolences which I can hear the sincerity of in your voice, Thank you my friend. I know you are in a hurry so I'll let you go. These arrests will please the government and shut the baying press up. We'll talk when you get back.' DCS Barlow was gone, knowing that Max had more urgent business to attend to.

'Okay team, you have thirty minutes to do what you need to do, pack an overnight bag then get tooled up and be ready to move out to Yorkshire. Let's move.'

52

The smell of burgers and fries waffling up his nostrils took the world famous assassin's thoughts back to the United States, back to the diners that are on every highway junction and in the centre of every major town right across the country. Whatever oil they cook their fries in, it brings back the customers time and time again and in particular kids and teenagers almost to an addiction level. Brad Zimmermann needed to fuel his well-kept frame and burning off calories at his age and with his occupation wasn't a problem. He ordered and within five minutes was carrying away two double decker chicken burgers with melted cheese and garnish and, like most people, he left the soggy lettuce.

While eating he considered the intel and extensive dossier he had received from Tazi Emir about Max-Catt which told the Yank that he was dealing with no ordinary dude and he felt he should really be charging double for the hit but with four million already paid to him by the IRF plus his little excursion on the Thames, this all made him feel he'd done good.

Max-Catt has made Phonoi feel patriotic as it was a US Navy Seals versus a British SAS soldier, the bragging rights of which had been contested for many years and there was a loving hate between the two special forces of two great military nations. Phonoi was not prepared to go below his 98% plus risk rate so he decided that the hit must be a clear, unrestricted shot.

The courier who was sent to the Harrow Road newsagent delivered an order for all the river agents to make contact immediately but, as his shop was empty, he called the courier back. 'A message had been delivered only this lunchtime for a meeting at the Peter Pan statue in Kensington Gardens so why is another message coming in just forty minutes after that request? Take this message to Kamal immediately. Go!'

Hafeez dismissed the courier and read the rushed message from the newsagent. I am sure something is wrong. Did you send a message this morning because I received one delivered by a courier at lunchtime. The message instructed all the rivers to meet at the Peter Pan statue in Kensington Gardens. Confirm if that was you and another thing, the courier didn't speak or take his helmet off. I fear the worst!'

Hafeez called in his deputy and explained the shopkeeper's anxiety and alarm. 'What can we do Kamal?'

We can do nothing until we know the fate of the river agents, unless you have any bright ideas.' The sarcastic tone was apparent in Hafeez's voice borne out of frustration in not knowing what was going on with the IRF's river agents investment. 'We are in troubled times.' Hafeez mused and he guessed right and put his and the IRF's troubles down to his nemesis Max-Catt and was now relying heavily on Phonoi to remove this obstacle.

53

It was unseasonably cold for a late April evening and Jade blew into her hands to stop them tingling with the cold. It was almost twilight as the Bastion field team of four left for Bradford using one of the organisation's fleet Jaguars and Callum, who loved to drive, volunteered his motoring skills that were readily accepted. Max wasn't going to drive as he needed to concentrate on the forthcoming raid at the mosque.

When they reach the M1 motorway the volume of traffic just to get on to it was almost deadlocked and was just about moving so much so it took over an hour and ten minutes to crawl past the Watford Gap.

Once on the outskirts of the main conurbations of London and given the dilution of late evening traffic, their progress started to improve and they made up some time, reaching Wakefield by 23:50.

They continued on the M1 motorway to East Ardsley then drove the short distance to pick up the A650 into Bradford, arriving there just after 00:15, much earlier than they anticipated when they were stuck in traffic south of Watford. Their in-car satnav directed them to the Halifax Road mosque and Callum didn't need to be told to stop as he drove past the religious building.

The mosque was a facade as it had more sinister undertakings since the previous kindly imam was disposed of by the IRF to replace him with their own radical man,

Mousa Alami, who was now the IRF's communications coordinator and he was the main target of the Bastion team's mission as well as getting the mosque closed until the correct supervision was in place to return it purely to a place of true Islamic worship.

Since the unaccountable absence of the courier and more alarmingly the disappearance of Tazi Emir, one of the river agents, all the IRF cells including the mosque had their security increased to two armed guards on twelve hour shifts day and night so the Bastion agents assumed this and Dani Quibi had passed back intel saying as much. Max didn't want Jade put in any danger but at the same time he didn't want to have her think she was a passenger so he decided that he must treat her as any front line field agent.

'Okay, Jade and Callum you skirt around the back and on my signal you will both will affect an entry through the rear window. We can't use our friends, the stun and smoke bombs as there could be innocent people in the building. However all the occupants should be asleep apart from a guard or guards on duty who will probably be armed and I sure the place will definitely be alarmed. Mason, you are our electrics expert so check out where the electricity supply is and cut it which will kill the alarms and sensor lighting and send me a thumbs up emoji when you are ready to cut as we will all be in position to enter by then.'

'Keep your phones open as within five seconds of Mason's affirmative I will ping you with the message to go! On that signal I will crash through the front window and Callum and Jade will do the same at the rear using your busting ram as I will. We all have bullet proof vests and head bands with night infrared vision and our biggest and only advantage will be surprise as they will not know how many we are. If you are confronted by an armed guard shoot him in the legs but use your machine pistols with restraint as we don't know what our target looks like and we don't want to kill an innocent cleric. Okay, Let's get to our positions.'

Mason broke open the external meter box and, with insulators at the ready, was just about to send the confirmation text message when a noise prevented him from opening his phone which would have illuminated his position so he stood still and slowly dropped to a creeping position. He saw the silhouette of a man with a rifle slung over his shoulder who was about to light his cigarette and was coming straight towards where Mason was along the path leading to the front of the building and he nearly stepped on Mason before the SAS man pounced upwards directly in front of the guard who had no chance as Mason's special forces issued knife was quickly around the throat of the shocked smoker.

The guard didn't struggle against the cold steel pressing against his throat as he knew that any increase in pressure would draw blood by the razor sharp blade. Mason was now behind his victim and dragged him to the ground and tightly taped his mouth, wrists and ankles and secured him to a fruit tree at the back of the mosque. Callum and Jade looked on bemused at what they saw and Mason put his fingers to his lips and calmly returned to the meter box. Without any further interruptions Mason sent the thumbs up emoji and waited for the anticipated reply! The sound of smashing glass in a noisy pub sounds loud above the background of chatter, but in the dead of night, where only a distant vixen could be heard calling for her mate, the sound was deafening!

Shouting came from somewhere above the team, but toothy had to clear the ground floor first. The two pairs of agents moved inwards and met somewhere in the middle then moved on together but spread out, stealthily sweeping the ground floor and entering the prayer hall that made up two thirds of the building's footprint. The noise from upstairs had ceased but the producers of the sounds must be still there.

The ground floor was cleared and next it was time to move up to the first floor. Max asked Jade to cover the ground floor area and protect their backs then he led the two guys upwards while placing a finger to his lips for dead silence. Max spun on the first step of the return flight of stairs and was thrown back with an intense pain in his stomach that warmed to heat in an instant. Max knew he'd been shot but the shooter was soon taken out by Callum who fired from behind Max. With the help of his night laser-sight, Max let off a burst of rapid fire along the line of the shadow and screams were replaced by silence. Mason called down to Jade to see to Max, who had been thrown halfway down the main stairway. Perkins then joined his teammate, Callum, as they gingerly cleared the front bedrooms which were evidently used as offices then they moved on the middle rooms of the substantial house that was once the Bradford and Bingley Conservative club. How ironic!

'I'm okay Jade so go and cover the ground floor and that's an order!'

'But Max, you….'

'No buts Jade, go!' Max moved back up the stairs just in time to see a dark figure moving up behind Callum and Mason and Max made light work of him in a similar fashion to what Mason had done outside but without the aid of a knife then gagged his victim and secured him to the staircase's newel post. Max then moved to the back rooms and saw his two agents in the last room which appeared to be empty. The three teammates left the man strapped to the stairs and went down to check the ground floor more thoroughly to see if there was a basement. There was, but Jade was not at her post.

'Both of you check out the basement and I'm going to check where Jade is. Go!' Max moved out of the building to see the final throws of resistance being offered by a man who was being attacked by Jade. By the time Max had reached the noise the man was face down on the lawn with Jade straddling him and forcing his arms behind his back and with one hand and help from her teeth, she taped her captive. The show was over and Jade had her Smith and Wesson now jabbed in a man's back. She took his wallet and phone from his pocket and threw them towards Max who winced with pain as he stretched his arm outwards and upwards to catch it. 'Ouch, that fucking hurt!' Max recovered his composure and rifled through the wallet which belonged to none other than their target, Mr. Mousa Alami who, but for the quick reaction of Jade Jackson would have escaped through the main gate. 'Bloody hell Jade, remind me never to mix it with you. What speed you have in unarmed combat.'
'But I am armed Max.' She wiggled her Smith and Wesson in the air making that very point.

Mason brought down the armed occupant who had been taped to the stairs while Callum released the first guard from the fruit tree. 'Jade search him for his phone, he must have one.'

Two of the captives were taped and put in the boot of the car and the other one went in the back of the car between Callum and Jade. Max had calls to make in the front passenger seat and Mason was driving this time. They left for London with blue lights flashing as time was of the essence as they needed to try and locate the headquarters of the IRF before they got wind of the raid on the mosque. Max rang Tim Barlow, his old Scotland

Yard pal. 'Bloody hell Max, do you know what the time is?'

'Sorry Tim I…' Barlow stopped him and whispered back.

'I don't want to wake or worry my wife as she's sound asleep so I'll go downstairs.'

'Right Max, you were saying?'

'My Bastion team have just raided the suspect mosque in Bradford and we have three captives including our target man, Mousa Alami, the bad imam. We are bringing them back to Bastion for now but I need you to take this number and check with the phone provider who the phone belongs to.' Max gave Tim the mobile phone number. 'I need it urgently because once the IRF bosses at their London headquarters find out about the closure of the mosque which was also their communications hub they may close down their current headquarters which I suspect is somewhere in East London. Can you check it out Tim as no one argues with Scotland Yard's guv'nor.'

Tim Barlow grunted a chuckle and agreed and after just a few moments he rang Max back. 'Max it's registered to a Mrs. Zamara Ali of 347 Rorke Street, Limehouse, London E14 9JD. Can I go back to bed now oh master?'

'Sorry Tim and thanks but I'll probably need your boys tomorrow though.'

'It is tomorrow already and I'll do anything to catch those bastards that murdered thirteen of my brave officers and you be careful Max!'

The team got back to Bastion and placed the three captives in one holding cell as that was all there was available but it was only for a brief period of retention.

'Okay you three follow me.' They didn't even stop for coffee as Max led his team to the armoury. 'Okay guys sign out for two stun and smoke grenades and a machine pistol if you haven't already got one and a grappling hook and rope.' All kitted out and with their backpacks full, the team got back in the Jaguar whose bonnet was still warm from its recent speedy drive back from Yorkshire with their expeditiousness was validated by the greasy smearing of splattered moths.

54

The Jaguar driver had switched back to Callum and he drove a hundred yards passed the target and stopped. Max explained why they were doing this raid without resting after Bradford and they all understood well enough. 'Okay, same teams. I will enter the front with Jade and you two go around the back. This time we won't bother about the alarms as it will add to the confusion. We will set our watch timers for sixty seconds and start them when I say go! Callum you have your smash-ram ready to break through the window so don't bother with the door as it'll be reinforced for sure. Our main target is Kamal Hafeez, the IRF boss, and I want the murderous bastard alive if we can. Okay get ready to set your timers and we break through at zero. Now go!' All four cleared the dwarf wall with Callum and Mason jogging to the back garden.

The team were becoming specialists in shock entry tactics and at 04:55 the house was in darkness as was expected. Callum and Mason had to climb a wooden fence to get to the rear of the house but were soon standing next to the chosen window to smash and enter. All four had donned their breathing apparatus and night sights with their machine pistols over their shoulders. Ten seconds to go and both teams were eager to get the job done. At zero time two windows simultaneously smashed wrecking the silence. Jade threw one stun bomb and one smoke bomb into the massive hole made in the shattered glass and Max climbed through in great pain from his stomach wound. Jade followed noticing the grimace on her boss's face.

To say there was confusion was an understatement with smoke, coughing, rapid gunfire and screaming everywhere, all the things that the SAS and Bastion agents take in their stride which is why they are the best in the world at what they do. Max stealthily moved through the smokey fog and confusion.

Like the at Bradford mosque, the guards were armed but had nodded off and the lack of discipline on their part cost them their lives. Before they could reach for their weapons the three defenders were cut down by a hail of gunfire. Like at the mosque, shouting came from the first floor he lights on the landing were switched on. A big mistake. Max lobbed up a stun grenade up to the landing followed by Jade's last stun. One defender holding his ears and totally disoriented fell into the banister his weight shattering the spindles and unable to hold back his forward momentum. He finished at the base of the stairs in heap and holding his broken leg, screaming Arabic expletives.

Ear defenders that incorporated the smoke mask protected the raiding party. The house battle was in full swing as Max led the team up the stairs. Again telling Jade to cover their backs and defend the front entrance. Also shoot the deaf broken-legged man if he moved. The team moved to the landing Max threw a stun to the rear and asked Callum to lob one to the right front of the top landing. The grenades went off within three seconds of each other. Max threw both his smokies one left and one right. The leader indicated through SAS sign language he was going left to the rear and indicated he wanted Mason to go right along the landing towards the front. Callum to stay central at the top of the stairs and stop anyone coming out of the dormitories.

Two stunned IRF men came staggering out of the smoke behind Mason who had missed the bedroom on his left. Callum had him covered and before either stunned defenders could raise their weapons Callum had dealt with them.

Mason rolled his last stun along the landing, as if bowling. Three seconds and the grenade exploded. The signal was given for Mason to throw his last smokey. He ran through his smoke and rapid fired at the coughing noise.Then at the end on the right he came to a locked door. He had no grenades of either type left. He had been taught never to stand in front or behind a locked door in house-to-house combat.

Max at the rear of the property had similar skirmishes and had taken out two men on the landing as they ran through the smoke clutching their heads form the stunning.

Max also had a type of stand-off with a locked room scenario. Callum had the last stun grenade so Max went back and took it from him, returning to the locked room this time with Callum. More sign language between then and Callum shot rapid fire to for a circled hole to be created a size of a football. As the perforated centre fell through into the room Max lobbed in the stun explosive. Both ex-SAS men stood back from any blast. Max kicked the door open but on halfway. There was a bullet riddled body stopping the door from opening. The man was unfortunate to be standing in the way when Callum was hole making. There were four others that were shocked and and out of the affray. The hapless four held their hands up. Max squeezed into the room followed by Callum and between them taped their wrists and with a coil of rope tied them in a line and pulled them to the landing. Max shouted down to Jade to join them upstairs. 'Hold on to this little lot if any one of them does something he shouldn't, should him or them.' Max passed over the rope end to Jade and joined in the skirmish at the other end of the house.

Mason had them trapped but quite rightly didn't go in. Max shouted through the door: 'The house is surrounded. We have orders to shoot to kill if you do not surrender in thirty seconds. We will first shoot a hole in the door and throw in two stun grenades; we will come in guns blazing. Your choice but you are on a thirty second timer from now.'

'Don't shoot, we are coming out!'

'Open the door slowly and throw out your weapons. Do it now!' The door opened and all types of weapons made a clatter on the landing. The door opened wider and five men, all well built and could pass for body guards, all with beards and dressed almost the same, stepped out one at a time. 'Which one of you is Kamal Hafeez?' Max demanded.

'He left when he heard the windows breaking down stairs, he told us to fight to the last brother.' He has a room up here that has a rope ladder he drops out of the window and locks the door behind.'

'Show me.'

Max allowed the talkative IRF member to lead the way down the corridor to a rear bedroom that led to another small one that was locked with at least four locking bolts. Max asked for the smashing ram and asked Callum to break the locked door down. Was a specially reinforced one but eventually the bolts pinged off and they were in the small almost cupboard size room. Obviously an emergency exit. The window was open and a rope ladder was hanging down to the ground into shrubs for a covered escape accessing the side boundary wall. All preplanned for circumstances such this. Hafeez you murderous scum you've outfoxed me for the second time. Max was damned annoyed with the sly fox slipping through his grasp again, here and Shelly Street. In total they had taken nine terrorists. Max wasn't interested in these and called Tim Barlow to collect the scum and clean up. Max was more interested in

Hafeez's office to see what he can find. The nine survivors who staffed the Rorke Road HQ Were huddled into the largest room on the ground floor where they were watched over by the three Bastion field agents. Five of the nine will be deported as they were illegal entrants into the UK. Four are second and third generation British citizens that sadly hated their adopted country enough to involve themselves in treacherous terror attacks. They all looked pathetic now and knowing their fate was certain. Amongst them was the deputy leader Hussain Badir. He was very much pissed off with his boss for leaving him to the Bastion wolves!

Max was in Kamal Hafeez's office, a crude attempt was made to burn documents in the fire place. Half were grey ashes but the fire had fizzled out prematurely. One file was of interest, however, that had reference to 'Operation Maealim Almadina' Max knew this was the name they had for the Central London atrocities carried out from the Met-Hopper. There were at least twenty pages in the folder and although the bottom of the pages were burnt, the top half of the pages survived with most of the content. As Max carefully flicked through the charred hard copies, he realised this is the extra proof DCS Barlow will need when presenting a case to the CPS against the IRF.

After a further five minutes of tipping draws out and folders Max came across what he was looking for. The name of Phonoi, the assassin brought over from the US to kill him. Bradley Zimmermann! Now at least I have a chance to get to him before he gets to me. Max thoughts had lifted his spirits just from that one burnt piece of paper!

All the documents will go to Tim Barlow when his team arrives. Max took a photo shot of the man he was now going to be hunting down SAS v US Navy Seals. An interesting prospect if one was a neutral.

Max continued his search and came across a framed picture faced down in the desk draw. It was 23cm x 8cm, too big to carry when in a hurry climbing down a rope ladder. It was a family photo of a man, women three girls and a boy. All the females wore a hijab but not face covering. Max guessed the man must be the boss he wants, none other than Kamal Hafeez. This will be another breakthrough as this will be the first picture the authorities will have of the most wanted terrorist in present time! Tim Barlow will be ecstatic with this ID. Max pondered the finds whilst in thought he heard increased chatter downstairs and assumed it was Barlow with his rapid response quad. He went to the landing and his guess was correct, the cavalry had arrived. Max owing to the status of Bastion, would remain superior in rank to his DCS friend but he wouldn't ever show disrespect and Max always treated Tim Barlow as his boss when together.

Max removed the family photo from its gilded frame and printed on the back was the photographer's studio.

Usama Shakeel, Photographic artist. Bethnal Studios 155 High Street, Bethnal Green. Tel: (020) 7749 6541.

'Bingo, bloody bingo!' Max couldn't help shouting his delight out loud. A voice from behind startled the Bastion man.

'Max-Catt you need to rest. Now you are talking to yourself! I see you have been busy again my over-active friend.' It was DCS Tim Barlow standing in the doorway of Hafeez's office. 'Bloody hell Tim, you shook me, creeping up like that! Take a seat and I'll bring you up to speed with the night's work. By the way my sincere apologies for phoning you at that ungodly hour, earlier.'

'That's not a problem, we picked up those three, including the bad imam from your Bastion cell. They are in custody ready for questioning along with the five river-agent spies who you tricked at Peter Pan in the park.'

Max explained in full the raid and although there were casualties, another nine more were alive to add to the DCS' collection.

In twenty-four hours The Bastion agents had closed down the IRF communications hub in Bradford, smoked out six river-spies from sensitive material sites and closed down the southern HQ of the IRF. This will at least bring to a halt the activities of IRF terror organisation for the foreseeable future if not finish them off in the UK altogether. If the IRF's proactive plans to disrupt the UK government and cripple the British economy had succeeded, anarchy was only just around the corner for the citizens of Britain. Bastion had paid back a massive slice if not all of the tax-payers investment with interest. Max handed over the charred file of Operation Maealim Almadina that included the missing name of the marksman that shot the thirteen Met officers. In total twenty-one terrorist in custody and another five dead.

'I suggest you and your guys get some sleep Max you must be hanging!'

'Yeah the team haven't stopped for nearing twenty-four hours but we had to keep going otherwise once the river-spies had been caught, the whole IRF network would have been aware and dispersed into their labyrinth of sympathisers around the UK. Thankfully we won that race against time.'

'It's a damn pity you didn't get the head honcho, Kamal Hafeez, although getting his deputy Hussain Badir and of course the chief communicator Mousa Alami, the two and three in the pecking order is a damn good!

55

Max-Catt and his team returned to Bastion and after signing their heavy weapons back into the armoury, Max sent his field agents home, by order! The tired leader was himself heavily fatigued, worsened by the bullet that had hit him in his stomach and he was desperate to see the damage it had done. Gingerly he removed his bullet-proof vest and could see that the bullet hadn't broken his skin but the developing bruising had already turned black in the epicentre of the hit and was changing to red with a yellow peripheral band like an image of Saturn. It hurt desperately when he breathed in deeply and he wondered if he had some internal damage but he thought he'd wait for a couple of days and see how it developed. It was 04:35 by the time Max drove his Porsche out of the Bastion garage. He slammed on his brakes and stopped which was not by design but because he had fallen asleep and the jerk caused by the panic breaking sent an excruciating pain to his bruised guts.

Max sensibly returned to Bastion's sleeping quarters and his head hit the pillow at 04:55 and didn't wake until 11:10 when he had to see his boss. 'Come in! Ah Max-Catt I hope you can explain why my office phone hasn't stopped ringing with congratulations and praise for Bastion and I just had a five minute call from an ecstatic home secretary! Bloody hell Max, I couldn't say I didn't know what they were all so excited about so I guessed you'd been putting the world to rights again so I winged my replies. Please help me out here as I am the bloody director!'

The dishevelled Max-Catt was unshaven and with a body odour that had been produced through nervous and physical sweating replied by explaining in three-quarters of an hour what took place in the last thirty six hours. Julia didn't interrupt once, in fact her face had frozen into a stare of incredulity. Even with the power of stale stench emitting from her lead field agent Julia Deakin went around her desk and hugged her lead field agent.

'No wonder all security departments were full of admiration and praise for Bastion and I think at last that we've won our spurs Max. Bloody well done to you and your team and no Bastion casualties. Brilliant!'
'Well I took a bullet in the guts.' Max pulled up his shirt to expose his Saturn image. 'But I now know that our standard issue bullet proof vests work as mine stopped a bullet from two metres!'

'Hell Max, I'd go to Accident and Emergency or ED as they call it now.'
'I'll see how it goes for a couple of days but for now I need a favour. I know we've all but killed the monster and the enemies within but the big IRF boss, Kamal Hafeez, escaped our raid in Limehouse and I really want to get him and cut the head off the IRF monster once and for all.

'I have one of the world's top three contract killers after me, a US navy seal called Brad Zimmermann. I need to draw him out to have an even chance of a…well a showdown. In the charred records in Hafeez's office I found that Zimmerman has been paid up front and these hitmen want to fulfil their contracts or their reputations and kudos are finished. Also you did give me until Friday to complete my mountain of reports so I want some free time until then.'

‘Maximus isn’t your life ever going to settle down? Yes of course take the time that you need. My God Max, you deserve a medal.’
‘Nah, I’ve got the only one I ever wanted. The same one my great grandad Neville Hainsworth-Catt received who was a true war hero!

The Bastion leader drove home to Chiswick, showered and made himself beans on toast and coffee for what was now lunch. While shovelling the food in, he studied Kamal Hafeez’s family picture and the photographer’s address which was where his first work of the day was going to start albeit that it was now afternoon.

There is never a place to sodding well park! Max cussed under his breath. He pulled up on double yellow lines and stopped an overzealous overweight traffic warden in his tracks. Max flashed his Bastion identity card and the Crown motive on it did the rest. ‘How long will you be parked here sir?’
‘Don’t know, depends how long it takes!’ Max hated pontificating traffic wardens and walked passed him and just about refrained from him giving a large middle digit.

Max entered the Bethnal Photographic Studio where a lady in a hijab was behind a display of selected photos.
‘Good morning sir, can I help you?’
‘Yes, I would like to speak with Mr. Usama Shakeel please. He’s the photographer isn’t he?’
‘Yes that’s right, do you want some photos taken sir?’
‘I need to see him for an extended photo shoot but I must see him now!’
He’s having his morning tea and manakish at the Islamic cafe two doors up. Shall I call him?’
‘No, I’ll get myself a coffee there. By the way, what’s a manakish?’

‘It’s a flatbread with a za’atar spicy mix topping.’

‘Thank you’ Max went into the cafe that had a strong smell of garlic and curry. There were only three people seated and he guessed the man he wanted was the well dressed guy sat in the window seat. Max approached. ‘Mr. Shakeel?’

‘Uh yes! Do I know you?’

‘No but you are the photographer that took Mr. Kamal Hafeez’s family portrait.’

‘No, no I don’t know that man!’

‘You do. Look,’ Max showed him the now crumpled family photo with his very own stamp on the back.’

‘Listen I want to assume that you are an innocent hard working guy but Hafeez is guilty of leading an extreme Islamic terror group called the Islamic Republican Front who are responsible for killing thirteen London police officers that you would have seen all over the news this week so don’t come the innocent with me and anyway I don’t have time to argue the toss with you. Under the table right here where we are sitting is a Glock19 handgun that is pointed straight at your bollocks. I am a zero-rated agent which means I’m uncategorised while working for the secret service which in short means I can kill people for fun and if I choose to do so I can without fear of legal consequences.

‘Of course I wouldn’t make a mess here but we would go for a little ride in my car that’s just around corner. So tell me the home address of Hafeez and he won’t know you told me, I promise. As I said, I believe you to be an honest businessman so the address if you please.’

‘I’ll have to get it from my studio and please don’t say anything to my wife about this.’

‘No problem, let’s go.’ The photographer led the way out of the café and into his studio shop. He spoke with his wife and went to a book on the counter which he opened and allowed Max to photo the address. Kamal Hafeez 29 Silver Street. Bermondsey. (020) 3546 7013.

Max wished the man goodbye and left after quietly warning him not to alert Hafeez or the police would arrest him within the hour.

Max was in his Porsche driving towards Bermondsey and on his hands-free dialling facility he asked for 020 3546 7013. The phone rang and a women answered. 'Yes hello.'

'Mrs. Hafeez?'

'Yes.'

'Your daughter Yasmina feels sick, there's nothing to worry about but we think she'd be better off being at home just as a precaution.'

'Yes of course, I'll be there in ten minutes.'

Max ran to the front door of 29 and rang the bell hoping that Kamal Hafeez would think it was his wife who had forgotten something. Somebody was coming to the door and Max was standing the other side of it with his Glock 19 in his hand. The door opened 'What have you forg….'

'Nothing!' Max put two silenced shots into the chest of the terrorist leader. He then unfolded and unzipped a government issue body bag and as Hafeez had spun back into the hallway that was where he was loaded into the bag and zipped up. Max reversed his car on to the driveway, lowered the cabriolet top and then squeezed the IRF's leader's body into the back covering it with his Stewart tartan car rug.

The Bastion agent stopped around the corner and took off his red-haired wig, beard and black rimmed glasses and dumped Hafeez off at the police morgue before informing DCS Tim Barlow: *The orchestrator is dead!*

56

The Bastion boss had done his final deed of that day, a deed that Max had waited nearly a year to complete. That deed was a self proclaimed pledge to take out Kamal Hafeez, the heartless killer of so many innocent people. Max was now going to have a decent dinner and watch some television from his new recliner sofa with only Miss Lochavennie for company and she was all he wanted that night.

What Max-Catt was oblivious to was that Brad Zimmermann had been lying in wait in the cover of the garden shrubbery at Thames Mews since 16:45. An attribute for any top hitman was patience and that is what Phonoi had in abundance. He saw the first signs of life from Max's penthouse at 19:07 when the lights went on and guessed he would have a bit longer to wait but he had brought refreshments with him for a long wait.

After three over generous Lochavennies and while going over his draft report of the tour bus operation, he started to nod, a sign of over tiredness so he brushed his teeth which was about all he could muster and when he had finished his shortened ablutions he crashed out on his king size bed.

His movements were being watched by Phonoi who saw the light go off in the living room and go on in the master bedroom. It was time to prepare so he shook himself and stretched each major muscle after being in his cramped observation position for so long. Another hour and he would enter Max's apartment thinking that it would be an easy kill and he could claim the bragging rights of the US navy seals versus the British SAS.

Max was asleep in under ten minutes and there was no worry about insomnia when he had only slept for seven hours in the last thirty-six.
Phonoi looked every part a night intruder, completely dressed in black and wearing nothing reflective. He skirted the perimeter of the apartment block to avoid any eyes, a mark of professionalism, and avoided the paths and moved through the bushes until he reached Max's block and with his duplicate key he entered the locked building. Phonoi knew how noisy lifts could be to the trained ear of a special forces soldier which might just give Max time to prepare for a visitor. Zimmermann climbed the stairs to the penthouse floor and walked the few paces to Penthouse number three.

With the stealth of a cat burglar he fed the duplicate key into the lock and stopped, waiting and listened intently for any noise from inside. Two minutes of listening phase elapsed before he slowly turned the key, hearing each of the ten point lock tumblers open. Another wait for any noise from inside then Phonoi continued with two more softly manoeuvred turns of the key and the door was free and the slightest touch opened it ajar.

He was in and Max was dead to the world. The armed intruder moved stealthily over the footprint he's memorised from his earlier reconnoitre, moving slowly but purposefully towards the master bedroom and from the open casement window Phonoi felt the night breeze brush past his face. For a whole minute he stood at the foot of Max's king size bed watching for any movement that didn't come. He laid his rifle against the bedroom chair and unholstered his handgun while fitting a silencer to it and moved to the side of the large bed. Max stirred and changed sleeping sides and that was when a cold metal silencer touched his face which triggered an immediate reaction from the sleeper who jumped up in bed but still with a gun barrel pressing into him.

The startled Max hadn't a clue where he was and what was happening although the cold gun barrel made things clearer.

'Get out of bed and stand over by the main wall and take off your pyjamas, top and bottoms,' Max wondered what was going to happen and why he was being ordered to strip off.

Max had spent a lot of time in the 1st Rifles and more recently in 22 Regiment where all inhibitions and dignity were lost by sharing communal showers and open toilets. So as long as the intruder didn't want to roger him he had no aversion with having his private parts stared at. The scene was set with Max-Catt standing naked facing Phonoi. 'So Max-Catt I have read all about you from a detailed personal dossier that Tazi Emir prepared for me.'

'So here we are, US navy seals versus the SAS. What odds would you get for your survival chances at this moment? In the States I can tell you that all bets would be on me but I'll tell you what, I'll give you five minutes for a last request, a cigarette or a beer or whatever you want but only if you admit that the seals are better than the SAS and allow me to record it. I think that's a damn good deal for you. So say it. I'm recording your execution so speak up, there's a good chap.'

'Go fuck yourself Yank! Your seals can't hold a bloody candle to the SAS or our SBS so you can do a double fuck from both regiments!' This angered the edgy psychopathic professional.

Max had come to terms with his fate, realising that this time there was no way out as he was starkers and against the wall in his bedroom with a professional hit-man just three metres away aiming a gun straight at him. Even with these unlikely odds though, Max was determined to at least try something even though he knew he'd die in the attempt. He had thoughts of diving over the bed at Phonoi but calculated that the paid killer would get at least two, well aimed shots at him before he had got anywhere near hm..

He visualised getting shot in the air like a moorland grouse trying to escape in vain but better to die attempting to save one's life than just rolling over and accepting a meek death or losing face by not standing his ground for the SAS. He was almost ready for the Geronimo-moment and felt tension creep into his body with adrenaline fuelling the now or never leap of death. Max had already estimated his chances as being next to zero but any second now the leap was going to happen Then and any further delay would lessen Max's odds even further! Prayer time Max-Catt!

'Come on Max-Catt just say those few little words for an extra five minutes of life! Come on say US seals are better than the SAS.' Max had had more than enough and he would never betray his regiment or lost comrades to this Yankee jerk!

Max kicked off from the wall forming an aerodynamic bascule dive over the bed towards Phonoi. Before his dive had reached the target, three shots had been fired at point blank range from a crack shot killer and found their target along Max's torso!

Phonoi couldn't believe what was happening as he'd had a career in the US military and shot many targets, all of whom had finished in a heap and stone dead! Not this time, not Max-Catt who screamed like a banshee as he reached Zimmermann. The killer had got one more shot away but still it didn't stop Max who threw his naked body at the shocked intruder locking them together in a moving maul. Max managed to lean back and flick the light on as he hated fumbling in the dark!

Zimmermann pulled his cosh out and started thrashing at Max and both men were now on the floor, two well matched killers in physic and unarmed combat skills but the best boxing skills went to Max courtesy of his training in Patrick McCoubrey's gym. It was a strange sight, a naked man bare knuckle boxing another man of equal physic. Max's speed was sensational as he ploughed into Phonoi with a barrage of left and right jabs with his arms moving like oiled pistons. Zimmerman went down but from the floor was able to land a wicked blow to the side of Max's knee which gave him time to get back on his feet and get to his rifle, Max could only look on as he was reeling from the coshing as Phonoi aimed from his hip slipping the rifle's mode onto automatic. There was lots of noise but only cardboard and bits of plastic spluttered out of the gun! Astounded that he wasn't dead, Max quickly recovered by bringing Phonoi down and biting a quarter of the hitman's ear off. He spat the blooded gristle out onto the floor and with speed fuelled by angered adrenaline, his next series of punches pummelled Zimmermann's face. The blooded Yank was losing the scrap and Max went in for the kill by repeatedly banging the face of his opponent on the marbled floor.

Max stood up, leaving Zimmerman unconscious, he had heard the rattle of keys turning in his front door that sent him scurrying for his Glock and dressing gown, in that order!

57

Approximately twelve hours earlier

Jade called her team mates over to her car. 'Please get in you two. We have to help Max! When I was backup on the ground floor at the Limehouse raid, I was nosing around and saw a screwed up ball of paper which was thrown away in a hurry. It was a note from Phonoi saying the Max-Catt killing would be in the next three days and that he had keys to Max's apartment and that's how he would get to Max. The note was written on The Wellington hotel's note paper in Chiswick.'

'We know Max is stubborn and will not go into hiding nor will he allow us to help him so I think we should check Phonoi's hotel room when he goes out. We can use our Bastion badges to demand access to the room and swap all his ammunition for blanks and he shouldn't notice the switch as the guns are certain to be already loaded, the only difference is that the blanks are filled with a wad of paper, plastic or cotton. We will take away all his live ammunition and watch him in shifts for the next two or three days if he hasn't moved on Max in the meantime. What do you both think?'

Perkins answered first. 'I think it's a brilliant idea. Max knew he had to somehow draw Phonoi out to make a fair fight of it so it would be rude to interrupt Phonoi's mistake. You get my vote Jade so when do we do it?'

'I'm in of course, anything for that bastard Max.' Jade and Mason smiled at the SAS style banter.

'We'll get some sleep and we all have been given a day off tomorrow, or later today should I say so let's meet in the Wellington hotel in Chiswick at 13:00?' Both Mason and Callum concurred.

The Wellington hotel was a quality five star establishment and the manager, after seeing the Crown insignia on the Bastion badges, agreed to help. He checked the passport details for Brad Zimmermann but told the team that he was checked in as Charlie Faulkner, an American estate agent. Jade asked to be kitted out in a housekeeping uniform and opened the door to room 20, Charlie Faulkner's room. She shut the door behind her and checked for weapons and ammunition. The fold-up sniper rifle was wrapped in a spare duvet on a shelf and a handgun was wrapped in Kelvin Klein boxers at the back of a deep drawer with all the ammunition in the safe which Jade opened with ease as she had a master combination number that opened all safes. She asked Mason to go back to Bastion and sign out blank ammunition of the same calibre and amount to replace Zimmermann's live stash.

Mason got back to room 201 in just over an hour and Jade swapped the ammunition and left everything the way she'd found it after taking photos and notes of the room. She then locked the room and the team watched for the return of Phonoi from the hotel bar but he didn't turn up so they decided to keep a round the clock surveillance on Brad Zimmermann, alias Charlie Faulkner. Jade opted to go first so she stayed in the Wellington reception. The main reason for watching Zimmerman was to make sure he doesn't go to a gun shop and buy live ammunition which if he did that would mean that he had checked his loaded guns and Jade would see by his body language if he'd noticed the switch. The other two left the hotel and would be on standby on their day off to take over from Jade Jackson when it was time for their shift.

Zimmerman alias Charlie Faulkner passed Jade in reception and went straight up to his room. *Would a professional hitman be different with his guns, more thorough perhaps? Will he carry out a final check on the ammunition? I will soon know.* Jade pondered these thoughts. She also knew her team couldn't just steam in and take him out as, for all intents and purposes, he was just an innocent American tourist at that stage. Max wouldn't want that either as Bastion's main suspect for the tour bus killings was Phonoi but so far they had no proof. Jade was now getting concerned about her plan and started to question it and thought that perhaps they should have told Max but she realised, and Max had actually said so himself, that Phonoi would need flushing out which didn't make things any easier for Jade.

Present Time.

It was 15:00 when Brad Zimmermann came down from his room carrying a large backpack. Mason had replaced Jade on surveillance duty just an hour ago and Charlie Faulkner was checking out of the hotel. Mason assumed he would be calling a cab but waited to see exactly what he did next. Predictably Phonoi called a cab and Mason followed the taxi that Phonoi was in. Mason phoned the team to say the target had left the hotel and was in a taxi which he was following.

Jade and Callum went to their vehicles and headed for Chiswick as that was the assumed destination of their target. At 15:40 the taxi dropped Phonoi off at Strand-on-the-Green and Mason waited for the hitman to walk fifty metres before he locked his car and walked towards the river and, while keeping his distance, Mason gave Jade and Callum a road name to put in their satnav, both being only fifteen minutes away

Adjacent to the Thames was a luxury gated residence called Thames Mews with landscaped gardens and Mason watched Phonoi use a key to enter it. Mason hurried to the fence and pulled himself up to peer over it and saw Phonoi heading not for the building but towards the shrubbery and he didn't reappear.

Mason met up with the other two of his team and they all thought they should call the concierge and when he came to the gate Jade flashed her Bastion badge and they were in. The concierge allowed them to use his office but really they had commandeered its use. Mason had an idea and remembered asking Max if he needed a hand to move into his Thames view apartment but Max had said that Joseph Carmichael had booked a day off work to help him so he wondered if Joe had keys to Max's apartment. Mason phoned Julia Deakin and asked for Joe's number.

'Mr. Carmichael you do know me and we met after our operation in Aden when your ZX3 agent got us out of there. Anyway that's not why I rang. Did Max give you spare keys to his pad at Thames Mews by any chance?

'Yes, I have keys. Why?'

'Max is in danger as a contract killer is about to attack him so can you get to Max's now with the keys and I'll meet you at the gate.'

'Of course, I'll be about twenty minutes.'

At 18.15 the contingent of four comprising of Joe and the team were in the concierge's office and Jade was the first to see the lights go on in Max's apartment followed by Callum using his night binoculars. 'Shit, Phonoi has got to Max and right under our noses. How did he do that without us seeing him?' The team and Joe raced to Max's penthouse and as they got to the door they heard shots being fired. Joe rushed to the door and used his keys to get in and as the door flew open Max turned his Glock towards them before realising it was his pal Joe and the Bastion team. The still unconscious Zimmermann was face down on the cold marble.

'I shouldn't be here! Zimmermann fired blanks at me. Why? I dived at him assuming it to be a suicide dive as he was going to kill me anyway but he didn't and I hit eight bells of crap out of him and all this while I was naked!'

'Did you show him your pert arse sir?' Jade forgot herself and got a suspicious stare from Callum and Perks. Jade changed the subject by explaining the bullet swop at the Wellington hotel. Max was flabbergasted but thanked his loyal team for saving his life.

'Bloody hell Jade Jackson you saved my life, what the hell made you think of doing it though?'

'Well Max our field team are well aware, and with respect, how stubborn you are. By your own admission you wanted to draw this scumbag out to have a decent chance against him. I found out at the Limehouse raid on a scrunched up piece of Wellington hotel paper written by Zimmermann/Faulkner that he was going to move on you in the next three days. We didn't know where or when he would strike so as insurance I replaced all his live bullets with the plastic and cardboard blanks we use for practice at Bastion. That's about it apart from I have to ask you if it's a Hainsworth-Catt ritual to fight starkers.'

'Don't push your luck Miss Jackson. Seriously I'm very grateful to you all and the fact that you've hardly slept for days is a tribute to your spirit and loyalty. Thank you team and to you Joe.'

Max rang his pal, Tim Barlow, at Scotland Yard.

‘Tim we got the hitman from the killer bus, the guy who actually pulled the trigger on your officers. His DNA should match that taken from the concealed bus compartment and I have his rifle so that will provide evidence when your ballistic forensics team check the rifling marks against the ones used at the carnage.’

‘I’ll be over to you in twenty minutes to pick him up and I expect he’s well bruised, knowing you Maxy.’

‘I’ve left some of him for you Tim, don’t worry.’

‘Is that a piece of ear down there?’ Callum pointed to a blooded piece of gristle lying by Max’s bed.

‘I bit a piece of his ear off when I was most pissed off with him as he wanted me to say US seals were better than the SAS and he wanted to record it which was never going to happen.

‘Sir I’m taking you to Uxbridge hospital to get a tetanus jab and to clean those weeping spots so get dressed.’

‘Yes Miss, right away Miss but can we all have a double Lochavennie first?’ Jade hadn’t replied before four tumblers of amber Malt were poured. ‘Cheers to you all and here’s to the total demise of the IRF from the bottom to the very top and most importantly ***the enemy within!’***

THE END

Epilogue

The IRF in the UK were all but finished apart from some isolated pockets that didn't have the planners to cause and further problems and eventually they fizzled out.

Brad Zimmermann alias Charlie Faulkner alias Phonoi was charged with the tour bus shootings and the murder of Mr. Tandi Formento as his DNA was found on the river cruiser and the statue where the murder took place.

The five remaining river spies were exposed, arrested and sentenced to spend many years in prison.

The two million pounds Max embezzled out of Kamal Hafeez was shared out with half a million pounds going to the wife and family of Dani Quibi and bad balance shared between the families of the thirteen brave police officers slain in London. Max, unbeknown to the authorities, got hold of Phonoi's millions and shared them out between the 1st Rifles and 22 Regiment SAS orphans and widows fund.

The cross channel migrants had all but stopped but Max knew that like the tide, they'll be back but his estimation was that it would be a good six months before the boats could be reorganised. Max-Catt made it blatantly clear to Sir Crispin, now high in government circles, that until the UK government removed all the incentives the illegal migrants would keep coming into the UK by the thousands and what Max-Catt and his Bastion team did would only create a respite for the UK!

OTHER TITLES IN THE MAX-CATT THRILLERS.

The Beginning

Vengeance is mine

No turning back

Rotterdam

Bastion

The Yalta Project

Enemy within

Rogue kill

Printed in Great Britain
by Amazon

61002757R10178